tur
en

OPERATION CODE BREAKER

ILKKA REMES

OPERATION CODE BREAKER

A LUKE BARON ADVENTURE

ANDERSEN PRESS

First published in 2012 by
Andersen Press Limited
20 Vauxhall Bridge Road
London SW1V 2SA
www.andersenpress.co.uk
www.lukebaron.com

2 4 6 8 10 9 7 5 3 1

The right of Ilkka Remes to be identified as the author of this
work has been asserted by him in accordance with the
Copyright, Designs and Patents Act, 1988.
Copyright © Nordic Media Ltd., 2012
British Library Cataloguing in Publication Data available.
ISBN 978 1 84939 119 1

Printed and bound by CPI Group (UK) Ltd, Croydon, CR0 4YY

PART ONE

1

When Luke headed back into the Sistine Chapel, leaving his classmates souvenir shopping in St Peter's Square, he knew his teacher might tell him off, but he didn't expect to get arrested.

The echoing coolness of the immense, world-famous church offered welcome relief from the heat outside. He gazed at the dramatic fresco by Michelangelo high above, where the Hand of God reached out to touch the hand of Adam, giving him life. Muted voices and footsteps reverberated in the lofty space. The current pope had been elected here by the College of Cardinals, but right now the place was full of tourists.

A sudden flash made Luke jump. He knew cameras were forbidden – there were signs about it everywhere – and sure enough, a pair of guards came charging through the throng and loudly told off an American tourist. Waving his hands, the tourist tried to explain himself to the guards, but they grabbed him by the arms and marched him out.

Luke was about to leave when he caught sight of a weird-looking man he'd noticed earlier in the square outside. Dressed in an old raincoat several sizes too big for him, partially bald, with deep-set eyes, the man followed the forcible removal of the tourist with an intense stare. He reached for something under his raincoat and, as he did so, his eyes locked with Luke's, who quickly turned away, feeling his heart begin to race. What was the man up to? Why was he wearing a raincoat on such a hot day?

No doubt just some harmless local nutter... Yet Luke felt uncomfortable standing so close to him. The man scratched his curly hair, which formed a wreath around the naked dome of his head. He had a massive, hooked nose, and a chin so weak it barely existed. His neck was thin and somehow askew. Sweat glistened on his bald forehead.

Luke glanced at his watch. The hour's free time was almost up. He decided to go back to his friends and not risk missing the bus. When he reached the doors through which the guards had just dragged the American tourist, he glanced over his shoulder. The strange-looking man had disappeared into the crowd but there was something wet on the floor near the spot where he'd been standing, and Luke detected a strange chemical smell... A trail of drops led towards Michelangelo's *Last Judgement* on the altar wall. Suddenly alert, Luke rushed after the stranger, shouldering his way into the crowd. A woman's scream rang out in the direction of the altar wall, behind the throng. People craned their necks to see.

Luke squeezed through a group of small Japanese women then stopped in his tracks, stunned by what he saw: the man had bounded onto the altar and now pulled a flat white container from under his raincoat. Without a second's hesitation, he splashed the contents onto the figures at the bottom of the fresco.

4

'Stop him!' Luke yelled out, lunging towards the vandal. 'It's acid!'

Michelangelo's fresco had to be saved. Luke knew that certain masterpieces, including the *Mona Lisa*, were kept behind bulletproof glass, but the *Last Judgement* clearly wasn't: dissolving paint was already dribbling to the floor from the patches where the acid had bitten. The man was racing across the altar, wild-eyed, swinging the small container. Drops of liquid flew onto the clothes and skin of the stunned onlookers, causing shrieks of panic and a chaotic stampede. People crashed into each other. One of the Japanese women slumped to the floor, trying to crawl away. Screams filled the air. Someone tried to pull the vandal off the altar, but he kicked out and wriggled free.

For the second time Luke met the deep-set eyes of the chinless, big-nosed weirdo – eyes that were cold and leering and devoid of all feeling. Then the man tossed the empty container into the crowd and ducked out of the chapel through the door to the right of the altar.

Glancing in the opposite direction, Luke saw the guards who'd expelled the American tourist returning. They had to fight hard to force a passage through the terrified crowd that was rushing towards them.

An alarm began to scream in a relentless, ear-splitting wail, but the damage was done: the *Last Judgement* hissed and bubbled, dripping onto the floor. Having survived for more than four and a half centuries, the masterpiece of the Italian Renaissance had been destroyed in an instant. Only a second Michelangelo could save it.

Unable to believe what was happening right in front of his eyes, Luke shifted his attention from the fresco to the door through which the vandal had escaped. What motive could explain such an insane action? Would the man be caught and punished?

'*Calmarsi, calmarsi!*' the guards shouted. 'Calm down, calm down!' Although they looked almost wild with despair themselves.

More personnel had appeared from somewhere and tried to shepherd the tourists out in an orderly fashion, arranging people into groups, ordering them to wait for the arrival of the police. All eyewitnesses would be asked for statements. Some of these people would be staying in the Vatican for longer than they'd expected, Luke thought to himself. Already a few voices could be heard protesting. He himself had a plane to catch early the following morning. Not to mention his bus, right now.

He stopped to help an old lady to her feet. The acid had burned holes into her clothes but luckily it hadn't damaged her skin. She thanked him over and over again, unable to control her shaking hands.

A wall of tourists now stood in a semicircle before *The Last Judgment*, staring at the guard who was dabbing it gently with his jacket. At last the deafening alarm stopped and a babble of different languages rose up like a loud storm as the shaken tourists all spoke at once.

Looking back at the altar wall, Luke realised that the damage done to the Michelangelo was actually less serious than he'd thought: the splashes of acid were small and dispersed and, from a distance, the fresco looked almost unharmed.

What, Luke wondered, was the point of attacking a painting? Was someone trying to destroy Italy's tourist industry? Or was it an assault against art? Luke's Vatican guidebook told the story of a religious fantasist, claiming to be Jesus, who'd taken a sledgehammer to Michelangelo's *Pietà* sculpture in St Peter's Basilica. Like the *Mona Lisa*, the sculpture was now kept behind bulletproof glass.

'Hey, watch out!' Luke called to no one in particular when he saw the empty container being kicked along the floor by the blindly rushing crowd. It was important evidence . . . He bent over, managing to reach it and, as he did so, he realised it was probably best not to be seen handling it. Made of ridged white plastic, the container was empty, but it smelled unpleasant. Holding it with the tips of his fingers, he placed it on the altar.

Suddenly there was another burst of activity. A guard grabbed his tall colleague by the shoulder and pointed at Luke. Both men stared. A heated discussion began.

Luke tried to melt into the crowd, but it was too late. The tall guard strode up to him, clutched his arm and let out a flood of Italian, of which Luke didn't understand a word. The other guard took the container from the altar.

'What were you doing with this?' the tall man asked in heavily accented English.

'I found it on the floor.'

'You come with us. Move, boy!'

Luke found himself being led towards the door through which the vandal had escaped.

'I'm here on a school trip . . . The bus is waiting.'

'Where is your accomplice?' asked the tall guard, taking the flat container from his colleague. 'Why did you do this?'

Luke felt as though a strong electric current had passed through him. He couldn't believe it. He was now a suspect accused of destroying a landmark of western civilisation. It was ridiculous, but also oddly exciting.

'I want to talk to my teacher.' Luke's attempt to add a few years to his voice failed miserably, and he ended up emitting a high-pitched squeak.

'*We* decide who you talk to,' the tall guard snapped with a hostile stare.

'*Beh, lascia stare, Federico,*' the other guard cut in, his voice calm. '*Non lo sospetto di niente. Pero lo visto tutto da vicino. Dobbiamo interrogarlo.*'

Luke's cheeks blazed with shame as he was led out through the door to the right of the altar. He tried to maintain a sense of direction, but it was hard to concentrate with his heart beating like a hammer. Excited voices echoed in the richly decorated rooms packed with guards and police officers.

And then the strangest thing of all happened. Another guard came sprinting towards them, waving his arms in a wide arc, bellowing in Italian. The alarm began its shrill, yapping music once more. Like a stampeding herd, all the uniformed figures went rushing in the same direction, and Luke was surprised to find himself alone.

His mind was racing. He could run away now, join his classmates outside and catch the bus back to the hostel . . . But fleeing the scene might only make matters worse for him. Besides, he was curious. He joined the general rush and burst into a room whose walls were lined with enormous paintings set in gilded frames.

A crowd of police officers and guards stood staring up at one of the frames. There was complete silence. Luke swallowed.

The frame was empty.

2

The tyres of the Fiat van screeched as it rounded the corner from the Via Pandolfini onto the Via della Condotta, almost flattening an old-age pensioner who was hobbling across the street with his walking stick. The name of a plumbing firm was written in orange on the van's sides.

'*Pazzi!*' The pensioner shook his stick, yelling after the vehicle: '*Maledetto bastardo!*'

But the van was already speeding in the wrong direction down a one-way street. It caught the side mirror of a carelessly parked Lancia, which snapped off and went clattering into the dust. A scooter heading up the one-way street had to swerve to avoid the van. The shaken rider screamed after it, making an obscene hand gesture.

When it reached the very end of the Via della Condotta the van finally slowed down, swinging another turn, onto the Via dei Banchi Vecchi. Advancing at a more sensible pace, it meticulously stopped at the next pedestrian crossing to allow a woman with a pushchair to cross the street. Even the keenest observer would have struggled to notice the precise moment when the van had lost its orange livery. One of the passengers had pulled a fishing line that ran through the bodywork, peeling off the name of the non-existent plumber, revealing an excellent imitation of the yellow and red DHL courier company lettering beneath.

The van followed the street, lined with old blocks of flats, for a kilometre or so then carefully turned into a deserted courtyard, rolling gently into a waiting garage. The double doors silently closed behind it. Minutes later the doors of the adjoining garage opened and a colossal 1967 Cadillac SSV Hearse came rumbling forward, its black paintwork polished to a bright sheen. The broad windows revealed a wooden coffin with a flower arrangement on top.

The hearse turned ponderously into the street, swaying slightly as it stopped at the first set of traffic lights. An old lady dressed entirely in black crossed herself and tottered to the other side of the street, tipping her head respectfully at the driver and his bald, weak-chinned passenger at the front. They returned her greeting with solemn nods.

Luke didn't struggle, but he protested in English as the guards half dragged, half carried him out of the galleries behind the Sistine Chapel. No one paid any attention to what he said. Complete mayhem had broken out when the empty frame had been discovered.

Shouts in Italian echoed in the vaulted space of the museum's entrance hall. Discontented tourists murmured as they queued for questioning and identity checks conducted by the red-faced officials sitting behind a row of makeshift desks. Luke could feel the stares of the onlookers, clearly wondering why he'd been singled out for special attention. He wiped his face on his sleeve.

With a clunk the heavy door opened and Luke was dragged outside by the guards. The heat, strangely intense for early spring, enveloped him like a stifling blanket. The late-afternoon sun made long, hazy shadows under the people in the street. After another burst of excited talk, the guards ushered Luke round a corner.

A police car came hurtling towards them, lights flashing. It drew up, screeching to a shuddering halt. Luke was dimly aware that in different circumstances he might have enjoyed participating in this spectacle, but what with his burning thirst, the scorching sun and the tight grip of the guards, not to mention the guilty discomfort triggered by their accusations, he felt totally miserable.

The doors of the police car swung open and two policemen wearing peaked caps stepped up to the guards. Moments later Luke was hurled into the back seat and the guards simply left.

It was hot in the car, even hotter than outside, and he was desperate for a drink. There were no inside door handles for the rear passengers, and a scratched pane of Plexiglas separated the back seat from the front of the vehicle.

Closing his eyes, Luke visualised the fountains in St Peter's Square. His parched tongue stuck to his palate. How could he talk himself out of this situation if his tongue wasn't working? The two police officers sat in the front, acting as though they'd already forgotten his existence. The one behind the wheel was speaking into a radiophone and the other scribbled in a black Moleskine notebook. Luke had to shade his eyes against the glare of the pitiless sun.

His shirt was drenched with sweat and his face felt sticky. He looked at his watch and felt a stab of misery when he realised that the deadline set by his teacher to meet back at the bus had now passed.

Suddenly there was a sharp rap on the Plexiglas. The police officer in the passenger seat had put away his notebook and was studying Luke with an ominous frown. Luke braced himself. Somehow or other he had to explain what had happened and get himself freed.

'You tell the truth or you're in trouble,' the severe-looking officer said in English. '*Capito?*'

'*Capito, capito,*' Luke said, thinking, *I'm in trouble no matter what I say.*

'*Scusi?*' the officer barked. '*Come ti chiami?* What is your name? English? *Bist du Deutsch?*'

Luke squared his shoulders and tried to project dignity. 'My name is Luke Baron. I'm English.'

'*Luca Baroni.*' The officer scribbled in his notebook. '*Documenti.*'

Luke pulled his passport from the thigh pocket of his combat trousers and searched in vain for a way to pass it through the glass. The officer shook his head as though filled with agonising despair, then gestured for Luke to place the passport flat against the glass and began slowly writing down the details.

'What were you doing with this?' The officer produced the white container, which was now sealed inside a transparent plastic bag.

'Nothing! It was being kicked along the floor. I thought it might be an important piece of evidence.'

'You saw the man who destroyed the fresco?'

'Yes.'

'How long have you known him?'

'I don't know him.'

'What is his name?'

'I don't know! I had nothing to do with any of it.'

The driver raised his radiophone to his ear. Luke took a deep breath and told himself to calm down.

A cortege of at least five police cars went speeding past, racing towards St Peter's Square, sirens blaring. Tourists stared as a team of men dressed in fluorescent yellow vests began closing off the street by means of a steel and barbed-wire barrier. A narrow alley leading off the street was also barricaded, although surely the vandals had escaped long ago.

What would Monty be thinking? Luke dreaded having to face her. She didn't tolerate lateness in class, let alone on school trips in foreign cities ...

A few blocks away, Mary Montgomery stood with her hands on her hips beside the revving bus. She had heavy, almost masculine features and tied her hair in a bun. Even in the Italian heat, she was wearing a tweed jacket and matching skirt, and her massive calves were encased in brown tights. All but one of the names on the list in her hand had been crossed out. Sirens blared in the distance. A police motorbike went flashing past.

'Monty' was seething. Luke was one of her favourite pupils, and she felt sick with worry, but she was careful not to let it show. Generations of kids had called her 'Monty', after her namesake, Field Marshal Montgomery, and that was now what she also mentally called herself. She slipped the list into the pocket of her tweed skirt and heaved her tired bones up into the bus.

The kids were bickering and fidgeting in the heat. Everyone was keen to get back to the hostel to pack. The flight home to Brussels would be leaving early the next morning.

'Jack, did Luke mention anything else to you?' Monty said quietly to a boy with prominent buck teeth.

'No, Miss Montgomery.' Squirming in his seat, Jack buried his hands into the pockets of his khaki shorts.

'But he definitely said he was going back into the Sistine Chapel?'

'Yes, miss. He said he was too hot.'

'And when was this?'

'An hour ago. Maybe more.'

'Anything else?'

'Well, there was a man there. Funny-looking. We were kind of laughing at him.'

Monty's heart missed a beat. 'Did he seem... dangerous?'

'No, miss. He was just an odd-looking man in the crowd.' Jack drank some water and wiped his big-toothed mouth as he stared at his headteacher. 'Maybe Luke's watch is slow?'

Monty ended the interview with an ironic grimace – as Jack well knew, Luke was famously punctual, always appearing in the classroom at the last possible moment but never even a second late.

Frowning, Monty went back to the front of the bus and tapped the driver on the shoulder. 'Let's go.'

3

The black Cadillac hearse crawled ceremoniously along the Viale Tiziano, the flashing blue lights of the oncoming police cars reflecting off its shiny doors. The driver straightened his tie and his white collar. He had a thin pencil moustache and his black jacket was slightly too small for his broad shoulders. He glanced at the police cars in his rear-view mirror.

'*Calmasti*, Giuliano,' Lorenzo, beside him, said in a soft voice. 'We're doing fine.'

'Easy for you to say.' Giuliano fumbled for a throat lozenge from the packet in his breast pocket. 'I'll be the one who has to talk.'

'Just say what we agreed.' Lorenzo spoke like he was calming an animal. 'The rest is in the hands of the Almighty.'

'Convenient religion you have.' Giuliano grinned, scratching his little moustache. 'Thou shalt not steal, but if you do, don't worry, the Lord will bail you out.'

'That's no way to talk to a cardinal.' Lorenzo chuckled, rustling his red robes.

'Why not dress as the Pope and draw even more attention to yourself?'

'The secret of successful disguise is distraction; the more flamboyant the better.'

Lightning flashed on the horizon, followed by a slow rumble of thunder, as the unusual spring heat wave gave way to a storm. A flurry of large drops struck the big windshield and Giuliano switched on the wipers. *Yes, let it rain*, he was thinking. *It will dampen the zeal of the police.*

Lorenzo's hand shot to the tiny button speaker in his left ear. He listened for a moment.

'It's Achim . . . He says we're all over the police radio.'

'Remember to take off that thing if they pull us over,' Giuliano snapped. 'And stop messing with it. I've never seen a cardinal with an iPod. And, wait a minute, what's that on your finger?'

'Right . . . ' Lorenzo chuckled uneasily. 'Good point.'

Giuliano shook his head as Lorenzo pulled off the wedding ring and slipped it into the pocket of his trousers under the scarlet robes.

'Temporary divorce,' Lorenzo said, then cupped his hand over his left ear again. 'Oh, no . . . '

'What is it?'

'Road block on Santa Trinita.'

Giuliano turned white. Neither of the men spoke for several seconds. They had rehearsed the situation over and over again – it was no surprise that the major exit roads were being controlled, yet it suddenly felt like one.

An orange light flashed in the rain ahead. Giuliano squinted and saw a police officer standing in front of a roadblock, flagging him down.

'Keep calm. He might just wave us through.'

Giuliano braked slowly and composed his face into an expression of funereal gravity. The policeman came splashing through puddles to the driver's door. He held his hands to his brow, forming a visor against the rain.

Giuliano wound down his window. 'Is something wrong?'

'Excuse me, but we're checking all vehicles. Without exception.' Glimpsing the cardinal in the passenger seat, the policeman gave a small bow and seemed to speed up his routine. 'Forgive me for this formality. I'll have you on your way in no time.'

With a sigh, Giuliano stepped out of the car and went round to the back, opening the hatch under the eyes of the police officer, who crossed himself before shining his torch into the gaps on either side of the coffin.

'*Grazie*,' said the officer and trotted off to the next vehicle.

Luke jumped at the sound of the familiar ring tone – his mobile was still with the police officers on the other side of the Plexiglas partition. He could see it flashing beside the packet of cigarettes on the small tray between the two front seats. The display said 'MONTY'.

More thunder growled across the sky, directly above the car. The rain poured, drumming the roof.

'For the last time. What were you doing with this container?'

'I already told you. I picked it up off the floor. It's important evidence, isn't it?'

'Leave the evidence to us. Tell us more about your companion.'

'What companion?'

'Your friend who vandalised the Sistine Chapel.'

'He's not my friend.'

'Where did you meet him?'

'I never met him or spoke to him. But I thought he looked odd. I thought it was weird he was wearing a raincoat on a hot day.'

'Cosimo, you won't believe this.' The police officer in the passenger seat leaned over to his colleague. 'We've picked up Sherlock Holmes!'

The officers laughed. Luke wondered whether there was any point even trying to be constructive: these men were just out to torment him.

'How and why did you travel to Rome, Mr Holmes? And is Doctor Watson travelling with you?'

The officers laughed some more, then waited for Luke's answer, big grins on their faces.

'I'm on a class trip organised by my school.'

'And where are your classmates now?'

'I don't know. They're probably waiting for me out there in the rain somewhere. We were supposed to meet at the bus.'

'And where can we get hold of you if we let you go?'

'If you give me that mobile back, you can ring me.' Luke's voice was starting to quiver. 'I'm flying home tomorrow.'

'OK, Luca.' Having noted down Luke's number, the officer in the passenger seat gave a wink and snapped the elastic on his notebook. 'We'll be in touch after we've compared the statements of all the eyewitnesses.'

'Thanks,' Luke said, almost tearful with relief.

'One more thing. We'll need your teacher's number as well.'

Luke's heart sank, but he gave Monty's number, which all the class had been told to memorise, then turned to let himself out of the hot car, quickly realising he had to wait until the door was opened from the outside.

'Can I have my phone back?'

'What phone?' the officer said as he opened Luke's door.

Luke's jaw dropped, but then he realised that the officer was pulling his leg. With a mocking wink, the man tossed the handset to Luke.

'*Grazie*.' Luke tried to smile, but his face felt numb.

The officer escorted him through the police checkpoint. On shaky legs, Luke trotted off into the warm rain. More thunder cracked in the sky above St Peter's.

Deep puddles had gathered in the gutters, which foamed and burbled like mountain streams. Heavy rain lashed his face, but he welcomed it after all the stress and the day's heat.

He hastened to the meeting point, but as he expected, the bus was gone. He quickly sent Monty a text message, saying he was all right and that he'd make his own way back to the hostel. He tried to make it sound light and casual, although a cold knot of anxiety had tightened in his stomach. His troubles weren't over yet. Far from it. He had no idea how he'd ever get to the hostel without any money.

4

Rain dripped from the overgrown vegetation in the courtyard of the Trastevere youth hostel, an ancient stone building near the River Tiber that resembled a monastic cloister. Monty let out an audible sigh and slipped her simple mobile back into her skirt pocket. Luke's text message had flooded her with relief and anger, and it was only the anger she intended to show when the boy reappeared.

Then the phone rang again and Monty was stunned to find herself speaking to an Italian police officer. Luke had witnessed some incident in the Sistine Chapel. Monty smiled fractionally. Typical. The boy seemed to run into the strangest adventures wherever he turned.

'And we need to talk to him again at four o'clock tomorrow afternoon.'

'Tomorrow he'll be at home in Brussels. Our flight leaves in the morning.'

'You don't understand. He is forbidden to travel. We let him go, but my superiors now insist on a full interrogation.'

Monty wasn't smiling any more. 'Would you hang on a second?'

She quickly stamped across the courtyard, knocked on

the door of the dormitory that her colleague shared with some of the girls, and explained the situation.

'Interrogated?' Miss Hart blushed with shock, bringing her hand to her mouth. 'What has Luke done?'

'Don't be so melodramatic, Anne. He's just been in the wrong place at the wrong time, as usual.'

'But our flight . . .'

'He'll miss it. Someone has to accompany him home. You.'

'But—'

'Be sure not to take your eyes off him until he's safely back in Brussels.' Monty glanced at the large bouquet of roses on Miss Hart's bedside table and put her phone to her ear.

'Hello? Mary Montgomery here again. Luke will come at four tomorrow, as instructed, accompanied by one of his teachers. Kindly repeat the address. *Slowly.*'

She scribbled down a few words, then cut the line and sat down heavily on Miss Hart's bed.

'These Italians! I'm exhausted.'

'Thank God Luke's OK,' Miss Hart said. 'Poor thing.'

'Are we missing any others?'

'They're all in the refectory.'

There was a pause, then Monty narrowed her eyes and said: 'Nice flowers.'

Miss Hart blushed to the roots of her hair.

With a grunt, Monty stood up and lumbered across the courtyard towards the refectory, where the hostel staff were already beginning to lay the table for the evening meal.

Luke put the map into his pocket and wearily slipped through the gate of the youth hostel. The courtyard was

21

deserted and some of the windows had shutters on them. He hastened inside. Tall doors led from the vestibule into the various rooms and halls. His footsteps echoed off the tiled floor and the bare walls.

He headed towards the clatter of plates and cutlery in the refectory, where he found his classmates tucking into semolina pudding and fresh figs. As he stepped into the long room, the cheerful hubbub came to a sudden end. Luke took a deep breath and walked towards Monty and Miss Hart, who were seated at the far end of the wooden table that spanned the length of the refectory. He passed the familiar faces of his grinning classmates as though in a blur.

'Our lost sheep,' Monty said.

Right on cue, Bernie, the class joker, emitted a series of loud bleats. The huge room exploded into laughter, whoops of delight and more bleats. The floor shook under stamping feet.

'We've been *so* worried.' Miss Hart stood up and patted Luke's arm. 'What happened?'

'Someone vandalised *The Last Judgment*. The police stopped everyone. I'm a key witness, it seems.'

'What took you so long?' Monty remained sitting and her face was blank. 'You texted two hours ago.'

'I didn't have any money.'

'Then how did you get here?'

'I found some coins in one of the fountains. Then I took a bus.'

Miss Hart smiled. 'Resourceful as ever.'

'He'll need to be if he's prosecuted.'

'What do you mean?' Luke's heart missed a beat.

'The police phoned.' Monty stood up. 'Miss Hart, take

charge of this circus, will you? Follow me, Luke.'

As Luke followed his teacher towards the TV room, Bernie started bleating again, but this time he only got scattered laughs.

'Bernie, do act your age, if you possibly can,' Monty snapped without even looking in the direction of the bleating.

There were a few pupils in the TV room watching a football match. Monty sent them scurrying with a flick of her hand and closed the door. She folded her arms and fixed her gaze on Luke.

He lowered his eyes. Monty's legs, he told himself, in fact her entire physique, would have struck envy in Arnold Schwarzenegger.

'You better tell me exactly what happened.'

Luke gave a detailed account of the events in the Sistine Chapel and the treatment he'd received at the hands of the police afterwards.

'They want to question you again tomorrow.'

'Tomorrow?'

'You are wanted for interrogation at the police station at four o'clock.'

'But the flight—'

'Change of plan. They were very firm about it. Miss Hart will keep an eye on you, and I fear that this Paolo she's been seeing will be keeping an even closer eye on her…'

'But the tickets are unchangeable.'

'I have booked new tickets, and you will personally pay for them if it turns out you're in any way to blame.'

'Yes, Miss Montgomery,' Luke said. 'But I swear I was only—'

'That's all for now.' Monty lowered her massive bottom into an armchair and switched on the news. 'Go and ask the kitchen staff if there's any pasta left. Then get yourself to bed. You look exhausted.'

As he slipped out of the door Luke caught a glimpse of *The Last Judgment* and then an excited journalist, holding a red microphone, on the flickering screen.

He walked through the refectory into the kitchen and returned carrying a tray with a plate of spaghetti, a basket of bread and a Fanta on it. Some of the others had already retreated to the dorm rooms to finish their packing. Bernie greeted Luke's arrival with a ragged laugh, but Jack, who was Luke's closest friend at school, clamped the much larger Bernie in a headlock.

'We want to hear from Luke, not you.'

'Let me go . . .'

A ring of faces gathered around Luke as he gave his account of what had happened. There wasn't even any need to embellish the story: it was a genuine adventure, although it unfortunately had the potential to turn into a nightmare.

'The Italians take art pretty seriously,' red-faced Bernie said when he finally tore himself free of Jack. 'I think you're looking at ten or twenty years.'

Half an hour later, on his way to bed, Luke glanced into the dorm room occupied by the girls. A small group sat on the floor leaning on one of the bunk beds, giggling at the video clips on Laura's iPhone.

Suddenly Bernie shot into the room, snatched the iPhone and scurried up the ladder onto the top bunk. Lying on his back, he scrolled through the contents. The girls attacked from all sides, but Bernie got to his feet on the bunk and hurled the handset in Luke's direction. Luke fumbled his catch and the precious phone rattled to the floor. Laura let out a scream.

'Don't panic, it's not broken.' Luke picked the phone off the floor. On its small screen, a gaggle of girls could be seen pulling faces in St Peter's Square.

'Give it here, right now, or I'm telling Monty.'

'Wait!'

Luke held the iPhone out of Laura's reach. He was looking at a shot of himself: a tall, skinny teenager strolling in St Peter's Square. And then he saw something more: a brief flash of the man in a raincoat.

'Oh, grow up!' Laura said, wrestling the iPhone from Luke.

'It's him! It's the guy who threw the acid!'

'What are you talking about?'

Luke rewound the film and brought the tiny screen closer to his eyes. It was impossible to see much detail, but the clip might be useful to the police. The first thing would be to hook up the phone to a proper screen.

'Give it back!' Laura yelled.

'Just five minutes, please, Laura,' Luke begged. He rushed out with Jack, Bernie and Laura at his heels and headed straight for the TV room, which was now dark and deserted: Monty had gone to bed. Luke switched on the lights and checked the back of the old-fashioned TV. As he feared, it had no USB port. In any case, he needed more than just a screen: the clip on Laura's phone had to be enlarged and slowed down, and any background noise had to be eliminated.

'What's up?' Jack asked.

Luke didn't answer. He jogged down the corridor,

stopped outside a large oak door and raised his fist.

'Are you nuts?' Jack had gone white. 'That's Monty's room!'

'I know...' Luke knocked. 'I can't believe I'm doing this.'

After a long wait, Monty appeared in a tightly belted dressing gown, feet planted wide apart in the manner of a Bulgarian shot-putter.

'Luke. Naturally. How can I be of service to you at this late hour?'

'It's important. I need a computer. Do you think the people who run this hostel would let me into their office? I saw a desktop in there.'

'I wouldn't touch that computer with a barge pole,' Bernie piped up. 'They let me go online yesterday, and it took almost an hour just to download my email. That thing belongs in the Science Museum.'

'I don't believe anyone asked for your opinion, Bernie.' Monty turned to Luke. 'And you've caused quite enough disruption for today, Luke Baron.'

'Please. I think Laura caught the vandal on her mobile. But I need to enhance the clip on a computer to get a proper look.'

'It's a brand-new iPhone!' said Laura. 'There's no way I'd trust you with it.'

'I promise not to look at your messages. Or to use it. You can even take out the SIM card.'

'No chance. I'm not letting you mess up my diary of this trip.'

Luke thought he could sense hesitation on Monty's face.

'Please, miss,' he said. 'I need that video when I go to

the police station tomorrow.'

'Laura,' Monty gave the girl one of her hard looks. 'Perhaps you should leave the iPhone with Luke. He'll bring it back to Brussels tomorrow evening.'

'But, miss! The boys are just clowning around. They already threw it on the floor once. Ask Bernie.'

'Is this true?'

Bernie rolled his eyes. 'It wasn't me, miss.'

'It never is, is it, Bernie? It never is. Luke, give Laura back her phone. Off you go. Everyone to bed.'

Laura went rushing back down the corridor towards the girls' room. At the door, she stuck out her tongue and tauntingly waved her iPhone at Luke. With a disappointed sigh, he went back to his own dorm, Jack still on his heels.

5

In a soundproofed, claustrophobic cellar deep under central Rome, Marcello Bari, a lieutenant of the *Polizia di Stato*, spun a paperknife in his quick fingers. The others in the room were liaison officers from the Ministry of the Interior, the Ministry of Culture and the *Carabinieri*. Also present was Cardinal Guido Falcone, curator of the Vatican Museums, dressed in a charcoal suit. Once everyone was seated the lieutenant pressed a key on his laptop.

A crowd of tourists appeared on the screen, their necks craned as they gazed up at the frescoes covering the walls and ceiling of the Sistine Chapel. Then, in a storm of shocked screams and shouts, the crowd broke up, scampering for the exits. Behind the fleeing tourists a figure stood on the chapel altar, swinging a white container.

Lieutenant Bari zoomed in on the right side of *The Last Judgement*, where the damned were shown suffering the torments of Hell. The figures along the lower margin of the picture began to melt as the acid dissolved the colours into a grey blur. Then there were more shouts, and guards could be seen darting this way and that. But there was no sign of the chinless man in the raincoat.

'*Attenzione!*' the guards could be heard barking over the clamour of the blindly rushing tourists. Seconds later a tall guard wearing a peaked cap frogmarched a tall, skinny boy towards the exit.

Lieutenant Bari's fingers danced on the keyboard and he showed the men a blank screen. They shrugged their shoulders and looked at each other. Bari drew their attention to the black square at the bottom right-hand corner of the screen. It said: CAMERA 12.

'What the hell?' The *carabiniere* captain waved his arms.

'That's right. They put camera twelve out of action right before the attack.'

'All that fuss with the acid was just a smoke screen,' Cardinal Falcone added. 'While the guards were distracted, the raiders struck in room seventy-three. They stole a masterpiece – the *Burial of Christ* by Caravaggio.'

'Gentlemen. Officers.' Director Romano Simonis of the Interior Ministry stood up. His gold-rimmed spectacles flashed as he surveyed the room. 'The Italian government is ready to assist this investigation in any way it can, as requested by the Holy See.'

'The Holy Father is grateful,' said the cardinal. 'Now, I have two questions. Who was the blond, German-looking boy who was arrested and then foolishly released? And why didn't the guards in the surveillance room react in any way when the camera died?'

Hiding a sigh, Lieutenant Bari clicked on his mouse and replayed the scene of the boy's arrest. He fully expected the bureaucrats to do what they always did: blame the police. 'Allow me first to sum up the sequence of events. The Caravaggio was removed from its frame, rolled into a cylinder and smuggled out through a service exit normally only used by the museum staff. There were two thieves. One of the cleaners saw them bursting out of a door onto the Via Leone IV, but she didn't see their faces. They melted away into the traffic. They probably had a car or scooter waiting on the Piazza Risorgimento.'

'So they knew the service routes,' Simonis said, with a glance at the curator. 'Inside help…'

'Exactly,' Lieutenant Bari said. 'We'll have to interview the entire staff. As for the camera, the guards who were on duty in the surveillance room at the time are being questioned by the police as we speak.'

'Two men, you say?' Anna Buretti, the expert from the Ministry of Culture, said dryly. 'That's all we know?'

'Unfortunately, yes.' Lieutenant Bari made a gesture of supplication with his fingers then leaned over his laptop once more. 'Turning to the foreigner who was held at the scene, we know the following… He's a schoolboy called Luke Baron. He's English but lives in Brussels, and he's in Rome on a school trip. He will be formally questioned tomorrow afternoon. We're not sure what his role was, if any, but he seems to be our best eyewitness.'

'Squeeze him for everything he knows, Lieutenant.' Director Simonis began to collect his papers. With a frown at his watch he stamped across the parquet floor, glancing back only to say: 'I want regular updates night and day… I will brief the Prime Minister myself.'

The clouds drooping low over the Valle del Treja glowed a strange shade of purple in the light of the half moon. Every few minutes the quiet murmur of the river at the bottom of the valley was drowned out by the sound of a car accelerating on the road between Civita Castellana and Faleria. It was hard to believe that this drowsy spot was just fifty kilometres from Rome.

The light-green blinds of the crumbling villa hung at crazy angles, and branches thrown by the winter storms had dislodged some of the roof slates. The ochre paint had fallen off in great slabs, revealing the masonry of the eighteenth-century stone walls. Beyond the river, on the opposite side of the valley, stood an ancient castle, whose gaping windows stared over the forest like the eyes of a skull. Just south of the castle the lights of the little town of Faleria twinkled in the gloom.

The villa's large living room was furnished with a threadbare sofa, a few sagging rattan chairs and a rough-hewn oak table. In one corner stood a small TV on an upturned orange crate. The news was on.

A muscular young man with close-cropped hair dropped to a crouch in front of the TV and turned the volume all the way up, so that his companions down in the cellar could hear the newsreader's voice.

'... *The thieves that struck in the Vatican Art Museum this morning were exceptionally audacious. To distract the guards, one of the gang threw acid onto Michelangelo's* Last Judgment. *Taking advantage of the ensuing chaos, another entered room seventy-three and removed Caravaggio's* Burial of Christ *from its frame...*'

The reporter turned to interview Lieutenant Marcello Bari of the *Polizia di Stato*, who urged the public to remain vigilant, as the stolen painting was probably still in the Rome area. Then a dog-food advertisement, featuring a blonde supermodel, brought the newsflash to an abrupt end.

The young man trotted down the stairs to the cellar where a white-haired figure, wearing an immaculate linen suit and a bow tie, stood holding a cardboard cylinder in his rubber-gloved hands. A digital camera and a pair of glasses hung from the old man's neck. Together the two men removed a rolled-up canvas from the cylinder and gently spread it on the table, pinning down the corners with map weights. A Leatherman knife lay next to it.

The younger man put on a pair of dark ski goggles and a balaclava, picked up the knife and brought the blade close to the centre of Caravaggio's painting, stopping inches above the figures carrying the crucified body of Christ.

'Not so close, Achim.' The old man raised the camera and took a dozen shots in quick succession.

He studied the shots on the small screen on the back of the camera. The painting was clearly visible behind the gloved hand holding the knife.

Achim folded away his knife and pulled off the goggles and the balaclava, leaving on his rubber gloves. He rolled his strong shoulders, impatient with such fiddly work.

The old man took the memory card out of the digital camera and slipped it into the computer on a brightly lit desk in the corner of the vaulted cellar. He chose the best pictures and printed them out in colour, studying each one carefully. The texture of the painting had come out well.

'Good.' He crumpled up all the pictures. 'Burn them.'

'But—'

'I've touched them. I'll print the best one again. We mustn't contaminate the letter.'

With a nod to his boss, Achim set light to the A4 sheets and tossed the smouldering pictures into a metal bucket.

The old man leaned over the painting on the table. He was in his seventies, but in good shape physically.

'Shall we roll it up?' Achim said, picking up the cardboard tube.

'Leave that,' the man said sharply. 'I've barely started.'

6

Luke lay awake in the hostel dormitory he was sharing with a dozen other boys. Through a gap in the curtains he could just make out the ruins of the ancient Roman baths outside. They reminded him of the Ravenglass Roman Bath House, which he'd seen on a trip to Hadrian's Wall.

On their first day in Rome they'd toured the baths, and Monty had told them about Julius Caesar's expeditions to Britain in 55 and 54 B.C. It was odd to think that the Romans had been vastly superior builders and soldiers compared with the Celtic tribes that had lived in England at the time. The Romans even had spas with pools, steam rooms, under-floor heating and other such luxuries.

At midnight Luke was still tossing and turning. The hostel didn't cater much in the way of breakfast, so Monty and Miss Hart had detailed some of the pupils to prepare the morning meal at eight o'clock. Luke was on the last day's shift, which meant he'd have to be up at seven. All the other boys were asleep.

His mind kept rehearsing the strange events of the day... He'd once seen a children's game designed by the Munch Museum in Oslo, which revolved around the theft of Edvard Munch's *Scream* and *Madonna* in 2004.

He remembered thinking that such a game was likely to inspire more art thieves.

He couldn't just lie here any more. He threw off the blanket and sheet, swung his legs out of the bed and looked through the window. At that moment the half moon scudding behind the clouds floated free, like a round lantern, flooding the dormitory with its brilliant glow. It was hard to believe it was just a reflection of the sun's light.

Moving as quietly as he could, Luke eased himself down from the bunk bed, pulled on his clothes and tiptoed to the head of Jack's bed, which was next to the radiator. He gave him a firm shake, trying to make as little noise as possible. Bernie was sleeping in the bunk right above Jack's, snoring so loudly it was a wonder he didn't wake himself up.

'Mum, it's too early…' Jack groaned and tried to roll onto his other side.

'Shut up, Jack!' Luke hissed, moving to one side, so that the moonlight poured onto Jack's face.

Jack sat up blearily in his striped pyjamas.

'It's Luke. Not your mum. Get up – we've got something to do.'

'Go back to bed.'

'Listen to me.' Luke spoke in an urgent whisper. 'I need to take a closer look at that clip. We'll borrow Laura's iPhone and find an internet café where we can watch it.'

'Are you out of your mind?' Jack's protruding front teeth glowed in the moonlight. 'It's the middle of the night!'

'This is Rome, mate. They've barely finished supper! The city will still be heaving.'

With an inward smile Luke saw Jack's eyes light up with excitement. The idea of a nocturnal adventure in Rome was just too tempting. Within a minute his friend was in his jeans and hooded jacket. They crept out into the corridor.

The girls' dormitory was on the other side of the building. To get there the boys had to pass the hostel reception. A lamp inside the little office cast a weak beam through the open door. A table lamp with an old-fashioned green shade stood on the desk beside a counter bell. The small office opened out into another room, where Luke could see the end of a folding bed. In all likelihood the night porter was asleep in the back.

He tiptoed past the reception door and stopped to wait for Jack, who promptly crashed into him in the dark. At that moment a phone rang in the back room, and a grumpy male voice answered in Italian, then switched to English, giving curt replies, explaining that the hostel was full. Moving as silently as he could, Luke led the way to the girls' dormitory. There was a night light above the closed door.

'Does Miss Hart have her own room?' Jack said.

'No, she's in there with the girls.'

'In that case I'm not sure this is such a good idea.'

'If Monty was in there, we wouldn't have a chance. Old people wake up easily. But Miss Hart's young. Well, kind of.'

'Don't talk about Monty.' Jack's eyes were round and bright. 'I don't want to see her in her nightie again.'

'Stay here.' Luke pushed the door gently. 'I'll get the phone.'

Luke hastened into the dormitory – he had to act

before Jack lost it completely. He was worried that the light in the corridor would rouse one of the girls, so he closed the door behind him. It had made no sound when he entered, but it now emitted a raw screech. Someone stirred and gave a sleepy moan. Luke crouched still in the darkness, listening to the thudding of his heart.

He advanced on all fours between the bunk beds. The moonlight found a path into the room, but it entered at a slanting angle, leaving most of the floor in darkness. Luke had to stand up briefly to locate Laura's bed. He saw her handbag hanging from the corner of the top bunk.

He opened it and felt inside, but it contained nothing that was big enough to be an iPhone. Then he saw the handset on the pillow beside her head. To reach it, he had to stand right in the moonlight. Girls, it seemed to him, made much less noise than boys when they slept – assuming they all were indeed sleeping... Luke feared that one of the girls or Miss Hart might leap up at any moment and scream.

The beautiful phone felt solid in his hand. The latest model, it would be expensive to replace should anything happen to it. But Laura wouldn't miss it during the night. He quickly checked that it wasn't password protected. It wasn't. He felt uncomfortable taking something so personal, but it couldn't be helped, and he certainly wouldn't read Laura's messages, or anything.

It was impossible to advance on all fours with an iPhone in one hand, so Luke dropped to a crouch and scurried silently between the bunks to the door. He inched it open without making a sound – and almost bumped into Jack, who was now lying on his back in the corridor outside the dorm room.

'What are you doing?'

'Snoozing.'

'Get up, you nutter. We're going straight out.'

The front door of the hostel was made of wrought iron and glass. Luke took a deep breath and prepared to press the electric button in the door jamb. He knew this was the critical moment: there would be a loud buzz and the mechanism would rattle enthusiastically as the security lock opened.

He pressed the button and pushed the door ajar. It was as heavy as a gate. They waited for a few minutes. No one stirred. As they closed the door, Luke took a pencil from his pocket and wedged it between the spring-bolt and the door jamb. If no one used the door while they were out, Luke and Jack would be able to get back in without a key.

'This is almost too easy,' Luke said. 'By the way, do you have any money?'

'Some.'

'Brilliant. We'll hail a taxi on the main road.'

At that instant an outdoor light turned on, and an angry voice shouted from the reception.

7

The white-haired man pulled a disposable raincoat over his linen suit, and covered his head and face with a shower cap and a surgical breathing mask. Finally he tugged at the latex gloves on his hands, finger by finger, to ensure a snug fit.

'You've thought of every detail, Dietrich,' Achim said, cracking his knuckles.

Dietrich Grimmer shot an annoyed glance at his assistant, then pulled down the breathing mask and forced himself to speak in a mild voice.

'If my father taught me one thing, it was the value of meticulous preparation.' He adjusted his cap. 'Talking of which, as agreed, let's not mention any names unless absolutely necessary.'

'You mean this place could be bugged?'

'I've swept it for bugs twice a day. No, it isn't bugged. But we must make a habit of caution.'

'Sorry, boss.' Achim made a series of swivelling movements with his head, stretching the thick muscles in his neck.

'Routine and inattention are the enemies of control.' Grimmer pulled up his mask once more. 'I want one hundred per cent control.'

Grimmer knew that his assistant had come from a poor background and that his main asset in life had always been his physical strength. But he was also very intelligent and didn't like to be patronised. The old man used his rubber gloves to open a fresh packet of paper then printed off one photo of the Caravaggio, Achim's gloved hand and the Leatherman knife. Then he opened the case containing an old mechanical typewriter and typed a short letter. Achim watched him throughout, shifting and fidgeting.

When Grimmer had finished he tore open a packet of envelopes and smiled. 'You write the address.'

'But—'

'It's OK.' Grimmer handed Achim a marker pen and an envelope. 'I'll spell it for you.'

Achim's jaw tightened. Grimmer knew perfectly well that he wrote like a child, and was ashamed of it. But that was just the point: the police could never trace a handwriting that didn't exist.

'Use your left hand. Capital letters.'

Encased in the rubber glove, Achim's hand was even clumsier than usual. It took him ages to scrawl the letters that Grimmer dictated to him:

SIGNOR TENENTE MARCELLO BARI
POLIZIA DI STATO
DEPARTEMENTO SPEZIALE
VIA DEL QUIRINALE
00185 ROMA

Grimmer slipped the letter into the envelope, which he put into a transparent plastic bag and handed back to Achim.

40

'You know the drill?'

'Why wouldn't I? You briefed me three times.'

Grimmer listened to Achim's heavy tread as he climbed up the stairs. The front door of the villa opened and closed and the car purred away.

First the young man would drive to Roma-Nord railway station. Then he'd take the metro to Rome's central railway station, the Stazione Termini, and leave the letter in a luggage locker, memorise the number and toss the key into a rubbish bin. Then he'd drive back. Simple.

Still dressed in his protective garb, Grimmer turned to the small shelf behind the brightly lit computer desk. On it was a small aluminium suitcase. Grimmer opened it, carried it to the table and folded out a tiny field laboratory. The minuscule bottles and tubes containing liquids of different tints were neatly labelled. He laid everything out. Then he fetched the lamp from the computer desk, unscrewed the scalding bulb with the aid of a handkerchief and replaced it with an infrared one. Heart pounding, he switched off the main light and leaned over the table. He held his throbbing head in his hands for a moment.

Caravaggio's *Burial of Christ* seemed to glow in the pool of dim infrared light. With a deep intake of breath, Grimmer reached inside the field laboratory and took out a surgical scalpel.

'*Vater, Vater, siehst du mich?*' he suddenly said to himself in a slow, strangled whisper. 'Father, Father, are you watching me?'

Bernie Sidebottom let out a huge snore, so loud he woke himself up.

He looked around and realised it was still the middle of the night, so he climbed out of bed quietly and started towards the bathroom, bare feet slapping on the cold stone floor. As he got to the end of Jack's bunk a tempting thought came to his mind: why not give that goofy rabbit a good fright? Bernie felt wide awake and he was famous for his pranks – celebrated, he himself believed – and Jack was his favourite victim.

He reached up to his bunk, stripped the pillowcase off the pillow and draped it over his head, leaving just a narrow slit for the eyes. Then he bent down to the bunk beneath his own and leaned close to Jack's head.

'Boo!' he said.

But as he tried to shake his classmate awake he realised there was no one in Jack's bed.

'Bernie Sidebottom, what on earth are you up to?'

Bernie swung round and saw Miss Hart standing behind him, dressed in a silk nightdress and a pair of slippers. She folded her arms and shook her head.

'I thought I heard something…'

'You take that thing off your head and go back to your own bed right now.'

Bernie pulled off the pillowcase. 'It's Jack,' he said. 'He's disappeared.'

'Keep your voice down.' Miss Hart's eyes flashed with anger. 'He's probably in the bathroom. Why are you always teasing him? Day and night!'

Bernie skulked back to his own bed. He could hear Miss Hart's footsteps as she checked the boys' bathroom, then the TV room…Bernie rose onto his elbow and peered across from his bunk and suddenly realised that Luke wasn't in his bed, either. He rushed out of the dormitory and found Miss Hart in the corridor outside.

'Miss! Luke's disappeared as well!'

'Are you sure?'

'What if they've been kidnapped?'

'Don't be ridiculous.'

Miss Hart followed Bernie back into the silent dormitory and checked under the beds of both missing boys, then told Bernie to wait in the corridor while she went to tell Monty.

Two minutes later Miss Hart was sitting at the foot of Monty's bed. The loudly ticking, old-fashioned, folding alarm clock on the night table said quarter to one. There was a vaguely medical smell in the room – Vick's chest rub, or something.

'I used to think that lad was destined for public service,' Monty said, dialling Luke's number on her mobile phone, squinting over her glasses. 'That he could be prime minister one day.'

'Full-time public nuisance, more likely,' Miss Hart said. 'Still, I hope he's OK.'

'It's ringing...No answer.'

'Let's try Jack instead.'

Operating her cheap phone with slow deliberation, Monty dialled the other missing boy. Again the phone rang, and again there was no answer.

'I can hear a phone...' Miss Hart got to her feet. 'Now it's stopped.'

Moments later Bernie appeared at the door, with Jack's travel bag in his hand. 'This started ringing,' he said, pulling a phone from the bag. 'I thought you should know.'

'We are indebted to you, Bernie Sidebottom.' Monty stared expressionlessly over her glasses. 'Now tell me, what is *your* home phone number, again?'

Bernie went white. 'Why, miss?'

'I want to talk to your father.'

'What, now?'

'No, Bernie, not now. Unless you think now would be a good time? Just give me the number.'

Still holding Jack's bag, Bernie dictated his phone number.

'Thank you. That will be all. You can leave Jack's belongings with me here.'

Bernie put the travel bag on the floor and handed the mobile to Monty. 'I don't see why you're giving *me* a hard time. I'm not the one who's gone missing.'

'More's the pity.'

Bernie looked stunned. He let out the first few notes of his customary nervous giggle, then made a quick exit.

'Why did you ask for his parents' phone number?'

'Keep him on his toes,' Monty said. 'Intolerable brat.'

8

Luke and Jack jogged down the Via del'Amba Aradam, towards the Basilica of St John Lateran. The night air felt pleasantly warm and the honking traffic made it easy to forget the lateness of the hour. Unfortunately the night porter at the hostel had seen them leave, which would mean problems later. Jack had stopped in his tracks like the frightened rabbit he resembled when the porter had called after them, but Luke had pulled him into the shadow of a tall hedge.

In the taxi Luke had watched the video clip over and over again, searching for clues until his eyes were sore. He was absolutely sure that the stranger caught on Laura's iPhone in St Peter's Square was indeed the acid attacker, but it was impossible to see much detail on the small screen of the phone.

'We should have stopped at that internet café the taxi took us to.'

'No, we need up-to-date software and a fast connection.'

Luke glanced at his friend. Jack's exhilaration had worn off as soon as they'd arrived in the city centre, and now he looked scared out of his wits.

'Listen, Luke,' Jack sighed, cheeks red, buck teeth jutting. 'Shouldn't we be talking to the police?'

'I'll have that pleasure tomorrow. It would be nice to actually have something to report.'

'Look!'

They stopped to peer through the window of a café, where yet another TV screen showed footage from St Peter's Square, followed by close-ups of the vandalised fresco and the stolen Caravaggio. Luke felt a pinching in his stomach, but he disguised his nerves by walking even faster.

'Wait for me!' Jack was starting to talk in a wheedling voice. 'If we hadn't been seen I wouldn't mind... But Monty's probably throwing a fit...'

'Go back if you like.' Luke knew that facing their teachers now rather than later wouldn't change anything. 'As for me, I'll watch that clip on a proper screen tonight, no matter what it takes.'

'But—'

'Where's your curiosity?' Luke spun round and gave vent to his feelings. 'If everyone was like you we'd still be sitting around in caves wearing loin cloths and eating grilled mammoth. In fact, we'd be eating it raw.'

They arrived in the square in front of the Basilica and the Lateran Palace, where a huge obelisk stabbed at the moonlit sky. From here, Luke knew, they could take the Via Merulana to the Papal Basilica of Santa Maria Maggiore, which was just a few blocks from Termini railway station. The station attracted thousands of backpackers, and there would surely be lots of all-night cybercafés there.

'OK, you win.' Jack gave an uncertain grin. 'Let's do this thing.'

'Good man.' Luke slapped him on the back. 'That clip could solve this whole case. Besides, when else will we get to hang out in Rome in the middle of the night?'

At that precise moment back at the hostel Miss Hart pressed the reception bell and smiled apologetically as the night porter, Signor Sordi, clambered from the back room to the desk, his face crumpled with sleep.

'Sorry to disturb you,' she said. 'We're missing two boys.'

'That explains it.'

'Explains what?'

'I saw them slip out. Some time after midnight.'

'Why didn't you stop them?'

'*Signora*, this isn't a prison, you know.'

Miss Hart suddenly felt as though she might cry. Luke and Jack were lively boys, sometimes even boisterously wild, but they were two of her favourite pupils. She felt bitterly betrayed by them and she feared for their safety. Where on earth had they gone at this hour?

Signor Sordi took a swig of water from a glass behind the desk.

'Here in Italy,' he said, wiping his mouth. 'Boys that age don't go out alone in the middle of the night.'

'Not just in Italy,' Miss Hart said. 'I need to tell my colleague.'

Miss Hart went back to Monty's room and told her what Signor Sordi had seen.

'I knew it. They're somewhere in central Rome, larking about, leaving a trail of disaster behind them.' Monty lay back on her pillows and pulled up the covers, bedsprings squeaking under her fearsome weight. 'This city has survived the Sabines, the Barbarians and the Nazis. But can it survive Luke and Jack?'

'Shouldn't we . . . call the police?'

'I already have. They said to call again in the morning if the boys haven't turned up.' Monty heaved onto her side and closed her eyes. 'My guess is they will. I also left Luke another message. We've done what we can. Go and get some sleep.'

Miss Hart turned out the light and tiptoed back to her bed in the girls' dormitory.

Luke and Jack stood in front of the service desk in a 24/7 internet café on the Via Principe Amedeo. Most such establishments in the area, of which there were dozens, were run by Indians and Pakistanis. This one seemed to be an Indian place, Luke noted, looking at the red bindi between the eyebrows of the beautiful woman at the counter. He knew the round mark was a Hindu tradition.

'*Ciao*,' the woman said, fluttering her heavily painted eyelids. 'How can I help you guys?'

Luke saw Jack blush deep red, and he felt his own face change colour as well.

'We'd like to use a computer . . .'

'Number four is free.'

'Thanks. And would you happen to have a USB cable?'

The woman pulled out a drawer and dug around in the chaos inside, then just handed Luke the whole thing.

'Good luck! There should be one in there somewhere.'

Luke quickly spotted a FireWire cable, and Jack helped him to extract it from the tangle. They went over to the computer, which was next to a row of telephone booths where travellers and immigrants from all corners of the earth were busy speaking to their loved ones in a multitude of languages. Others were Skyping. The keyboards clicked hectically under the bright lights.

'I'm thirsty,' Jack said. 'You want something?'

'A Coke, please.'

Jack selected drinks from the fridge beside the service desk.

Luke took out his phone. He had a message from Monty ordering the boys to return to the hostel by taxi immediately. She sounded more and more like the legendary field marshal every day, Luke thought to himself. He was pretty sure the police had already been contacted, but it was best not to worry Jack with that particular detail.

Luke put down his phone just as Jack returned with the cold cans.

'Monty tried to ring again,' Luke said. 'She's missing us, but she's not panicking, so don't worry.'

'Oh, no . . . We should ring back.'

'No,' Luke said. 'Let's just text to say we're all right. Do you mind doing it?'

'I guess. She'll go ballistic, you know.'

Luke handed his phone to Jack, took the iPhone from his pocket and reached behind the workstation to attach the cable.

Jack showed him what he'd written:

In town, safe and sound. Back soon. Jack and Luke.

'Short but sweet.' Luke switched off the phone and winked at his friend. 'And now . . . Let's concentrate.'

Sergeant Gianni Calabrese, on duty at the *polizia* headquarters, leaned back in his chair. On the scuffed desk before him a small television blared, whipping up excitement for the forthcoming thriller between AS Roma and SS Lazio.

The sergeant pulled up his sleeve to look at his watch. Almost one o'clock. The new girl at the adjacent Bar Marco had yet to bring him his nightly espresso.

He was about to phone the bar to announce he'd henceforth take his custom elsewhere when the telephone rang under his hand, giving him an unpleasant jolt. The number of the duty officer wasn't listed. The only calls that came through were from other police units working on cases of national significance.

'*Pronto*,' he said.

There was silence on the line, and then a male voice dictated a few words in a tone so flat it had to be a speech-simulator. '*Stazione Termini. Luggage locker number two hundred and eighteen. A letter concerning the Vatican Museums.*'

That was all. Sergeant Calabrese's eyes shot to his computer screen. He called up the telephone log. A pre-paid mobile. Untraceable. Breathing quickly, clutching the handset, Calabrese pressed the fast-dial button for Lieutenant Marcello Bari.

Luke could feel his hands shaking slightly as he enlarged the video that was now streaming from Laura's iPhone onto the large, flat screen in front of him. He rewound it a little, then froze on a frame that showed a man wearing a beige raincoat.

'That's it,' he said. 'His raincoat looks much too big for him. It was obviously for hiding the acid container.'

Jack leaned closer to the screen.

50

'It's definitely him,' Luke continued. 'Bald forehead, dark rings around his eyes, and that nose!'

'It's the chin I'm more worried about.' Jack's eyes seemed ready to pop out of their sockets. 'Did he, like, swallow it?'

The image leaped about at random. Laura had probably forgotten to switch off the video function on her iPhone between shots of her giggling friends. Luke pressed PLAY again. The phone swung round erratically. Moments later the man was in the frame once more, close up, but seen from behind.

'No close-up of the face,' Luke slapped his hands onto his thighs. 'Rotten luck.'

Jack kept glancing around. 'Main thing is this guy doesn't suddenly turn up here.'

'What are the odds of that happening?'

'The sooner the clip's with the police the better.'

Luke pressed PLAY once more, then took a pair of earphones from his pocket, plugged them into the iPhone and listened to the soundtrack. The chatter of the crowd, car horns, an American voice, Laura complaining about the heat... Then something strange happened. The man in the scruffy beige raincoat brought his sleeve close to his mouth and said something in Italian. His face wasn't in the frame, but his words were clearly audible.

'We've got his voice!' Luke leaned closer to the screen.

He rewound the sequence and cupped his hands over his earphones, straining to hear.

'What's he saying?'

'It's in Italian. Wait!'

Luke copied the voice onto his MP3 player, went to

the woman at the service desk and played her the sound, asking what the sentence meant.

'Play it one more time,' she said, and put the earphones in again. Her accent was Italian, not Indian, and her English was rudimentary.

'OK, now I have it. The man says: *"I'm ready to go in. See you in Faleria. Bow Tie is waiting in his cellar"*.'

'What is Faleria?' Luke said, trying to hide his excitement.

'No idea. Maybe a place somewhere. Or a restaurant, or something.' The woman turned to serve a new customer.

'The police better give me a medal for this tomorrow,' Luke said, patting the pocket containing his MP3 player. He pulled out the USB cable and put Laura's iPhone away too.

'Today, you mean,' Jack said, showing his watch. 'Let's go.'

9

Heavy tyres screamed on the asphalt as a pair of armoured personnel carriers raced up to the main doors of the Termini railway station on the Piazza del Cinquecento. Teams of *carabinieri* jumped out, their fluorescent belts shining in the glare of the flashing blue lights. The sound of the sirens echoed off the station façade. Twenty men in all sprinted into the station building and fanned out in an orderly fashion, taking the space under their control and beginning the evacuation.

A small unmarked lorry quietly pulled up beside the personnel carriers. It belonged to the bomb-disposal unit of the Italian Army's anti-terrorist unit. Chained onto the bed of the lorry was an Israeli bomb-disposal robot.

'Who called you?' the black-clad sergeant demanded.

Making no reply, the soldiers in camouflage jackets took their positions around the vehicle. The sergeant was about to repeat his question when he saw another figure leap out of the cab, Lieutenant Marcello Bari of the *Polizia di Stato*, who'd spoken on television about the attack in the Sistine Chapel. Then a man in a dark suit and gold-rimmed spectacles appeared: Director Romano Simonis of the Interior Ministry, the official at the very

53

summit of the Italian police hierarchy.

The sergeant stood to attention, boot heels snapping together. The two men ignored him and walked briskly towards the station. A small crowd of onlookers gawped at the proceedings from a safe distance.

Lieutenant Bari and Director Simonis pushed through the chain of *carabinieri* and stepped up to a stack of metal luggage-lockers. A bomb-disposal expert from the anti-terrorist unit zipped up his fireproof overalls and pulled on a pair of padded gauntlets that reached all the way to his armpits. The entire station had now been evacuated. The bright torches of the soldiers licked the walls. Radios crackled in the eerie silence.

Lieutenant Bari was quietly convinced that no explosives would be found in the locker, but the guidelines had to be followed. The bomb-disposal robot had climbed down the ramp at the back of the lorry and was inching its way through the deserted station towards the luggage lockers.

Luke stopped dead in his tracks and Jack bumped into him from behind. The pulsing blue lights of at least a dozen police cars cast lurid tints on the faces of the onlookers behind the fluorescent yellow safety cordon in the square outside the station.

'What's this now?' Luke said, tensing. His temples were pounding with exhaustion, but the unexpected nocturnal drama gave him an unnatural energy boost.

'Whatever it is, let's *not* stick our noses in,' Jack hissed. 'Got it?'

'No curiosity, that's your problem,' Luke said. 'Remember those troglodytes eating raw meat.'

Jack charged on ahead towards the taxi rank. Luke reluctantly trotted after him, glancing back at the severe-looking men guarding the station entrance. They wore orange reflector vests with P3/E stencilled on the back. Luke had long been planning a career as a crime detective or an intelligence agent, or maybe even an explorer. It seemed inevitable Jack would opt for librarianship or accountancy or some other boring office job.

'Ready when you are, *Tenente*,' said the expert from the bomb-disposal unit, saluting with his massive gauntlet. 'Shall we open the door?'

The hydraulic power-cutters were ready.

'This is easier,' Bari said, handing the man the universal key for the luggage lockers, which the station master had just brought him.

Director Simonis stood pointedly close to the locker but Bari drew him aside. They watched from behind the next row of lockers as the bomb-disposal expert took off one of his gauntlets to slip the key into the lock. He put the glove back on and used a device like a pair of long pliers to turn the key, standing well to one side.

The locker sprang open. There was no bomb. All that was required of the specially trained officer was to pull out a plastic bag marked with the logo of a Godiva chocolate shop. Inside was a light-brown padded envelope addressed to Lieutenant Bari in a childish scrawl.

He was about to step forward to examine the envelope when something emitted a buzzing sound behind him. The robot had reached the lockers and now came to a halt with a faint mechanical squeal. Bari barked an order and the machine went into reverse, retreating like an oversized toy.

'We must check for bio-agents.' The bomb-disposal expert was about to drop the envelope into a container that looked like a miniature aquarium.

'Stop your clowning around and open it.'

The man opened the padded envelope and pulled out a single sheet of paper: a colour print-out of a digital photograph.

Bari gasped as he saw the image on the sheet.

Caravaggio's *Burial of Christ*. And poised menacingly above the canvas was a gloved hand holding a Leatherman knife.

'Is that all?' asked Director Simonis, who had quietly appeared at Bari's side.

Bari and Simonis looked at the bomb-disposal expert, who shook the envelope in his hand. Another A4 sheet came floating out. Bari caught it in mid-air and saw immediately that the letter had been hammered out on an old-fashioned, mechanical typewriter.

Luke was sitting beside Jack on the small bench in front of the hostel reception. Monty towered before them in her tartan dressing gown, gazing over her half-moon glasses. Miss Hart, who had pulled her outdoor jacket on top of her silk nightdress, was standing next to Monty with her arms folded and her mouth drawn into an angry line. Behind the reception desk, Signor Sordi had found a football match on one of the television channels. The green screen flickered high on the wall.

'You want me to call the police again, Luke?' Monty said in a voice that was pure ice. 'So you can have more fun? At this rate I'll be the next one to be arrested.'

Monty had just informed the police that the missing

56

boys had reappeared soon after two a.m. However, Luke had asked her to call them back, offering to hand in the clip from Laura's iPhone.

'It's not about fun, Miss Montgomery.' Luke stared at the tiled floor. 'The face of the acid attacker is on the tape. It's vital evidence.'

'Then give it to the police when you are interrogated tomorrow.'

'But it's urgent—'

'What's urgent is that you reflect hard on your misconduct.' Monty pulled the belt of her dressing gown tighter. 'Rome is a dangerous city at night, and we have rules, which you appear to ignore.'

'We're really sorry, Miss Montgomery,' Jack piped in.

'If Bernie hadn't alerted us it might have been hours before your disappearance was noticed. Luckily he has a sense of responsibility and we were able to report you to the police.'

Luke and Jack glanced at each other.

'Miss Hart, be sure to learn from this charade,' Monty said. 'Juveniles absconding into the night then trying to run rings around their teachers. The lesson is this: never trust a boy. Miss Hart? Are you listening?'

'I agree...' Miss Hart made a sudden movement with her hand, which was half inside her jacket pocket. 'Luke and I should take the video clip with us to the police station...'

'I'm sorry, but I think it's more urgent than that,' Luke said. 'I know what I'm talking about.'

'Common mistake among children your age.' Monty suddenly stepped up to her colleague. 'Miss Hart. Who are you texting?'

Miss Hart's eyes widened and her cheeks went completely red. 'I wasn't . . .' She pulled a mobile from her jacket pocket. 'I was just—'

At that moment the phone emitted a beep and Monty grabbed it from Miss Hart's hand, reading the newly arrived text.

'*Con amore, Paolo.*' She handed the phone back with a look of deep revulsion. 'I can only hope this amorous tryst will not interfere with your sense of responsibility tomorrow.'

'Paolo knows his way around Rome,' Miss Hart said timidly. 'We could use his help.'

Monty was already striding over to the reception desk. Senor Sordi stood up, nodding and blinking.

'Mr Sordi, I want that door locked for the rest of the night. Do I make myself clear?'

'Yes, *signora.*'

'Everyone to bed.' Monty waved her arm like a drill sergeant. 'Right now.'

As Jack and Luke filed past her Monty stared hard at them over her glasses. Even Miss Hart loped away with her head bowed like a guilty pupil.

'Good night, Miss Montgomery,' Luke said. 'And I'm sorry if my natural curiosity has caused problems.'

'Your problems are only starting,' Monty said. 'Should the Italian police find the slightest fault in your conduct, you will be expelled.'

'Phew!' Jack said as they padded down the corridor towards their dormitory. 'I hope I'm not expelled, even if you are. Dad wants me to go to Cambridge. If I stay friends with you, I'm more likely to end up in a juvenile detention centre.'

'It'll blow over.'

'Night, then.' Jack tiptoed to his bed next to the radiator.

Luke could hear Bernie stirring in the bunk above Jack's.

'Where have you been?' Bernie whispered. 'They almost called your parents – and mine!'

'You sneak, you almost ruined everything,' Jack said.

'What's going on?'

'The police were here.'

'Really?'

'Yeah,' Jack continued, lowering his voice to a hiss. 'Monty's been arrested.'

Luke strained his ears, grinning in the darkness.

'Monty…' Bernie said uncertainly. 'What for?'

'Money laundering,' Jack whispered. 'She's been laundering euros with her underwear. She's going to prison for a long, long time.'

'And you're an idiot.'

'Tomorrow, everyone will be told what *you* are.'

That silenced Bernie. In his bed Luke had to bury his face in his pillow to stop himself from laughing out loud. Soon Jack and Bernie were both snoring.

Luke's limbs were leaden with fatigue, but his mind wouldn't stop spinning. He felt as though he'd been given sections of a puzzle that didn't join up.

The words spoken by the vandal in St Peter's Square echoed in his brain.

'I'm ready to go in. See you in Faleria. Bow Tie is waiting in his cellar…'

What was 'Faleria'? Some murky café or restaurant where secret meetings were held? 'Bow Tie' sounded like

59

a nickname. What could be done with these leads? Not much. Nevertheless Luke began to formulate a plan of action in his head. Rome was a huge, chaotic city, and the only hope of making progress was to proceed systematically.

The birds were already clearing their throats in the olive trees outside the hostel. He resigned himself to a completely sleepless night. In the morning he would go online and search for 'Faleria'. The phone book and the Yellow Pages for Rome would be the obvious place to start, he decided.

Then he had a vivid falling sensation as sleep swept him away.

10

Dawn had broken over the old villa on the outskirts of Faleria, colouring the hazy sky light pink. Cicadas chattered in the stand of fig trees. Every few minutes a tomcat somewhere in the distance let out a furious yowl.

'Ninety-eight, ninety-nine, one hundred.' Achim rolled onto his back after the last push-up to catch his breath. Having been woken by the cat, he was exercising even earlier than usual. He sprung to his feet and did a couple of squats, but the floorboards squeaked under the weight of his muscular body – Grimmer was still asleep in his own room, so Achim lay down on the carpet and did a hundred sit-ups instead.

Yowl, went the cat in the distance. Another one seemed to reply, close by, then another. The whole region was infested with them.

Achim pulled on his jacket and trousers and crept down the stairs to the ground floor. He slipped out of the back door and walked across the burgeoning garden towards the plane tree in the corner of the plot, where the tip of a cigarette glowed in the milky light.

'I'll take over.'

'You're early.' Lorenzo stepped up to meet him, an extinguished torch in one hand, a cigarette in the other.

'I woke up before the alarm. Those wretched cats should be shot.'

Lorenzo handed him the torch. 'All this watching is pointless, if you ask me. I fell asleep on my feet.'

'I wouldn't mention that to Bow Tie. And you've left the balcony door open again.'

Achim watched as the bald-headed, chinless Lorenzo entered the villa via the back entrance. A light was turned on in an upstairs window, then Lorenzo closed the balcony door and the light was switched off. The balcony was impossible to access from outside without a long ladder but Grimmer nevertheless insisted that all windows and doors be kept shut at night, including upstairs. The man was obsessive, Achim thought. Obsessive and driven. It was a wonder he slept at all.

In fact, Grimmer was awake. Down in the cellar, he was studying the results of the chemical consistency analysis he'd completed during the night. Lying on a sheet of blotting paper on the table before him was Caravaggio's masterpiece. A microscope stood on the floor beside a coffee cup and a Thermos flask. The old man's white hair glowed in the light of the infrared bulb.

Caravaggio, the Baroque genius, had changed his mind several times over, painting half a dozen layers on the same canvas, taking particular pains with the tormented face of the dead Christ. Dietrich Grimmer knew that multiple layers were often found in ancient oil paintings and that, sometimes, pre-existing sketches of some completely different subject were preserved under the finished work.

But something was wrong with this specimen. The results obtained from the cross section taken from the corner of the canvas were surprising. And they told Grimmer he was on the right track. He rubbed his eyes and took the top off the Thermos flask at the foot of his chair. Empty. He pushed the metal flask away, knocking it over. It fell with a sharp rattle, rolling across the floor. He'd been up for twenty hours straight and it was beginning to show. But he had the stamina to keep going as long as was needed.

The canvas was strangely thick. Why? He reached for a digital micrometre and, in order to be sure, measured the thickness in five more places. The result was clear.

There were two canvases, one glued on top of the other.

'Boss . . .'

Grimmer leaped up in his seat. 'Achim?'

'I thought I heard something, boss. What are you doing?'

Grimmer pointed at the flask on the floor. 'Go and make more coffee.'

Achim kneeled to pick up the Thermos and stopped beside the table, watching the old man work. Grimmer reached for the surgical scalpel he'd slipped into his shirt pocket and eased it between the two canvases. Only the edges were attached. He took a deep breath, taming the slight tremor that had appeared in his hands, put on the glasses that hung from his neck and moved the blade in a slow, sawing movement.

'This will take a while. Bring me my coffee.'

By the time he heard Achim's springy athlete's tread descending the cellar stairs once more Grimmer had separated the two canvases. Caravaggio's *Burial of Christ* remained on the table, and the other painting, which had been glued to the back of the Caravaggio, was already rolled into a separate cardboard tube.

'Is there a second painting?'

'So it would seem.' Grimmer marched to the safe at the back of the cellar and put the cylinder inside. He locked the safe by typing in the right combination and heaved a sigh of relief. Then he stretched his arms and straightened his bow tie. 'But the Caravaggio is the one we wanted.'

'And will they pay up?'

'Oh yes.' Grimmer blew into the coffee in his enamel mug. 'Get the mattress from my bed, would you? I need a nap.'

'You'll sleep down here?'

'I will.'

Achim trotted up the stairs as told. Grimmer unscrewed the infrared bulb from the desk lamp and replaced it with a normal one. He knew he wouldn't be able to sleep – not after what he'd just discovered – but he was worn out, and didn't trust himself to handle the precious materials with sufficient care until he'd rested. As he'd assumed, a dark secret was hidden inside Caravaggio's painting. It was more or less what he'd expected, yet it felt completely unreal. It was grand, terrifying, masterful . . . And no one else knew about it.

Achim brought the mattress and Grimmer lay down on it, taking off his shoes and bow tie and undoing the top button of his shirt. Outside, the birdsong was getting louder and he knew the sun would soon be high in the sky, but down in the cellar, complete darkness reigned, even at noon.

The Italian police believed that the masterpiece had been stolen for purposes of blackmail. Had they known the real reason, their blood would have run cold and they too would have had trouble sleeping.

'*Vater, Vater, siehst du mich?*' Grimmer murmured to himself, his brow creasing into an anguished frown. 'Father, Father, are you watching me?'

A large retractable screen covered the back wall of the conference room in the Palazzo Quirinale. Lieutenant Marcello Bari would have liked to have rested his eyes on the exquisite hunt motif of the ornate wallpaper behind the screen, but this was not the time for aesthetic pleasure. The crisis group overseeing the investigation of the Caravaggio heist was again meeting on the lavish premises of the Interior Ministry, a privilege that reflected the national significance of the crime.

The Italian government wanted everyone to know it was very, very tough on art theft. This was not a country where you could get away with a cultural crime like the successive Munch thefts in Norway, or the theft of Van Gogh's *Poppy Flowers*, a painting valued at thirty-two million pounds, from a museum in Cairo. Italy relished its cultural heritage, which sustained the country's tourist industry and had to be protected at all costs. Michelangelo, Caravaggio, Da Vinci: these were great names, deeply engraved in the Italian soul.

Director Simonis nodded at his secretary, who pressed a key on the laptop, beaming the *Burial of Christ* onto the screen. Inches from the precious canvas a gloved hand brandished a sharp knife. The photo, found together with the ransom letter in the luggage locker at the Stazione

Termini, contained no indication of the date it had been taken, but the experts had deemed it genuine. Alas, Caravaggio's masterpiece was in the hands of a highly professional gang.

'Item nine A,' Simonis said, leaning forward in his Rococo chair.

The letter appeared on the screen. The characters were uneven: a mechanical typewriter had been used.

The secretary read out the words:

'We have the Caravaggio. We will destroy it unless you pay a ransom: nine hundred grams of Aerangis *orchid petals from Madagascar. We will provide delivery instructions by eleven o'clock tomorrow morning.'*

Lieutenant Bari immediately looked at his watch. Five to ten already.

'Orchid petals?' snorted Bari. 'What's this, a joke?'

'If only. Do you know how much just under a kilo of those petals cost? Three million euros. These are professionals. They know exactly what they're up to.' Director Simonis fished his gold-rimmed glasses from the pocket of his shirt and prepared to read from a printed email. He paused for effect, flourishing the sheet of paper before reading from it.

'The petals of the Aerangis *orchid are used as a natural fragrance ingredient by the perfume industry. This rare flower is particularly rich in ethereal oils, and a thriving black market has sprung up. The perfume industry has no mechanism for tracing the origin of this precious raw material.'*

Silence filled the conference room.

'Tricky.' Anna Buretti from the Ministry of Culture was the first to speak. 'If we meet the demand we're encouraging future blackmailers. Yet what can we do?

The Caravaggio is a national treasure. The credibility of the government is at stake.'

'The Holy See agrees,' said Cardinal Guido Falcone, stroking the sleeve of his dark suit. 'As the curator of the Vatican Museums, I take responsibility for the lapse in security that allowed this outrage to happen. We will review and upgrade security without delay. Meanwhile, His Holiness has authorised the payment of the ransom. The only problem is it will take a miracle to find such a huge quantity of petals at such short notice.'

'That shouldn't be a problem for the Holy See,' Bari quipped, but no one laughed.

'In fact, we've solved that.' Simonis took off his glasses and waved them around. 'We already have half a kilo from a French perfume manufacturer in the Grasse area, and we're negotiating with an Indian wholesaler for the rest.'

'It's a lot of money.' Cardinal Falcone plucked a handkerchief from the breast pocket of his dark suit and wiped his brow. 'A lot of money for the Vatican.'

'Look on the bright side!' Anna Buretti was smiling. 'If all goes well, the events will only increase the value of the Caravaggio.'

Buretti was an attractive woman. With an inward smile, Bari watched her basking in the attention of the men around the table.

'What do you mean?' Cardinal Falcone said.

'Think of the precedents.' Buretti's voice was almost cheerful – she was clearly relieved that the Vatican would foot the entire bill for the ransom. 'The Tate in London paid 3.3 million to recover two stolen Turners. The publicity put a rocket under their market value – the price doubled.'

'Same thing with the *Mona Lisa*,' Simonis said, refusing to be upstaged. 'Stolen in 1911, and the centre of worldwide fascination ever since.'

'Exactly,' Buretti laughed. 'It's surprising no gallery has faked a robbery, just to attract fame and visitors.'

Cardinal Falcone cleared his throat and said in a mock-serious voice, 'What are you insinuating?'

'My dear cardinal!' Buretti fluttered her eyelids, practically flirting with the man. 'The Holy See is above such conniving. And your collections are priceless, being the finest in the world.'

'So the Pope will pay the ransom. That seems only fitting.' Simonis fixed the cardinal with a cold stare. 'Let us not forget, however, that the Ministry of the Interior has also incurred expenses.'

Cardinal Falcone nodded. 'The Holy See is most grateful. Like Rome as a whole the Vatican benefits from the tourists who come to admire our collections of spiritual art.'

'While we're talking about money,' Bari spoke for the first time, 'can someone explain to me why the ransom is so small? Three million! The Caravaggio is worth at least double that.'

This brought a hush over the room.

'Be that as it may,' Simonis eventually said. 'I must reiterate the need for absolute discretion in this matter. On no account should we reveal that any ransom whatsoever has been paid.'

'Naturally, naturally…' Cardinal Falcone was all nods and smiles under Simonis's stare.

'Finally, let us not lose focus of the objective at hand,' Simonis said. 'Catching these criminals. Our best opportunity will be when we exchange the painting for the petals. The field operation is being led by the finest man we have. Lieutenant Bari.'

'Thank you, Director.'

'You have my full support,' Simonis replied. 'No one must know of the ransom. And if anything pops up in the media we'll know it came from somebody in this room.'

Simonis got to his feet and beckoned his secretary, who opened the double doors, admitting the catering trolley that had been waiting outside.

'While we wait let us refresh ourselves.' Simonis beckoned his guests towards the trolley. 'Sandwiches, coffee, biscotti and mineral water. No one leaves the building before we hear more from this gang.'

1 1

Grimmer dried his hands and adjusted his bow tie in the bathroom mirror. After a wet shave he'd splashed his face with ice-cold water, and his mind now fizzed with new energy. Neatly brushed as usual, his white hair was thinning in the middle, but his eyes were bright, like a child's.

He looked at his watch, wondering what the Italian police might be doing to catch him. *Let them try*... Out in the garden the cicadas made a relentless ticking sound. A cat screeched. Grimmer loved cats, and he used to have a dog, but his current lifestyle didn't allow for pets. He had two homes, one near Munich in Bavaria, and another one in Paraguay, South America.

He peered into the kitchen and saw Achim sleeping at the table, head resting on those powerful arms. Or was he sleeping? There was something unpredictable about the young man. Orders got obeyed, but there were searching glances, sudden questions and other signs of too much curiosity. And yet Grimmer trusted Achim more than he did his Italian assistants, having personally saved the Ukrainian youth from a Bavarian young-offenders' institution, almost adopting him as his own son, and training him over the course of many years.

In the living room the TV was blaring out a manic quiz show on Channel Five, but Giuliano Megúcci had obviously long given up following it. Tired out by his recent duties, he was fast asleep on the sofa, pencil moustache twitching to the rhythm of his dream. His brother Lorenzo was snoring upstairs, gathering strength for the night watch.

Moving with calm steps, although his mind was running at an exuberant sprint, Dietrich Grimmer switched off the TV, then padded softly down to the cellar. *Trust people, and distrust them too.* That was one of his father's sayings. Old Heinrich Grimmer had imparted many principles to his son, shaping the way he saw the world. Having darkened the boy's childhood, he'd also prepared the path that Dietrich would follow throughout adulthood and into old age. Sometimes it had felt as though the journey was too long, the path too perilous, the price too high. But tonight Dietrich Grimmer's step was light, for he knew he was about to reach his destination.

He'd been just ten years old when his father had died. Throughout his childhood the old man used to call him to his armchair beside the fireplace, asking him to solve a few multiplication problems, then moving on to calculus and algorithms... The beautiful discipline of mathematics, and especially its unsolved problems, were the old man's great love. He worked as an actuary, calculating probabilities and assessing risks for a major German insurance company, then joined a large bank. During the Third Reich, the bank had been taken over by the Nazis. Grimmer senior was then transferred to work for the German National Bank – the Reichsbank, becoming

Head Cashier. The Nazi leadership soon heard of his brilliant reputation – including Adolf Eichmann, the notorious transportation administrator who master-minded the mass murder of Europe's Jews…

At the very end of the war, when the SS had begun spiriting away the Nazis' massive stockpile of gold, currency and artworks, Eichmann entrusted Heinrich Grimmer with a secret task, the details of which his son Dietrich had partially uncovered in his father's archive…All he knew for certain was that Eichmann had assigned two assistants to support Heinrich Grimmer in his mission – SS officers Ivan Balanchuk and Otto Schmitz – men who had committed acts of unspeakable cruelty at the Treblinka death camp earlier in the war.

Grimmer's heart was beating too fast. What exactly had his father done for Eichmann? Was there some dreadful mystery hidden in the canvas behind the stolen Caravaggio? Like an archaeologist about to break the seal on a tomb lost for a thousand years he felt a thrill that seemed to light up his whole being – a thrill tinged with fear.

He sat in the chair next to the table and calmed his breathing before kneeling beside the safe once more. He punched in the code and pulled out the tube containing the canvas that had been glued to the back of the Caravaggio. It was this second canvas that interested him. Undoubtedly the *Burial of Christ* was a priceless master-piece, but it was impossible to sell, except perhaps to some stinking-rich oligarch or Mafioso. Even *trying* to unload such a painting would have been fraught with risk. *Kein danke*. No, stealing the Caravaggio had been just a small but necessary step on a much longer journey, and he'd be happy to hand it back – for a modest reward.

Before unrolling the second canvas Grimmer pulled on a pair of white cotton gloves. The painting was of an apple-cheeked shepherdess against a backdrop of three hills, with a clumsy, bright-yellow squiggle representing the sun – a sentimental scene done in the Romantic style of the nineteenth century. The signature was illegible, the artist unknown. And he deserved to be unknown, Grimmer reflected, turning the canvas onto its face and smoothing it against the wooden desk before reaching for his hand-held UV torch.

He slid the beam over the back, covering every inch of the painting. Then he repeated the operation.

Nothing.

He felt an unpleasant stabbing sensation in his chest. He thought he could hear his father's voice, taunting him...

Dietrich, you can do better than that...

Each night, at his father's knee, he had been humiliated. The routine never varied. First, the questions would be easy. Then they would be hard. Finally, right before sending his son off to bed, Heinrich Grimmer would ask a question that Dietrich had no hope of working out. Laughing, he'd reveal the answer and pinch his son's cheek, telling him he had to do better, much better.

Then, on his death bed, Heinrich had set his son a challenge 'to occupy' him after he was gone... Dietrich had spent almost his entire life working on this mystery, and in truth it had brought him close to insanity, suicide and despair. Sometimes he hated the memory of his father, yet he also had a strong sense that his father had cared about him deeply and that the mystery would confirm this, if only he could crack it.

Growing more and more obsessed, attacking the riddle like a man laying siege to an imaginary fortress, Grimmer had spent almost his whole adult life on it. But now, at last, at long last, the answer was near…. He wiped his forehead, put away the UV torch and reached with his trembling hand for the halogen lamp instead.

Again, nothing.

Suddenly he had the feeling that someone was watching him. He looked up at the cellar windows, but the blackout curtains were drawn as usual. He turned off all the lights. A stair creaked. Rising silently to his feet Grimmer slipped behind one of the brick pillars supporting the vaulted ceiling.

His Sig Sauer pistol was in the safe and the safe was locked.

The strip lights tinkled as they came back to life. Achim was standing at the bottom of the stairs in his tracksuit.

The younger man was the first to smile. They'd given each other a violent start.

'Morning, boss.'

'I suppose you're going to tell me you heard a noise again?' Grimmer ran his white-gloved palms over white hair. 'Your ears are too sharp.'

Achim grinned. He had a stealthy way about him – perhaps he'd learned it at the police academy in Munich, where he'd taken weekend courses at Grimmer's urging. The young man's eyes kept darting to the canvas on the table. At least he had some life in him, a healthy curiosity, unlike the mindless thugs slumbering upstairs…

74

'Let me show you something.'

Grimmer reached for the UV torch. He slid it along the dirty brown weave of the back of the canvas. Achim leaned closer, eyes narrowing.

'This was the canvas that was hidden behind the Caravaggio. Can you see anything?'

Achim tracked the pool of UV light as it stroked the canvas.

'No, boss . . . What can you see?'

'Nothing. I'm stuck.'

'Could there be a third canvas?'

'There could, but there isn't.'

'What's that?' Achim suddenly pointed at something.

Grimmer leaned closer. The young man was right. Down in the lower left-hand corner, at the very edge, the tint of the fabric was very slightly different in the light of the UV beam. *A patch had been glued onto the canvas.* Identical in colour and texture to the canvas itself, it looked like a patch used by a professional picture-restorer and was virtually invisible to the naked eye.

Grimmer felt like cursing himself. How could he miss something so obvious? Maybe his eyes were failing? He took off his glasses, wiped his face on his handkerchief and put on the glasses again.

'You're right. Hold this.'

Achim pointed the UV torch at the right spot and Grimmer used his scalpel to dislodge the piece of canvas, forcing himself to advance slowly, fighting the urge to rip off the patch like a piece of sticking plaster. Then he switched on the desk lamp, flipped the little square of fabric over with a pair of tweezers and studied it through a large magnifying glass.

The patch was about the size of a matchbox. Three words and a sequence of numbers had been written on it:

Schwartzberg-Todspitze-Elend

5-6-20-8-20-17-22-23-6-5-6-24-23-21-3-9-6

Grimmer felt a great heat spreading through his veins. The words and the numbers were written with a fountain pen, in an old-fashioned Gothic script also known as 'Blackletter'. Its German name was *Faktur*. It had been Heinrich Grimmer's favourite style of lettering.

The writing was tiny, but there was no doubt about it: *the strange note was written in his father's hand.*

'What does it mean?' Achim whispered. 'Is it some kind of code?'

Grimmer had completely forgotten about his assistant. He swung round.

'Achim . . . You've been a great help. But now I need to concentrate. Hard. You go for a stroll in the garden.'

Achim looked hurt but did as he was told, bounding up the stairs like a cat.

'Achim!' Grimmer cleared his throat. 'Thanks for your input!'

The young man paused on the stairs, smiled and continued on his way.

Grimmer returned his attention to his discovery, poring over it until his back began to ache. He knew his heart was beating unnaturally fast. He had to slow down. He must be meticulous.

He reached for a notebook and copied the words and the numbers onto a clean sheet. Then he switched on his MacBook Air and typed them into an email, which he sent to an address he'd created for the sole purpose of storing such information. Now if something happened to the piece of canvas, or to Grimmer's notes, his father's secret message from beyond the grave would still be safe.

He returned his attention to the writing. He thought he could see signs of haste in the way the letters were carved. That was no surprise. They'd been written in the final days of the Third Reich, even as the murderous machine created by the Nazis collapsed around its makers, burying them alive.

He turned the canvas the right way up and prepared to return it to the safe. It was then, when he wasn't really even looking, just as he thought the canvas had already given up all its secrets, that Grimmer's eyes fell on the illegible signature. Was it some trick of the light? Was it his over-excited state? Or was it the mixture of fear, fascination and shame that this particular name had always held for him? Whatever the reason he almost yelled out in shock when, to his horror, he was suddenly able to read the artist's signature without any difficulty at all: *Adolf Hitler, 1913.*

12

Strong chin jutting out at a determined angle, Monty counted her pupils on the platform, ticking off their names as they hastened past with their luggage and boarded the train for Rome's Fiumicino airport.

Luke was standing to one side with Miss Hart. Bernie was pulling faces from behind the train window but Luke ignored him.

Having warned everyone about pickpockets, Monty now set her pupils an example, standing with her small suitcase firmly wedged between her strong calves. Battered from years of use, the suitcase was secured with a rusty padlock and two wide belts, and marked with a sturdy luggage label, a piece of cardboard inside a leather contraption attached to the handle with a thick strap.

'...and fifteen.' Monty put her list into her skirt pocket. 'That's everyone.'

'Have a safe trip,' Miss Hart said.

'Oh, we will,' Monty snapped. 'It's you chaps I'm more worried about. Where is he?'

'Who?' Miss Hart said, turning deep red.

'Paolo.' Monty put her hands on her big hips. 'You texted him on the bus and now you keep glancing over your shoulder. Ah, that must be the irresistible young man.'

Monty had spotted her target behind a coffee stand and went after him like a grizzly bear, hauling him onto the platform by the scruff of his neck, to the immense gratification of the party of children, who applauded wildly behind the windows of the train.

'Now.' Monty had tossed Paolo in Miss Hart's direction like a scrap of meat. 'You two. You are responsible for this boy here. *Capito, signore?*'

'*Sì*,' Paolo said and seemed to shrink inside his leather jacket. He'd hooked his thumbs in the pockets of his jeans, and his long fingers drummed nervously on his thighs.

Miss Hart didn't seem to know where to look.

'You head straight for the airport and fly back to Brussels after Luke's interrogation. As for you, Luke, your future at my school will depend on how you behave during the rest of this trip.'

'Yes, Miss Montgomery.'

The imminent departure of the train for the airport was announced over the station's loudspeakers.

'Can I help you with your bag?' Luke offered.

'No, thank you.' Monty picked up the bag herself and charged onto the train, the last passenger to board. Then the carriages inched forward, screeching and thudding, and the train pulled out of the station.

Luke felt a wave of excitement rush through him. An extra day in Rome! Miss Hart and he had already deposited their own bags at the left-luggage office inside the station. He wasn't worrying about the appointment at the police station any more. Why should he? His conscience was clear. And he was itching to follow up his leads.

Miss Hart and Paolo were talking in Italian. Luke looked the other way, scanning the station crowds. The place had returned to normal after the previous night's activities, and there were the usual backpackers and other tourists around. Sick of being bossed about and chaperoned, he couldn't wait until he was old enough to travel on his own...But Miss Hart was OK. The young assistant teacher seemed to come from a different century compared to Monty. She wore normal clothes – jeans and a simple T-shirt today, plus pearl earrings and a touch of lipstick, presumably for Paolo's benefit. Monty had hired her straight from teacher-training college in England and she'd been an instant hit among the pupils, especially the boys. She got jokes, and stuff like computer games, music and pranks.

Right now, though, she seemed in no hurry to pay any attention to her young charge. She and Paolo were still talking – it was almost an argument, in fact.

Eventually Luke decided to cut in.

'So, we still have time to kill before my appointment at the police station,' he said. 'I have a suggestion.'

'No, you don't. You stay with us,' Miss Hart said, her cheeks red. 'You heard what Monty told us.'

'Sure, Miss Hart. I just need to do some emailing.'

'We'll see.' Miss Hart tossed her hair and glanced at Paolo, hesitating. 'Let's have a coffee, shall we?'

They moved to a refreshment stand and Paolo bought espressos for Miss Hart and himself and a Fanta for Luke.

'*Grazie*,' Luke said.

Paolo didn't reply. His fingers played with the tiny spoon. There was an awkward silence.

'Where's the best shopping?' Luke eventually asked Paolo. 'Miss Hart loves clothes shops, you know.'

'Luke! I can see right through that ruse.'

But Paolo played ball. 'Wait, Anne. It's a good suggestion. The Via dei Condotti isn't far. They sell all the Italian brands.'

'Armani, and all that?' Luke said. 'Dolce and Gabbana? Sorted!'

'Gianni Versace. Bellissima!' Paolo leaned forward and slapped Luke on the shoulder, grinning broadly. 'Anne will like it.'

Anne? It felt weird to hear Paolo address Miss Hart by her first name.

'And while you're shopping,' Luke said gingerly. 'I just want an hour to myself...'

'Dream on, Luke.' Miss Hart was fanning her cheeks with her slim hand. 'Monty will rip me to shreds if I leave you for a single second.'

'I just need to go online. There's an internet café round the corner from here. I went there with Jack last night. See, this is the receipt with the address on it. What do you say I meet you there in an hour?'

At this suggestion Miss Hart and Paolo burst into an animated discussion. Miss Hart's Italian seemed to be getting ever more fluent, hands flying all over the place. Luke had no idea what they were saying.

Miss Hart turned to Luke with a fierce expression in her bright-blue eyes. 'You and I must be at that police station near Quirinale in less than seven hours from now. There's no way I'm letting you wander off on your own again.'

'But—'

'Let me finish. My friend Paolo has kindly promised to show us some sights in his car. You and me, together. But before we set off you can have one hour for emailing. While you're doing that I'll go and look at one or two clothes shops with Paolo.'

'Great!' Luke couldn't stop himself grinning. 'You're a star, Miss Hart.'

'One hour, do you hear?'

'That'll be plenty.'

'Now where, exactly, is this internet café?'

Luke handed Miss Hart the receipt with the address.

'OK, we'll meet you there,' Miss Hart said. 'Off you go.'

'Miss Hart ... Slight problem. Can I borrow some money? Just until we get back to Brussels?'

'Some cheek you've got.' Miss Hart dug in her purse and handed Luke some notes.

'Thanks!' Luke sprang to his feet and walked away from the station. As soon as he was out of sight he began running. Every second counted now. He saw a taxi and waved it down. Luckily Jack had also lent him some money, and Monty had given him some as well, 'For emergencies only,' so in actual fact he felt loaded.

It took the taxi a painfully long time to negotiate the traffic, longer than it would have taken to walk, but Luke used the time to think. He had to be ultra-organised, and he had to keep Paolo and Miss Hart on side throughout. He paid off the taxi on the Via Principe Amedeo. The dark-haired girl with the red dot on her forehead had finished her shift and been replaced by a massively fat Chinese boy. Luke bought an extra memory card for his

MP3 player so he could make a copy of the video that would be easy to hand over to the Italian police, and then took a seat at a computer.

Within seconds he'd collected the essentials about Caravaggio's *Burial of Christ* from Wikipedia, a couple of academic sources and the official website of the Vatican Museums. Then he gathered the basic outline of the artist's life and works, and downloaded a floor plan of the Sistine Chapel. He printed everything, heedless of the cost, before turning his mind to the word he'd heard on the video soundtrack. It was his only lead . . .

'*See you in Faleria*,' the man caught on Laura's tape had said.

Faleria.

He did some internet searches. It appeared to be both a surname and a place name. He could find no restaurant called 'Faleria', but there was an amateur football club of that name, as well as a professional belly-dancer. He decided to focus on towns and other place names. There was a tiny village on Corsica called 'Falerria,' but as the spelling was different and it was far away, he discounted it. The region of Calabria also had a tiny parish called Faleria . . .

Then Luke perked up. Faleria was also the name of a small town situated fifty kilometres northwest of Rome, near the national park of Valle del Treja.

He found the local municipality's website and printed out the salient facts about Faleria. Many of its three thousand inhabitants commuted to work in Rome. Luke read on, using his knowledge of French to guess the meaning of the Italian words. The countryside around the town looked pretty in the photos posted on the website.

Looking for the clearest possible road map, he printed out a map of the Lazio region. There was a direct road from Rome to Faleria, and the timing would be good now the rush hour was past. Luke wondered what car Paolo had. It was unlikely to be a Lamborghini or a Ferrari, but even an Alfa Romeo wouldn't be bad.

Luke didn't need to speculate for long – an ancient Fiat Panda drew up right outside the internet café, provoking a storm of protest from the drivers behind. They hooted their horns and yelled at Paolo, who came sauntering into the café in his sunglasses.

Luke paid at the service desk and hurried into the back seat of the small car, which he had to share with what looked like a complete drum kit.

He complained, but Paolo just shrugged his shoulders and slammed the door shut. Miss Hart was sitting in the front passenger seat.

'New sunglasses?' Luke inquired by way of greeting.

'Did you get your emails done?' she replied coldly.

'More or less,' he said. 'Cheers, Miss Hart.'

By now the cars that had been backed up by Paolo's Fiat had invaded the left lane and were causing a blockage in the opposite direction. Paolo wound down his window, waved his arm and pulled out into the flow. Miraculously no one got even a dent. In Italy, it seemed to Luke, the main traffic rule was to signal your intentions boldly and to follow through, no matter what.

'Paolo's going to drop us off somewhere. I've decided it's best if you and I just have lunch somewhere close to the police station.'

'What about that sightseeing trip you were planning?'

'I rang Monty at the airport and she said no way –

I'm supposed to be keeping an eye on you, not roaring around sightseeing.'

Paolo looked bitterly disappointed.

Miss Hart put her hand on Paolo's knee. They were soon speaking in Italian again, but after a while, to Luke's relief, Miss Hart switched to English. The gist of the matter was that Paolo still wanted to show Miss Hart around, whereas Miss Hart was worried that they'd get caught in traffic and miss the police appointment.

'Miss Hart's right, there's a lot of traffic here in Rome,' Luke butted in, choosing his words carefully. 'Why don't we take a short trip outside of town, but not too far?'

'Luke! Are you deaf? Monty says no!'

'Just a short trip.'

'Just a short trip,' Paolo repeatedly eagerly. 'Anne, what would you like to see?'

'My Italian geography isn't that great, to be honest.'

'What about Faleria?' Luke said.

'Never heard of it,' Miss Hart said. 'No.'

'*Magnifico!*' Paolo cried. 'Faleria has a castle, wonderful views . . . And no traffic, Anne.'

'Beautiful spot,' Luke said.

'What, you've been there?' Miss Hart said suspiciously.

'Well, not yet.'

'How far is it?'

'Only fifty kilometres.'

'*Fifty?*' Miss Hart shrieked.

'Less,' Luke said. 'Open road. And we've got almost five hours left.'

'No,' Miss Hart said.

'Anne . . .' Paolo winked, brushing her cheek lightly with the back of his hand.

'Well . . .' Miss Hart was blushing again. 'As long as you promise we'll be back in good time.'

'My Panda will get us to Faleria in less than half an hour.' Paolo turned on the radio and reached for a packet of mints wedged behind the vanity mirror. 'Let's go.'

'Be careful. I'll get that for you.' Miss Hart grabbed the mints and passed them round.

The adults were soon immersed in another arm-waving, gesticulating conversation in Italian. Paolo took a course north of the Vatican towards the Via Cassia, the ancient road that led northwest out of Rome. Luke followed their progress on his map.

Paolo kept asking for help with directions, and Luke suspected that the man had never been to Faleria but had seized blindly on Luke's suggestion as a chance to spend a little longer with Miss Hart, even if it meant driving with a gooseberry in the back.

The drum kit kept shifting with the jolts and vibrations of the car.

'Are you a musician?' Luke asked.

'I am a podiatrist. You can also say chiropodist.'

'A foot doctor?'

'Yes,' Paolo said proudly. He had the English terminology down pat. 'I specialise in corns, calluses and ingrown toenails.'

'That must be a really satisfying occupation,' Luke said. 'I personally think feet are fascinating.'

Miss Hart turned round to give him a poisonous glance.

'What's with the drums, then?' Luke said.

'A hobby.' Paolo made a sweeping gesture with his thin hand. 'A dream!'

The tiny car had seen better days – it made Luke wonder whether Paolo was short of patients. There were holes in the upholstery, the engine had a strained note to it and the gear changes sounded like mechanical failure. Paolo handled the controls with fierce concentration, like a man dismantling some dangerous object.

While Paolo regaled Miss Hart with an extended account of his drumming activities Luke quietly stored some important numbers into his mobile: 113 for general emergencies and 112 for the *carabinieri*. Then he copied the video from his MP3 player onto the extra memory card he'd bought in the internet café.

Luke certainly didn't intend to confront the art robbers, assuming he even tracked them down. He couldn't help but wonder whether a podiatrist would be much use in a crisis, if something unexpected turned up in Faleria . . .

Roman history was full of mythological beasts, mad emperors and strange prophecies, but Lieutenant Bari took a cool and rational view of things. And, yet, as he strained his eyes to see what was happening up on the dome of St Peter's, he felt a wave of almost supernatural dread pass through him. Although he was standing on the roof of the basilica, at the foot of the immense statues that capped its Baroque façade, he had to lean back to see all the way up to the top of the cupola, 133 metres high.

How, in God's name, did the blackmailers think they could collect the ransom from the top of St Peter's? Would they swoop down with a helicopter? He thought of the famous opening scene of Fellini's *La Dolce Vita*, with the wide-armed statue of Christ suspended from a helicopter, blessing the whole city. An hour ago Bari and Cardinal Falcone had together overseen the careful preparation of the ransom package, which contained 900 grams of *Aerangis* orchid petals from Madagascar, packed in a Kevlar sack, attached to a loop made out of a garden hose.

The celebrated climber Silvio Knoll, member of the Italian Alpine Club, just back from an expedition to Tibet, had been hastily recruited to deliver the package to the summit of the immense church dome. Bari quickly raised his binoculars to his eyes when he saw Knoll emerge on the side of the cupola, having successfully dropped off the ransom.

Scanning the scene through narrowed eyes Bari glanced back at St Peter's Square, where the Pope delivered his annual Christmas message to the crowds of faithful and to the world. Right now the square was deserted, the police having closed it off indefinitely. Pigeons flapped around the fountains flanking the obelisk in the centre of the square. Black-clad *carabinieri* with sub-machine guns patrolled the security barricades, which barely held back a surging sea of tourists, onlookers and television cameras. Only part of the situation had been revealed to the media, and to Bari's relief the extortion plot had been successfully kept secret. No one in the crisis group had talked. So far.

'This entire thing is just smoke and mirrors,' Cardinal Falcone said. 'A prank or a stunt of some sort.'

'That's certainly a stunt,' Bari said, pointing up at the mountaineer now scaling down the dome of the basilica.

'Fearless man that Knoll. A great Italian. I think I'll ask for his autograph for my nephew.'

'So the ransom is in place,' Bari replied. 'But how will the blackmailers ever collect it from up there?'

'Hot-air balloon?'

'We've closed the airspace above Rome. But a hot-air balloon would suit us fine: slow and conspicuous. They'd never get away.'

At that moment there was a commotion behind them. The officer manning the field-communication and IT centre had seen something in the sky and was waving his arms, staring at a point right above the dome of the church.

A small remote-controlled helicopter.

Bari cursed aloud.

'What do we do now?' the cardinal whispered.

'We can disable the remote-control signal, sir,' the officer called out.

'No,' Bari said. 'They still have the Caravaggio. Let the helicopter go. They can keep the petals.'

13

On the main street in Faleria, fifty kilometres from the Eternal City, Paolo engaged the handbrake of the Fiat and Luke sprang out of the back seat, relieved to be separated from the drum kit. He felt slightly car sick, having read his various papers en route, and thanks also to Paolo's style of driving, which involved endless sudden accelerations and split-second lane-changes.

Scanning his surroundings, Luke flexed his cramped legs and inhaled the mountain air that smelled pleasantly cool and fresh after the scooter fumes of Rome. Behind a low stone barrier that skirted the main street the cliff plunged away into the Valle del Treja. At the bottom of the valley a small river snaked through thick vegetation. Luke had read in the car that the national park was home to wild boar and a whole host of lizards and snakes. Entering Faleria he'd glimpsed the picturesque central square, which offered a view of the ruined castle at the other end of the town. The valley was dotted with old houses and villas.

'Time for lunch. You are my guest,' Paolo said, leading Miss Hart by the arm. 'You too, Luca.'

The Trattoria Fenizia was full to bursting, and it took

a good fifteen minutes before the perspiring, out-of-breath waiter asked for their orders. Miss Hart and Paolo chose the pasta with truffles, but Luke went for a safe and familiar option: spaghetti Bolognese.

When he realised that Miss Hart was English, the waiter insisted on bringing a large plate of antipasti 'on the house', and Paolo countered by ordering a glass of wine for his companion, who clearly enjoyed being the centre of attention, constantly giggling and adjusting her hair. Luke picked at the cold vegetables, leaving the adults to talk, trying to decide on his next step.

Then the waitress came back with a basket of bread and informed them that they'd have to wait for at least another half hour as the place was so full.

Luke immediately seized the chance to go for a walk.

'Just going to stretch my legs,' he told them. 'I'm feeling a bit sick from the car.'

'Don't go far...' Miss Hart's cheeks were as red as the wine in her glass.

The tourist office was a white building with a tiled roof in Faleria's central square. Luke drew himself up and raised his chin as he entered, trying to look older, wealthier and more confident than he was. The young girl at the desk spoke excellent English.

'My dad is looking for a villa to rent,' Luke said. 'Something peaceful, a bit remote.'

'What sort of budget is he on?'

'The budget's not a problem,' Luke said, squaring his shoulders for emphasis just as he had seen Paolo and other Italians do.

The girl studied him with a look of amused fascination. Luke glanced at his watch, frowning fractionally.

'We're not an estate agency. And this isn't really the holiday-rental season. But you could ask Signor Moretti, who has an office next door.'

'Thanks,' Luke said. 'I'll speak to him, then.'

'He's a busy man, but you can always try.'

Without replying, Luke snatched a tourist map from the stand in front of the girl then walked out. The girl kept her eyes on Luke until he was in the street again. Not for the first time, he wished he looked a little older than his age.

Luke knew he didn't have a minute to waste so he marched straight to the massive mahogany door marked with a brass plate that read: MORETTI IMMOBILIARIA. He tried the handle. Locked. Photos of holiday homes with swimming pools and gardens were arranged in the window, and a picture of the grinning, moustachioed Mr Moretti was displayed in a small frame, with his phone number underneath.

Losing no time, Luke dialled it and introduced himself, speaking in the deepest voice he could produce. 'Mr Moretti? Luke Baron here.'

'*Buongiorno.*'

'I am phoning from London, on behalf of a British client who is looking for temporary accommodation in Faleria or nearby. Preferably a house.'

'*What type of house?*'

'It needs to have a cellar.'

'*A cellar? What for?*'

'My client is a photographer and he needs to set up a darkroom.'

'*I don't have anything with a cellar to let. But we have two houses for sale, and I think one of them has a cellar.*'

'But it's not to rent?'

'It is being rented right now, but the owner wants to sell when the current lease ends.'

Luke felt excitement stirring in his belly. 'Can you tell me more about it?'

'Well, the lease ends soon, actually. Let me see... Yes, it expires three days from now. The Villa Mariluce. Lovely old building. Bellissima!'

'Could I...?' Luke forgot to speak from the chest, producing a shrill note. He pretended to cough then continued. 'Could I visit it?'

'I thought you were in London?'

'Indeed...' Luke's mind went blank. 'But a friend of mine is in your area.'

'I suggest speaking directly to the current tenant – Mr Wintermann. You can tell him I sent you.'

Luke scribbled down the name and address of the villa. As he did so, he suddenly felt deflated; he knew how unlikely it was that this house had anything to do with the words spoken by the mysterious art vandal and thief in St Peter's Square. However, he went ahead and marked the location of the villa on his map. It was just outside town, within easy walking distance.

Moments later he was back at his seat in the Trattoria Fenizia, with a plate of cold spaghetti in front of him. The excitement had taken the edge off his appetite, but he forced himself to eat. Then he gave a start, almost choking on the food.

'I'm sure the Caravaggio is already far from Italy,' Paolo was saying, gesturing at the small TV screen at the bar, real grief in his voice. 'Some international drug baron has stolen it and Italy will never see it again.'

'You like art?' Miss Hart said. 'You *love* art – I can tell. It's so romantic!'

Paolo joined his fingers and thumbs and held his hands out to Miss Hart. 'I am an Italian.'

The TV showed a glimpse of St Peter's Square, still closed off for investigative reasons, then the newsreader moved on to another topic.

'We need to get back,' Miss Hart said, pushing away her unfinished plate of tiramisu, looking at her watch.

'You're right.' Luke wiped his mouth and finished his glass of mineral water. 'But shall we go for a short walk before we drive back?'

'Luke, you've just been for a walk!'

'We have plenty of time.' Paolo paid the waiter. 'And walking is good for the digestion.'

'I've got a map,' Luke said. 'The best views are in this direction.'

'Are you *sure* we have time?'

'*Senza dubbio!*' Paolo drummed the table top then sprang to his feet. '*Andiamo, Luca!*'

They drove a little way out of town, Luke guiding Paolo towards the road between Faleria and Calcata. The turning for the Villa Mariluce was easy to find: it was the only one for miles. A wire fence two metres high encircled the building, its mesh clogged up with ivy. Here and there a dog, or some other animal, had dug tunnels underneath it.

Paolo pulled into a rest area under a large yellow sign giving information about walks in the Valle de Treja National Park. The faded pictures showed snakes, wild boar and birds, and there was a sign pointing towards a marked footpath.

'Look, I know I'm in your way,' Luke suddenly said.

'If you'd like some time on your own, I'll just walk on the road and meet you back here in half an hour.'

Miss Hart's mouth opened with surprise and the blood rushed to her cheeks. 'Luke, what are you talking about?'

'Anne, don't be angry!' Paolo grasped Miss Hart by the hand and gave Luke a wink. 'This boy is a diplomat. He is more intelligent than he looks!'

Luke smiled.

'Half an hour,' Miss Hart said as she followed Paolo onto the grassy path beneath the enormous trees. 'Do you hear?'

Luke jogged towards the villa. The rusted gate hung lopsidedly on its hinges, the wrought-iron coat of arms in its centre covered in moss. A shiny new chain secured with a large padlock joined the two halves of the gate. Yellow ochre was crumbling off the walls as though the house had some devastating skin disease. The window frames could have done with a lick of fresh paint. The curtains were drawn.

Luke glanced at his watch. No time to hesitate. He could have climbed the fence easily, but he knew that he'd be less conspicuous if he slipped underneath it. Skirting the grounds of the villa, he chose his spot carefully: the right side of the house, where thick bushes grew along the fence. He took a deep breath, dropped to all fours and crawled, then squirmed, through one of the tunnels under the fence. When he resurfaced, his view of the house was blocked by a stand of oaks, beeches and plane trees. With pulsing temples and a heaving chest he struggled forward through the thick briars that tore at his clothes and scratched his hands and cheeks.

The silver car parked at the front door was a large Audi

estate with German number plates. Luke noted with appreciation that it was the latest model.

Then his heart almost exploded inside his chest.

A man had appeared at the door. Dressed in a light summer suit, he had white hair that was carefully brushed. *And he was wearing a bow tie!*

Luke eased himself onto his knees, keeping out of sight. Could it be a coincidence? Faleria, a house with a cellar, a man with a bow tie…?

What seemed certain was that this smartly dressed old man was Mr Wintermann, the tenant mentioned by the estate agent. Luke moved a little closer and watched as the man loaded two aluminium suitcases into his car. He must have been in his seventies. A pair of glasses hung around his neck on a chain, and he moved with slow, silent precision. He looked like a historian or maybe a surgeon – a gentle, educated person, and not at all the kind of man who might vandalise and steal paintings.

The man climbed the steps to the front door and slipped inside. Luke could hear loud voices, but it was impossible to make out the words, or even the language that was being spoken.

There was a dark object on the grass near the driveway. Luke's stomach lurched. It looked like a weapon of some sort. Or did it?

Peeping at a stranger in their own yard didn't feel right, and Luke's heart rate told him so. He almost wished he'd stayed with Miss Hart and Paolo. He squinted at the dark object on the grass. Suddenly the old man reappeared with a mobile phone held to his ear. Again, Luke couldn't hear what he was saying, but he didn't think he was speaking Italian.

Luke kept as still as he could. What should he do next? His mind swarmed with fear and curiosity. In twenty minutes he had to be back at the car. The police interview was only a couple of hours away now, but he still hadn't discovered anything worth reporting. He'd answer some questions and offer the police a copy of the recording from Laura's iPhone, and that would be that. He'd be on the plane this evening.

If he wanted to find out more, he had to do it now. But he felt childish, suddenly. Childish and ridiculous. The odds were that these people had nothing whatsoever to do with the events in the Sistine Chapel.

Luke stood up. There was no time for speculation. Brushing his clothes, he walked through the bushes and trees to the front of the house. Tall grass grew between the yellow tiles of the patio. Reason told him everything would be OK if he simply played innocent, but his heart hammered faster and faster.

The white-haired man almost jumped into the air when he set eyes on Luke, hastily slipping his mobile into the pocket of his linen jacket and slamming down the hatch of the car. Then he straightened his bow tie, glancing at the open door of the house.

'Giuliano!' the man called. '*Hergekommen!*'

So he's German, Luke thought to himself as he walked up to the man.

His legs felt wobbly under him and he had to strain every muscle in his face to produce a smile. He waved his hand in greeting. The old man took a step back, hesitating.

The blond head of the skinny boy was sharply drawn in the cross hairs of the telescopic sight.

Achim Voynovych rested his hunting rifle against a sofa cushion placed on the living-room table. The window was open and the sightline was good.

He took long calm breaths. He had the boy covered as a matter of precaution, ready to act if the boss gave the order to fire. He hoped he wouldn't. The boy stopped right in front of Grimmer, who shook his hand and gave him a thin smile. Then Giuliano appeared beside them.

'Sorry,' Luke said. 'Do you speak English? I'm a bit lost.'

'This is private property,' the man said. His smile lasted about half a second. 'How did you get in?'

Luke could hardly speak his mouth was so dry. For he had seen what the object on the grass was: a sub-machine gun. He had to use all his willpower to stop himself from looking at it again.

The old man made a small gesture with his hand and the dark-haired man who'd appeared from the house threw his jacket over the weapon and carried it back into the house.

'There was a hole under your fence.'

'You are trespassing.' The accent was definitely German. 'Explain yourself.'

'Sorry. I know.' Luke rubbed at the back of his hand, which was bleeding slightly from a thorn-scratch. 'I was on a hiking trail, but must have taken a wrong turn. I didn't want to go all the way round.'

What Luke had said made no sense whatsoever given that the man had seen him appear from the brambles, which grew on the side of the house that was diagonally opposite the wooded valley. And Luke wasn't dressed for hiking. He thought he saw the man looking at the thorns caught on his sleeves.

'Which way is Calcata?' Luke said, holding out his map.

The man paused, fixing Luke with a piercing stare, then took the map and put on his glasses.

'There.' The man had small fingers and neatly clipped nails. 'And now I must ask you to leave.' The man led the way past the Audi, down the paved driveway.

They arrived at the gate. The key was in the man's hand, but he didn't use it . . . He just stared at Luke, as though thinking hard. A cold feeling seeped into Luke's chest, spreading into his limbs. There was something terrifying about this man. He seemed *unnaturally calm.*

'Head back that way.' The man pointed. 'The town of Calcata is at the top of the hill.'

'Gosh, thanks!' Luke knew he sounded idiotic, but it was probably just as well. 'You've got a nice place. Someone I know is looking for—'

'Goodbye.'

The gate swung open and Luke walked out on shaky legs. The German went back to the front door of the villa, closing it behind him. Heaving a huge sigh of relief Luke strode off down the road. As soon as he was out of sight he reached for his notebook. Then he looked at his watch. Still five minutes to spare, perfect. He hurried away.

He was sure now. There was something badly wrong with the whole set-up at the villa. Why would a group of men have rented a place like that? They didn't look like they were on holiday. And what did they need a sub-machine gun for?

*

Achim calmly picked up the hunting rifle and bounded upstairs to get a better angle, keeping his target in sight for as long as he could.

'He's staring at the house,' Achim said to Grimmer, who'd silently appeared at his side. 'And he's taking notes.'

'He's just some dim little English boy.'

'What's he doing here?' Achim worked his jaw muscles nervously. 'Giuliano says he saw the gun.'

'He's just a tourist. And we're leaving the villa anyway. I thought I told you to fix those holes under the fence?'

'Lorenzo was supposed to do it,' Achim said. 'Have I ever left an order unobeyed?'

'OK, OK. Let's keep calm. We've reached stage C of the operation and this is our first hitch, if it even deserves to be called that.'

'Who's that now?' Achim said, indicating with the barrel of his weapon. 'See, two more people.'

An Italian-looking man and a blonde woman had joined the boy on the road. The woman was wearing jeans and the man had a leather jacket and shades. The three of them set off towards Calcata together.

'Could they be undercover police?'

'With a child? Come on. They're hikers. We're right next to the trails.'

'The adults don't look like hikers,' Achim said. 'Look at that woman's shoes. She can barely walk in those heels.'

'You're sharp, Achim,' Grimmer said. 'Maybe you should consider a career in the police...'

Achim lowered his rifle. He smiled at his boss's joke although it didn't amuse him. Within minutes the three strangers had disappeared down the road.

'Sorry for accusing you about the fence.' Achim felt Grimmer touch him lightly on the shoulder. 'It was unfair.'

Achim smiled. He respected his boss immensely. Without him he would never have got out of that young-offenders' institution. He'd be in prison, or worse.

14

Sitting on the hard wooden bench in the waiting room, Luke felt like covering his ears. The crime-investigation bureau of Rome's eastern police precinct echoed with shouts, phone calls, slamming doors and excited voices. He was grateful to have Miss Hart beside him. Paolo had gone out for a walk.

A stream of police officers and *carabinieri* came filing past, hauling in their arrests: women in heavy make-up, young men in flashy clothes, a couple of rowdy drunks... Luke heard a bark and saw a huge a St Bernard leaping up against a door. Then it came loping through the room, sniffing at the crowd with a friendly air.

A man in civilian clothes stepped up to Luke and looked in his file. 'Luca Baroni?'

'Luke Baron, yes.' Luke stood to his feet, his heart pounding.

'*Inglese?*'

'Yes,' Luke said. He glanced at Miss Hart. 'Where's Paolo?'

'I'll text him.'

The man led Luke and Miss Hart into a cluttered office. The desk was awash with paper, and there were files, newspapers and plastic cups all over the floor. They'd just sat down when there was a knock and Paolo appeared.

Luke reached into his pocket and took out two items: his MP3 player with the video from Laura's iPhone saved on it and a separate memory card containing the same file.

The officer presented Miss Hart with a document in Italian. Luke saw his name at the bottom.

'It's a sworn statement,' Paolo explained, putting his hand on Luke's shoulder. 'It says you were present in the Sistine Chapel yesterday and that you're willing to be called as a witness when the time comes. Are you prepared to sign?'

Miss Hart studied the short document closely. She looked at Luke and nodded. Luke took the pen offered by the officer and signed at the bottom of the page. The Italian police officer plucked the document off the desk, slipped it back into Luke's file and opened the door: the interview was over.

Luke couldn't believe it. They'd made him change his flight for nothing.

'But when will they question me?' he asked through Paolo. 'We're flying home today.'

'It depends,' Paolo translated the officer's reply. 'They have dozens of witnesses. You can stay in Rome if you want, at your own expense, but you're free to leave if you prefer.'

'But the video,' Luke said to Miss Hart. 'They need to investigate the leads.'

'Do you have a copy?'

'It's on this memory card. Tell him I want to play him the tape.'

'What tape?' Paolo looked at Miss Hart.

'Luke's classmate was filming in St Peter's Square,' Miss Hart said, rolling her eyes. 'He thinks the footage might interest the police.'

Luke nodded. 'And I also think I know where the thieves might be hiding.'

Miss Hart's eyebrows shot up sarcastically and Paolo gave Luke a patronising grin before saying a few words to the officer, who tapped his watch with a fingernail and threw up his hands.

'Give him the tape,' Paolo said. 'He'll watch it later.'

Luke handed over the tiny memory card. With a sigh the officer took it and tossed it among the papers on his desk. Then he rotated his arm like a traffic policeman and shooed them out of his office.

They were back in the din of the hallway, among the throngs of pickpockets and drug peddlers.

'What was that all about?' Miss Hart said, grabbing Luke by the arm. 'You know where the thieves are hiding?'

'I don't *know*. But I have a theory.'

'What theory?'

Luke mentioned that he'd seen a man with a bow tie acting suspiciously at the Villa Mariluce in Faleria.

'You're priceless. You know what the police call people like you? Fantasists. You'll get into trouble if you mislead the investigation.'

'Sorry.' Luke stared at the floor as they headed for the exit. 'You're right. You won't tell Monty, will you?'

'Let's see how we get on for the rest of the day, shall we?'

Unexpectedly, they now had four hours to kill before they had to be at the airport. Paolo promised to drive them there. Luke wasn't looking forward to getting intimate with the drum kit again. He wished he'd insisted on showing the officer the video, but what could he do if the man wasn't interested? At least he had handed it over. They hadn't given him a receipt, but Miss Hart and Paolo were witnesses.

He wondered whether the police really would call him back for a proper interview? From what he'd seen, the investigation seemed totally chaotic, and he had a strong feeling the call would never come.

Dietrich Grimmer – in Italy under the alias Hans-Martin Wintermann – sat in the passenger seat of his Audi in the parking lot of Césano railway station and watched as the stream of commuters returning from Rome got into their cars and raced each other for the exit leading to the Via Cassia and the suburbs. Achim stared tensely over the steering wheel. Sprawled in the back seat, Lorenzo was humming to himself and eating gum.

'What's keeping him?' Achim worked his jaw. His knuckles were tense and white on the wheel.

'There he is,' Lorenzo let out a rattling laugh. *'Mamma mia!* I've never seen my brother looking so smart.'

Dressed in a beautifully cut suit and a crisp shirt, Giuliano blended in perfectly with the crowd of doctors and lawyers marching out of the station. He advanced towards the Audi, thick briefcase swinging, face expressionless, and got into the back.

Grimmer searched for the man's eyes in the rear-view mirror. 'How did you get on?'

Giuliano scratched his pencil moustache and frowned, before his face slowly melted into a smile and he patted the briefcase lovingly. Laughing with relief Lorenzo pinched his brother's cheek. Giuliano swiped his hand away and burst into a flood of obscenities.

'Give it to me,' Grimmer said quietly.

Giuliano rested the briefcase on his knees, snapped open the combination locks and pulled out a flat package. He tore off a layer of shrink-wrapping and handed the white box to his boss.

Grimmer planted his glasses onto his nose and used his thumbs to prise off the tightly sealed lid of the box. Inside were two identically sized packets of orchid petals, just under half a kilo each. He allowed himself a small smile.

Without turning to face the Italians in the back, Grimmer handed them one of the two packets. Four hundred and fifty grams of *Aerangis* orchid petals from Madagascar – this was their reward. In silence Lorenzo stowed the box in the backpack at his feet. Then the two brothers got out and walked towards the station, Giuliano leaving his empty briefcase in the car. Everything had gone precisely to plan.

Grimmer looked at the dashboard clock. A train to Trastevere station was due to leave from platform two in precisely three minutes. Lorenzo and Giuliano would board that train and melt away amongst the millions of faces in the Italian metropolis.

At a nod from Grimmer, Achim drove a short distance then pulled up at a recycling station and stepped out of the car. Grimmer watched him reach into the boot of the Audi, walk over to the paper-recycling container and feed a long cardboard cylinder into it . . . Caravaggio's painting would be safe in the container until the authorities were tipped off to collect it. The call would be made in due course, using an untraceable pre-paid line.

If only the *next* task was as easy...

Grimmer braced himself for one of the riskiest moments in the operation: the meeting with Father Sebastiano. The priest worked in the Prefecture for the Economic Affairs of the Holy See, and it was he that had supplied the necessary information about the security systems in place within the Vatican Museums, including the Sistine Chapel.

Achim swung the car onto the Via Cassia and weaved his way through the traffic towards La Storta, a suburb of Rome.

'So you gave Giuliano half the ransom?' Achim said with sudden venom. 'Just for that? Sweet deal for him!'

'You think so?' Grimmer turned to look at his assistant, surprised by his tone. 'It took months of training.'

'What did?'

'Giuliano used a remote-controlled helicopter equipped with a camera to pick up the package from the dome of St Peter's and then landed it safely on the roof of his hotel in Borgo Pio and grabbed the petals. Then he flew the helicopter into the Tiber, rode a stolen Vespa to Trastevere and took the train to Césano, where we just met him.'

'But *half* the ransom?'

'Achim, trust me... The ransom is nothing compared to our coming reward. And, besides, money isn't everything.'

'It is, when you have none.'

Grimmer twisted round in his seat and took the briefcase from the back. He opened it and placed the remaining packet of orchid petals inside. Achim drove on silently, working off his anger with his jaw muscles. He glanced at the remaining packet of petals, obviously wondering what would be left for him if the rest of the ransom was handed over to Father Sebastiano. Grimmer smiled. He deliberately encouraged rivalry between the men he recruited – it kept them on guard and stopped them from uniting against him. Divide and rule: it was an ancient Roman tactic, tried and tested.

Father Sebastiano was a small, dark Spaniard with the eyes of a mouse. He looked very, very uncomfortable as he sat perched on his bar stool in the air-conditioned cafeteria of the Stazione La Storta. The moment he spotted Grimmer and Achim walking in he gave a visible start, but he stayed in his seat as agreed.

Achim took the stool beside Father Sebastiano's, and Grimmer marched straight into the men's room with the briefcase, followed by the priest several minutes later.

As soon as the man walked in and began to wash his hands Grimmer stepped over to the hand dryer, leaving the briefcase on the floor. He could see the small Spaniard rubbing his hands furiously under the tap – as though trying to wash away his sin.

'Take it,' Grimmer hissed.

Father Sebastiano scurried over and picked up the briefcase with his wet hand.

'So, we're done then?' the priest said.

'We'll never meet again.' Grimmer combed his white hair in the bright mirror. 'I need not remind you what we agreed?'

The priest nodded, blinking. 'I mustn't talk about this to anyone.'

'And if you do, my friend outside knows where you live.'

Grimmer rested his hand on the shoulder of Father Sebastiano's suit and, as the priest pulled away, he formed a pistol with his forefinger and thumb.

With a frightened gasp Father Sebastiano hurried out of the bathroom. Grimmer would have found the little man's skittishness amusing had it not posed such a risk. But a necessary risk: the operation would have been impossible without his inside information of the locks, alarm systems and security guards protecting the priceless collections of the Vatican.

A deeply religious man, Father Sebastiano was also a gambler, and sadly not a very good one. His Catholic vocation hadn't reduced his passionate love for sport, especially all the Italian classics, which he followed obsessively: Serie A, motor racing, alpine skiing... His rapid slide to financial ruin had begun on the day he'd discovered that placing bets on the events he watched in his sparsely furnished flat boosted his enjoyment a hundredfold. One thing led to another and now he was massively, massively in debt. Even before meeting Grimmer he'd more than once dipped into the coffers of the Vatican to fund his habit.

Grimmer firmly believed that breaking the law was something you should only do if it is unavoidable in the light of ice-cold intelligence and cast-iron logic. He detested gamblers, fraudsters and thieves. And the priest was all of these things.

Grimmer and Achim arrived back at their car and exchanged a relieved glance. The hard part was over. The next thing was to leave Italy as fast as possible.

But within minutes Achim was sulking again, jaw clenching silently. Grimmer let him stew in his thoughts.

They'd already passed Viterbo on the busy motorway when the young man finally spoke his mind. 'So you gave that priest all we had left?' Achim said, shaking his head. 'You kept nothing for us at all?'

'Achim, you have trusted me thus far,' Grimmer said. 'Trust me a little longer. This is just the beginning. You and I will now go after a far greater prize.'

'What prize?'

'Wait and see.'

Grimmer closed his eyes and took a deep breath. A feeling of warm satisfaction filled him from head to foot. The Caravaggio had been merely a side issue, almost an irrelevance. It just happened to be the place where Grimmer's late father had hidden the crucial clues that signposted the way to the hidden secret... That was the only reason the canvas had to be stolen. The theft had been outsourced to professional criminals and the only purpose of demanding a ransom for the *Burial of Christ* had been to recover the costs of the operation. Grimmer had decided from the beginning that he wouldn't keep a penny of it. His conscience was clean. Unlike Father Sebastiano, he took his morals seriously.

He allowed his mind to drift to the patch of canvas he'd removed from the back of the hidden painting, and the maddening mystery that still refused to yield to his intellect.

'Where now?' Achim demanded.

'To the Alps,' Grimmer said. 'Schwartzberg, Todspitze and Elend. Somewhere in those fearsome mountains our real reward awaits us.'

The car was loaded, the villa was empty and the path was clear. Grimmer settled down for the long drive. A drive that would lead to the crowning triumph of a lifetime's work . . . Or so he hoped. He wished that Achim could share his excitement, but it was best to reveal as little as possible and, in any case, this was mainly a personal quest.

Strictly speaking, Grimmer himself still didn't know precisely what his father had hidden in the secret Alpine location in the closing days of the Second World War – or where exactly that secret location was. But its value and importance would make Caravaggio's painting look like some worthless sketch in a junkshop.

PART TWO

15

Luke's fingers jabbed at the mouse pad, and article after thrilling article came cascading onto the computer screen in the corner of his small bedroom in Brussels.

According to Interpol, art theft was the fourth-largest sector of international crime, and a growing industry all over the world. Stolen artworks were used as collateral in many different kinds of illicit deals, including money laundering and drug trafficking. Laundering cash used to be easy, but ever-tightening anti-terrorism legislation and monitoring meant that even casinos and betting shops were now off-limits. Only the art trade still remained below the police radar. Dealers weren't interested in the backgrounds of buyers and sellers, and the provenance of a stolen artwork could always be fixed, if the price was right.

Artworks offered a way of hiding and transporting colossal sums of money in a compact form, and professional criminals had long ago got wise to the fact that museums were far easier to rob than banks. Stolen masterpieces were also used to purchase armaments and to fund terrorism. The ancient Greeks and the Nazis had done it. Al-Qaeda was still doing it. One of the most lucrative heists in history had targeted the Gardner Museum in Boston in 1990. Possibly hired by the IRA, the thieves had made off with canvases by Rembrandt, Vermeer and others, worth millions of dollars, which had never been recovered.

Perhaps cash-strapped terrorists had also struck in the Vatican? Luke thought to himself. It was a sickening idea.

He went into the kitchen, made himself a cheese sandwich and poured a glass of orange juice. Dad, who worked for a secret Europol unit in Brussels, was at some meeting or other, and the au pair had the night off. Mum was away at a science conference. So much the better. A mountain of information was available online, and Luke needed to concentrate or he'd never be able to sift out the relevant facts. The more he read about the murky, violent methods of international art thieves, the more determined he was to get to the bottom of the outrage he'd witnessed in the Sistine Chapel.

He turned his attention to Caravaggio's *Burial of Christ* and its background. The first article he read made him go cold all over. *The painting had been stolen by the Nazis from a Jewish collection and ended up in the Vatican as part of a large bequest.*

The Rubinsteins, a wealthy merchant family from Cracow, had bought the *Burial of Christ* in 1906. Being Jewish, they'd had their entire fortune confiscated in 1940, upon the orders of SS General Herman Fegelein, when the Germans were ransacking Poland. The next time the painting had been seen in public it had been on display in the Vatican.

What had happened in between?

Luke clicked on a link to an article about art treasures pillaged by the Nazis. Countless sculptures, canvases and other objects had been stolen from their Jewish owners all over Europe. The list of cases was almost endless. The SS officers had gone for it with a vengeance, cramming tonnes of art onto lorries and trains in Paris, Warsaw, Amsterdam, Cracow, Prague, Budapest and scores of other occupied cities.

The looted art was transported to Linz in Austria, the site chosen by Hitler for the Führermuseum. Today almost every major western museum contained some of these stolen works. One study covering the catalogues of 225 museums had identified more than 1700 works looted by the Nazis.

Many – but not all – museums had begun returning works to their original owners and their heirs. However, like the Soviet Union before it, Russia stubbornly refused to return items that Soviet troops had taken from Germany, including art.

According to the article even the Vatican Museums harboured treasures that the Nazis had taken from their rightful owners.

Suddenly Luke felt a chill pass through him. Was it just a coincidence that the tenant at the Villa Mariluce was German? The man was, of course, too young to have been a Nazi himself, yet he'd got the sense that there was something cold and heartless about him. Or was this just prejudice? Luke knew perfectly well that modern Germans couldn't be blamed for their country's past.

The lawful owner of the Caravaggio had been one Shmuel Rubinstein, a leather manufacturer from Bratislava, last heard of when he'd been locked up in the

Theresienstadt concentration camp in 1942. He had almost certainly been murdered in Auschwitz, in Poland. His descendants had repeatedly demanded the return of the Caravaggio, but the Holy See had maintained a stony silence.

Luke rubbed his eyes, which were starting to ache from staring too long at the screen. He took his notebook and found the car-registration number of the white-haired man in Faleria. *M-YE-3923*.

He stretched his arms and closed his sore eyes for a minute then plunged back online. He keyed the number into the web page of the German Automobile Association, but as he'd feared, there was a charge for the service. He hesitated before paying with his PayPal account. He received an instant result: *NICHT IM GEBRAUCH*. Not in use.

He swallowed hard. This could mean only one thing. The registration plates of the Audi estate were forged.

Luke took a deep breath, then dialled Miss Hart, who picked up almost at once and – amazingly – sounded happy and not at all surprised to hear from him. It was already three days since their return from Rome and Luke had only seen the young teacher in passing at school.

'Look, Miss Hart, I need a small favour from your Italian friend.'

'Paolo?'

'It's about that business in Italy, the art thieves—'

'Luke, drop it, will you? If your theories had any basis in fact you'd have heard back from the police by now.'

'I'll bet they never even watched that clip.'

Miss Hart sighed. *'What is it you want from Paolo?'*

'I'd need to know the home address of the tenant at

the Villa Mariluce, and as many other details about him as possible.'

'Paolo's a busy man.'

'I know, he's a podiatrist and a drummer, but you can always ask.' Luke paused. 'By the way, I think he's a really nice guy.'

That did the trick.

'You're a smooth one,' Miss Hart laughed. 'OK, I'll make a fool of myself and ask next time we talk.'

'When will that be?'

'Depends. It's his turn to ring. I rang yesterday.'

Luke thought he detected a touch of heartache in Miss Hart's voice. 'Well, maybe this is a good pretext for you to get in touch again today.'

'Do you think so?' She let out a lovelorn sigh. 'I'll let you know what he says.'

Luke slipped the phone into his pocket and bit his lip. He was working partly by intuition. He'd found Faleria and the Villa Mariluce and the white-haired German by a process of logical deduction yet, if he was honest, he still wasn't sure the man had anything to do with the events in the Sistine Chapel. But, having come this far, he wanted to be certain either way.

Dietrich Grimmer sat hunched up in the chair in front of his massive mahogany desk in the attic of his Alpine chalet in Bergstein, southern Germany, near the Austrian border. With a sudden, violent gesture he swept the papers and the glass of water off his desk, then buried his face in his hands.

'Vater,' he gasped. 'Vater, Vater . . .'

But, of course, his father wasn't listening. He took a

series of deep breaths, marshalling his emotions, bringing all sides of his being under the control of their lifelong master: his intelligence.

He kneeled on the soft carpet and retrieved the patch of material that he'd cut from the canvas behind the Caravaggio and stroked it with his long fingers.

Schwartzberg – Todspitze – Elend
5-6-20-8-20-17-22-23-6-5-6-24-23-21-3-9-6

The delight he had felt when he'd found the patch of canvas with this strange coded message had long faded, giving way to a sense of anguish. His father had been a tough parent, by any standard, yet this was cruel even for him. He was tormenting his son from beyond the grave.

With a shaking hand Grimmer picked up the glass, whose contents had made a dark stain on the cheap carpet. He padded across the room to the small bathroom in the corner and refilled the glass at the sink. A strange sense of dread had taken hold of him. *Schwartzberg, Todspitze and Elend*...All three places had an ominous ring. He was a cautious man. He wanted to understand more before he went to them.

A crackly football commentary droned on downstairs, interspersed with the sound of Achim's curses and thudding fists as he tried to improve the image on the cheap TV.

Normally Grimmer's desk was immaculately arranged but today he'd allowed it to get cluttered. He took a deep breath and began arranging the papers and books, but he lost concentration, gazing at two black and white photos that stared at him from a double frame. The first one showed a young, smiling, well-built man in a dark woollen suit, smoking a cigar in Berlin's Brandenburger

Square. In the second picture, the same man was sitting behind an office desk, grim-faced, dressed in a uniform whose collar bore the jagged SS insignia – runic letters that looked like bolts of lightning.

His hand still trembling, Dietrich Grimmer yanked out the stiff desk drawer and took a sheet of paper from under his pistol. His father, Heinrich Grimmer, had been a sublimely gifted mathematician with a promising future before him when he'd graduated with perfect grades from Berlin's Friedrich Wilhelm University in 1929. Then, after a short-lived research career, the mathematical prodigy had joined the Dresdener Bank in 1934. Times had been hard and he'd needed money to support his family. Shortly before the war the Nazis had seized the bank from its Jewish owners.

Dietrich's most vivid childhood memories of his father were from the time when he was around nine years old. By then his father, once a vigorous and promising man, had withered into a stooped shadow of his former self, a pale ghost with prematurely grey hair, who eked out a living for his family by doing accountancy for tradesmen and small firms.

It was only later that Dietrich had begun to wonder what his father had done in the war. Once, and once only, he'd asked what Heinrich Grimmer had thought of Hitler, and the angry flash that had appeared in his father's eyes haunted him to this day.

'When I die, I will tell you,' the old man had said. 'I will tell you who was the greatest German. And you will understand everything. I will set you a challenge and leave you a reward ...'

Heinrich Grimmer had been a distant, brooding

father, and the only interest he took in his son's education had been mathematical. He supervised Dietrich's studies, setting him ever harder and harder problems. The boy had inherited his father's gift, but only in part, and looking back at his father's private lessons still filled him with humiliation. Yet mathematics had also been a real bond between father and son, and Dietrich was grateful for the education it had given him. His father had opened his eyes, not just to the pleasure and fascination of mathematics, but to the interesting lives of the great pioneers in the field: men like Euclid, Isaac Newton and Carl Friedrich Gauss.

'Study the great mathematicians. You will not regret it.'

But Dietrich did regret it. Mathematics had destroyed him. For when death finally came his father had left Dietrich a puzzle that had consumed almost his entire life.

Now, at last, already an old man himself, he was close to the solution. Very close. And it filled him with fear and foreboding.

The first clues had been contained in an envelope that Heinrich had left with his lawyer, who had solemnly presented it to Dietrich on the day of his father's funeral.

For Dietrich Grimmer, read the note on the envelope. *The answer to your question.*

After a long and bitter search the clues had led Dietrich to Caravaggio's masterpiece, which in turn had the second canvas hidden behind it, on which a small patch of canvas had been glued. The numbers written on the patch contained a numerical code. But so far Grimmer had been unable to crack it.

He didn't think his father would have chosen a system that would have involved using some external table or device: too messy. He'd tried the old phone number of the family flat in Munich in the 1950s, his father's date of birth and even his shoe size. It all led nowhere. He knew the code was likely to be simple, but devilishly simple. *Einfacht ist schön*, his father had never tired of saying. Simple is beautiful.

Well, then, Grimmer asked himself. *What would be the simplest imaginable code?*

Suddenly an outrageous idea came to him. What if there was no code at all? What if the numbers simply referred to the letters of the German alphabet? He reached for a ruler and a notepad and quickly sketched a table with two columns: the 26 letters of the German alphabet, and the numbers 1–26 in Arabic numerals beside it. Then he sketched another table for the code, filled in the letters and immediately saw he was onto something...

5	6	20	8	20	17	22	23	6	5	6	24	23	21	3	9	6
d	e	r	g	r	ö	ß	t	e	d	e	u	t	s	c	h	e

Yes, that was it! So simple, it was insulting. He had it. The numbers translated into a written phrase:

Der größte Deutsche.
The greatest German.

What on earth did it mean? Who was the greatest German?

Grimmer's eyes wandered to the canvas he'd pinned to the wall beside his desk, then to the signature in its bottom right-hand corner... Suddenly he thought he was going to be sick. He closed his eyes and buried his clammy face in his hands. He didn't like the direction things were taking... All those years ago he'd asked his father what he thought of Hitler. His father had set him a trail that had led him to a painting by the Führer himself, on the back of which a secret message had been hidden, which read: *The Greatest German.*

So the greatest German was Adolf Hitler – was that his father's opinion? Had Heinrich Grimmer been a Nazi, after all? And was this the reward for his son: a horrible painting by Adolf Hitler? Even the sun floating over the landscape was a misshapen yellow squiggle, too bright in colour, weird-looking...

Returning his attention to the three place names on the patch of canvas, Grimmer took out an old atlas, printed in the 1940s, which he'd retrieved from his father's archive in the outbuilding at the top of the yard. A slip of thick paper was pasted onto the inside cover.

Ex libris Heinrich Grimmer, it said, over an engraving of a shield decorated with the mathematical symbol for infinity: ∞

Heavily annotated in his father's hand, with pencil marks and notes on almost every page, the atlas showed all the military and storage facilities known to have been constructed by the Nazis in the Alps, including the area surrounding the family chalet.

Grimmer swallowed.

Schwartzberg, Todspitze and Elend were all on the map... Low Alpine summits, they formed a perfect triangle. But why had his father listed *three* places? A glance at the old map told him they were fairly far apart. On a sudden impulse he tore off the piece of the map showing the three sites. Using a ruler and a marker pen he joined the three dots on the map, forming a triangle. Then he pinned it onto the wall next to Hitler's painting.

It was time to take the bull by the horns. He decided to start with Schwartzberg the very next day. But he now dreaded what he might find there.

16

Luke thumbed the red button on the phone and put his hands to his face. It wasn't hot, but his cheeks were blazing after the brief conversation with Miss Hart. Eager to please, Paolo had contacted the estate agent in Faleria and wheedled out the permanent address of the tenant at the Villa Mariluce.

But that wasn't all. The Italian police had just issued a stunning piece of news: the Caravaggio had been recovered unharmed. There was no word about any suspects or arrests, or a ransom demanded or paid, yet Luke felt certain that the canvas couldn't have been handed back for free.

Miss Hart had taken the announcement at face value and assumed that the new turn of events demolished Luke's speculations. He too felt an unpleasant sense of defeat. If the painting had been found, the case was over. Or was it?

The thieves hadn't been caught yet. And while they were still on the run it was too soon to call off the investigation. Surely they could be prosecuted even though the booty had been recovered?

He looked at the name and details on the sheet of paper before him.

Hans-Martin Wintermann
Schilderstrasse 12
40885 Ratingen
Germany

So this was the address of the white-haired man who'd rented the villa in Faleria. Paolo had even provided Mr Wintermann's phone number, a German mobile that started with the area code 0172.

Luke clicked on his favourite online map programme and typed in the address. The search took a second or two, then the result popped up on the screen.

His heart missed a beat.

There was no such street in Ratingen.

What was this now? Why had the bow-tied man given a false address? Luke looked at the phone number. He was reluctant to ring it. If he did the old man would discover *his* number, perhaps even his address. Maybe the safest thing was to ring from a public phone somewhere?

Then he had it. He could use the SIM card he'd recently bought when he stayed with Granddad in East Sussex. It was pre-paid and thus untraceable. He turned off his mobile, took out the battery, changed SIM cards and, with a racing heart, entered the number of the German mobile.

Luke counted seven rings, squeezing the handset harder and harder until, at last, a mild, elderly voice answered in German. It might or might not have been the man that Luke had encountered in the yard of the villa – it was impossible to be sure…

Luke fumbled with the keys of his mobile, abruptly ending the call. He wanted to probe further, but he needed a good excuse, and he knew his own voice was too childish to be credible. He needed someone else to make the call for him. Hans-Martin Wintermann – if that was his real name – was probably back in Germany now. Luke had seen him preparing to leave Faleria.

Then he had a real brainwave. The pretext for the call to Grimmer would be simple: the caller could pretend to be the new tenant. He could say that an official-looking letter had arrived in the name of Hans-Martin Wintermann. Could Mr Wintermann be so kind as to confirm his postal address? Brilliant!

Pure genius. The main thing was to stage everything credibly. Who could help? Paolo again? He was easily motivated. But there was a limit to how many times Luke could ask Miss Hart to get Paolo to do stuff for him.

Dietrich Grimmer studied the display of his yellow mobile. The call had come from a UK number, but the caller was untraceable – a quick check online had confirmed that. It made him feel extremely uneasy, although reason told him it was almost certainly just a wrong number. But then why had the caller simply hung up without saying anything? Just rudeness, probably.

He'd marked the handset with a piece of masking tape, on which the words WINTERMANN, VILLA, FALERIA were written in thick block letters. Grimmer calmly set the cheap yellow mobile down next to the three others – black, silver and red – on his desk. In Italy he'd done everything he could to appear as normal and respectable as possible. This was why he'd also made sure the landlord and the estate agent in Faleria could reach him even after he left, in case something came up. The last thing he wanted was to be 'A mysterious German'. No, Hans-Martin Wintermann had to be an impeccable tenant. Grimmer even carried a passport in the name of his cover – forged, of course, just like the plates on the Audi.

He went back to the simple rug in front of the fireplace, stoked the flames, lit the powerful halogen lamp and threw himself at his task once more, like a bull charging a brick wall.

At last he had something concrete: the three locations marked on the page from his father's old atlas, which he was going to visit, starting the next day. They were all known Nazi storage facilities. But why three? And what was the reference to 'the greatest German' about? Spread over the rug was a more detailed modern map of Austria and Germany. Crouching on all fours, Grimmer began scouring the surface with the aid of a magnifying glass, unsure what he was even looking for.

Suddenly the phone rang again. Dietrich rushed back to his desk and saw the yellow phone flashing. Someone was calling 'Hans-Martin Wintermann' again – and this time, the call was coming from Italy. He composed himself, forcing a smile so that his voice would sound friendly, and took the call.

'Signor Wintermann?' The voice at the other end had a strong Italian accent.

'Der bin ich. How may I help you?'

'My name is Paolo Monticelli. I am phoning from Faleria – I am the new tenant at the Villa Mariluce.'

'And?'

'There is mail for you.'

'Mail?'

'An express letter. It's a thick padded envelope. Where

would you like me to forward this?'

'The agent has my address.'

'Mr Moretti only gave me your phone number.'

Dietrich thought for a moment, weighing up his options. Having scrupulously avoided giving the address of his Bavarian chalet to anyone but his closest associates he wasn't about to reveal it to a complete stranger... He couldn't for the life of him think who might have sent him an express letter or what could be in it.

'Is the sender's name on the envelope?'

'No.'

Dietrich allowed himself a few more seconds to reflect. Much as he hated uncertainty, he was accustomed to overcoming it. His method never varied. The trick was to seek more information and to make choices on the basis of that information.

'I am travelling,' Dietrich said. 'Perhaps you would be so kind as to send the letter to the address I am about to give you? I assume you have a pen. *Poste restante*, 80820 Bergstein, Germany.'

'I'll post it right away.'

'By express mail, please, so that I get it by Friday morning.'

'OK.'

'I will send money to the agent to cover your expenses.'

'That is not necessary, Signor Wintermann.'

'Thank you. You are most helpful.'

Grimmer terminated the call and returned the yellow phone to its place on his desk. He had kept his voice calm and polite, but he was boiling inside, desperate to see this express letter right away... What on earth could it be? That such a letter had arrived at all made no sense. It could only mean one of two things: something trivial or something unpleasant. Then a weird thought came to him. Maybe Lorenzo and Giuliano were trying to blackmail him? Let them try. They'd pay a high price if they did.

Luke was standing in Miss Hart's small kitchen in Woluwe, Brussels, talking to Paolo on the phone about the letter to be sent to Mr Wintermann in Germany. It was Wednesday today and the besotted Paolo had agreed to post the letter from Rome that very evening to make sure it reached Germany by Friday.

The large pink clock above the kitchen table was almost at eight, and Luke knew he'd better rush home or his dad would lay into him for taking the metro too late in the evening. He knew from experience that the Brussels metro was perfectly safe – full of passengers well into the evening. But eight o'clock was the non-negotiable curfew set by his parents. He sometimes wondered whether it was his dad's police background and all the stuff he heard about at Europol that made him so overprotective.

'Thanks, Paolo,' Luke said and handed the phone to Miss Hart.

'And that better be it,' she said. 'Before you get into real trouble, pestering innocent people with your theories.'

'Appreciate it, Miss Hart. Really.'

'You better go home.' She turned her back on him and resumed her syrupy conversation with Paolo.

Luke had already decided to go to Bavaria, but he couldn't manage such a trip alone, so he had to somehow persuade someone to chaperone him.

Why not Miss Hart?

'Just one more thing—'

Miss Hart rolled her eyes at him. '*Go!*'

'I wanted to suggest something.' Luke picked up his school bag. 'What do you say we go skiing or hiking in the Alps this weekend?'

'Skiing?' Miss Hart took the phone from her ear and dropped her hand to her side. 'You're joking, right?'

Luke winked. 'Ask him.'

'Paolo,' Miss Hart said, her cheeks glowing suddenly. 'Now our young friend has yet another idea. He's suggesting we go skiing this weekend.'

'*Eccelente!*' came the tinny voice over the mobile in Miss Hart's hand. '*Amo le Alpi.*'

'Come on, Miss Hart!' Luke hissed into his teacher's ear. 'There are loads of cheap flights to Munich. A quick break will do you good.'

Giggling, she shooed him towards the door and continued her discussion in rapid-fire Italian. Motivation really was the key to all study, Luke said to himself, amazed by her fluency. He was about to slip out when Miss Hart rushed after him, mobile in hand.

'Actually, Paolo likes your idea. God knows why.' She touched her burning cheek with her fingertips. 'But he suggests Innsbruck or Salzburg, not Munich.'

Luke shook his head. 'Munich's cheaper.'

'Really?' Miss Hart knitted her brows. 'I'm a bit short of cash myself, actually.'

She spoke a few more words to Paolo, then concluded '*Ciao, amore.*'

'So it's on?' Luke said.

'Why not? If your parents agree.'

'Paolo's really cool.'

'Isn't he?' Miss Hart beamed.

'I'm off. I'll ring you tomorrow,' Luke said, keen to get going before his teacher changed her mind.

He managed to get into the house without drawing any comments from Dad. As soon as he reached his room he went online to check out the prices of the different airlines. The cheapest tickets were already sold out. He knew from experience he had to act fast. The best fare to Munich he could find was sixty-nine euros with Virgin Express. It was a lot, but he decided he'd blow his small savings, earmarked for a computer game. A real adventure was better than a virtual one any day.

He rang Miss Hart and asked her to book two tickets with her Visa card – he'd reimburse her in cash. Then he started researching flights for his Finnish friend Toni who was always up for a spot of excitement – and who happened to be eighteen. Luke's mum was from Finland and he usually spent the summer holiday with his Finnish granny in a small town called Porvoo. Toni lived nearby.

Yes, Luke knew he needed Toni at his side. His friend had a driving licence and could be counted on not to chicken out if things got interesting.

A brand-new budget airline had just opened a new route from Helsinki to Düsseldorf, but that was the wrong region altogether... The only cheap flight from Finland to Germany was from a place called Tampere to Frankfurt, which was miles from Munich by train. Luke was getting desperate when, at last, he struck it lucky. A grin spread over his face: Air Berlin had a special offer that would get Toni from Helsinki to Munich via Berlin for ninety-nine euros.

He grabbed his mobile and phoned Toni to inform him that an interesting weekend was in store. Refusing to give more than minimal details he told his friend which flight to book, what to pack and where they'd meet.

He still needed to get his parents' permission to travel, but that shouldn't be a problem, provided he presented things the right way…

17

A hare sprang into the road. Achim Voynovych swung the heavy old Mercedes Benz G-Wagen right then left again, barely staying on the road. The boxy 4x4 drove like a tank. Had he swerved too far the car would have tipped down a precipice.

Grimmer was supporting himself by the handle above the window. 'Achim, for God's sake, slow down! This isn't a Ukrainian potato field. This is the Alps. You'll get us both killed.'

Grimmer at once regretted speaking so harshly to his sensitive young assistant. He squirmed round in his seat, reaching for the small pill dispenser in which he kept his headache medicine. He could feel his pulse in his temples: the altitude was getting to him.

Achim reduced speed as told, but he gazed blankly ahead, face set in a scowl. Grimmer took a deep breath, searching for the right words.

'Achim, my apologies,' he said, giving the young man's arm a quick clutch. 'You're an excellent driver. I'm over-wrought, that's all. Not enough sleep.'

Achim nodded fractionally and his jaw relaxed. If he had a fiery temper, he was also quick to forgive.

'Almost there.' Grimmer turned his attention to the pile of notes in his lap. He gave directions to a gravel road that travelled east of Bad Goisern. It led to Schwartzberg – at 1500 metres, one of the lesser summits of the northern Austrian Alps.

'What do you think we'll find here, boss?' Achim said as the 4x4 roared up the gradient. 'Something valuable?'

'Let's wait and see. There are three locations – this is only the first one.'

Achim parked the car in a small lookout area. Dietrich leaped from the vehicle and hurried round to the rear and hoisted out two backpacks filled with tools. He knew better than to expect the final stage of the search to be easy, but it felt good to be doing something real. He watched Achim stretching and rolling his shoulders, enjoying the biting air. The day's outing would do them both a lot of good.

Why, he still kept asking himself, had his father pointed him to *three* locations, all former Nazi storage depots located near modest Alpine summits? Assuming only one of them was relevant, Grimmer knew he had a 33.3 per cent chance of success today. It was reasonable odds.

They swung the packs onto their backs and strode off up the mountain path that skirted the Alpine slopes. Within minutes Achim had left his boss far behind. He looked back and stopped to wait.

'I haven't done this for a while,' Grimmer said, breathing hard, hiding his exhaustion behind a smile.

'Can I ask you something?' Achim said, gazing out over the valley.

'Go on.'

'I heard the Nazi gold ended up in the Alps after the war.'

'Who said anything about gold?'

'I can read, you know,' Achim said sulkily. 'I'm not an idiot. I know what books you've been studying.'

'Then you know as well as I do that no one knows precisely how much treasure the Nazis hid here,' Grimmer smiled. 'Let me just say this. Even a small fraction of the hidden gold would make us rich for the rest of our lives.'

As he said this Grimmer thought, with crushing sadness, how little of his life remained and how much of it he'd wasted grappling with this challenge . . . But Achim was young. Dietrich had no children of his own, and the young Ukrainian had somehow come to symbolise his future. He'd been a loyal servant and deserved to be told a little more.

'Some of the gold bullion that the Nazis hid at the end of the war was brought to Kaltenbrunner here in Austria. The records show that two trucks loaded with gold set off from Altaussee, but no one knows where they went.'

Grimmer inhaled the cool scent of the pines. He could have gone on to say that his father Heinrich had been one of those men, but he didn't. Nor did he mention that the rightful owners of the gold were the descendants of the Nazis' victims, from whom the wealth had been looted. Or that the two lost trucks had been personally dispatched by the notorious Nazi, Adolf Eichmann. The thought caused an unpleasant tightening inside his chest, like an asthma attack. He loosened his collar.

Achim stopped dead in his tracks and pointed ahead. 'Look!'

A door.

It seemed to lead straight inside the mountain. Grimmer pushed past his assistant and hastened along the path, almost running now. He rested his trembling hand on the box-shaped barbed-wire fencing that protected the door. He knew what they were looking at: one of the strategic fuel depots of the *Reichssicherheitshauptamt*, or the Reich Main Security Office.

The yellow sign said SCHWARTZBERG ÖLLAGER A. KUNTZE AG. KEIN EINTRITT.

Schwartzberg Oil Depot A. Kuntze AG. No entry.

'This looks like it's still in use.' Grimmer felt the disappointment like a dead weight crushing him. 'Oh well, we better take a look inside just in case.'

He swung his backpack to the ground and took out a pair of pliers.

Luke had never been to Munich airport before, and he liked its modern look. Even the ventilation ducts were like works of art. He was a seasoned traveller, but today he had butterflies in his stomach.

He followed Miss Hart through customs, and politely looked the other way while she and Paolo exchanged an unnecessarily long embrace. Then the Italian offered Luke his hand. Luke went straight to the point, asking whether Paolo had sent the letter.

'Yes, the letter to Mr Wintermann must have arrived at his address in Germany this morning.' Paolo winked at Miss Hart, who had pulled a face. 'Secret mission accomplished.'

'You boys are so childish,' Miss Hart said. 'Let's get going.'

'Look at that sun!' Paolo spread out his arms, swinging

Miss Hart's little suitcase high in the air. 'Luca, having made us come all this way, are you sure there is snow in the mountains?'

Luke nodded. 'The season's coming to an end, but the top lifts in Kitzbühel are still functioning. I checked for you.'

'Luke is meeting up with a friend. Are you sure Toni is eighteen?'

'Yes, I told you. Don't worry.' Luke was peering up at the arrivals screen. 'Great, he's just landed.'

'Where are you boys off to?' Paolo asked, putting his arm round Miss Hart's shoulder.

'We'll do some hiking near a village called Bergstein.'

The lovebirds looked thrilled to be setting out on their own. Whispering to each other, they followed Luke to the arrivals area. There was no sign of Toni, even after his flight disappeared from the arrivals screen.

Luke was glad that his cover story involved no actual lies. His parents were fanatical in their praise of fresh air and exercise, which had helped when he asked for permission for this spontaneous 'hiking weekend' in the Alps. What, after all, was a hike? A walk with a backpack. Luke had one, so did Toni, and walk they would, unless it could be avoided. Miss Hart's company on the flight and Toni's presence had persuaded his mother that the trip was safe. Dad had finally grunted his approval when Luke announced that he was paying for the flights with his own money, but at the last minute, he'd silently slipped him some extra cash – just as Luke had hoped.

'You don't need to wait,' Luke said, smiling at his teacher.

'Oh yes, we do,' came Miss Hart's reply.

Luke's eyes locked onto a short-haired stocky figure. It was Toni, although he'd changed somewhat in the space of a few months. He looked much bigger and stronger than he had when Luke had last seen him, on a visit to Granny in Finland. Like Luke he was dressed for hiking: walking boots, cargo trousers and a fleece jacket.

'All right?' Toni shook hands with Miss Hart, Paolo and Luke in turn, reddening, and shifting his legs. 'Have you been waiting long?'

'What happened?' Luke said. 'You landed ages ago.'

'Be good, boys,' Miss Hart said. 'And text me twice a day, OK?'

'OK.' Luke grinned, full of appreciation for Miss Hart's cooperation. 'See you back here on Sunday.'

Miss Hart hastened off on Paolo's arm, and Luke led Toni to the bus for Salzburg. They boarded the vehicle just moments before it departed.

'What kept you?' Luke said, throwing himself onto the back seat.

'I followed a sign that said *TRANSIT*.'

'You wanted *EXIT*.'

'I know that now. I must have walked three miles since I got off that plane.'

'That's good.' Luke took a swig from his water bottle. 'Really useful.'

'You winding me up?'

'No, I mean it. Now we can say with a good conscience that we've been hiking.'

18

Luke leaped out of the creaky, old-fashioned bed and swung open the heavy curtains, revealing a stunning Alpine landscape. With a big grin on his face he opened the door and stepped out onto the balcony to breathe in the fresh, sweet-smelling air. It was damp but not too cold. The ancient Gasthaus Grosch had half-timbered walls, a mossy roof and an air of dispirited gloom. The guesthouse and the small village around it could have come from some sinister fairy tale by the Brothers Grimm.

But the setting was a glorious panorama, absolutely stunning. Beyond the river, Luke could see the soaring Alps, their snow-white peaks luminous under the stupendous bulk of the dark storm clouds. He took deep breaths, feeling slightly unreal.

Toni appeared from the room, bleary-eyed. 'So,' he said, with a yawn. 'Let's go get ourselves some wheels.'

Luke glanced at his watch. 'Seven o'clock. Too early.'

'Breakfast?'

'Yeah.'

They went down into the cramped little beer cellar where food was served, and helped themselves to rye bread, ham, boiled eggs and pastries, washed down with hot chocolate. There was a fruit machine in one corner of the room, and the place stank of cigarettes and stale beer; Germany's strict anti-smoking laws went unheeded here. With full bellies, Luke and Toni slipped out of the guesthouse, arriving at the car-rental office at precisely eight o'clock when it opened. The only car they could afford was a Volkswagen Lupo, the smallest of the range, which basically looked like a toy. Toni pulled a face and pleaded for a Polo, but Luke shook his head.

'Do you know what petrol costs?' he hissed. 'Not to mention food and drink.'

Toni signed the papers and took the keys, tossing them in the air and snatching them in his hand with the air of a show-off straight out of driving school – which was precisely what he was.

'Let's take this baby for a spin,' he said. 'Check out some of those hairpin bends.'

'Post office first,' Luke said. 'We have to be there when it opens at nine.'

Toni had to adjust the driver's seat of the tiny car to make room for his legs. Luke again noticed how stocky his friend was looking. He also seemed more mature, sort of. Gone was the attempt at a moustache – a total of fourteen hairs he'd managed, seven on either side. He'd been to the barber too.

'You're looking human for a change,' Luke said. 'The short hair's better than that mullet you had last summer. Have you been doing weights?'

'Aikido.' Toni started the engine, revving like Lewis Hamilton at the starting grid. 'It's an ancient Japanese martial art.'

'I know what Aikido is.'

'You should try it. I train four times a week.'

They weaved their way through the village and parked the tiny car opposite the post office. This was where Mr Wintermann would have to come if he wanted to collect the letter sent to him *poste restante*. Toni put on his sunglasses.

'Why the shades?' Luke said. 'He's never seen *you*.'

'I doubt he'll even show up.'

'If I had a registered letter, I'd be curious.'

The village of Bergstein lay tucked at the bottom of the valley, as though in a bowl, with thick forest on all sides that soared up to slopes of rugged rock. The secluded village had been spared wartime bombing. A Baroque church dominated the central square, and many of the ornate houses were decorated with splendid artwork. The fast-running river Wilher sliced the village in two. Luke remembered the accounts he'd read of the firebombing of Dresden. On a school trip there, he'd seen the rebuilt *Frauenkirche*. Destroyed by Allied incendiary bombs in 1945, it had been rebuilt after German reunification, and as a symbol of reconciliation the replicas of the golden orb and cross decorating the church dome had been made by an English craftsman whose father had been an airman in the bombings.

'Hope we don't have to give chase.' Toni eyed the controls of the Lupo in disgust. 'This tin can is no match for a great big Audi.'

'Go easy on the accelerator,' Luke said, suppressing a smile. Big, burly Toni looked ridiculous at the wheel of the small car.

'Acceleration isn't something this car can offer.'

'Good thing too. You're a novice driver and you don't know these roads.'

'Look at all those Beamers and Mercs,' Toni said enviously, pointing at the parked cars that lined the street. 'I love this country.'

It was almost nine o'clock. Luke felt a stab of excitement in his belly. He took his baseball cap from his pocket and put it on, pulling the peak down over his eyes.

The residents of the small Alpine village seemed untouched by its beauty, going about their morning errands with sullen faces, staring at the ground, as though suspicious of each other. In a place this small everyone must know everyone else, at least by name, but on this strangely brooding spring morning the villagers didn't even greet each other. They did, however, immediately notice the pair of foreigners in their Lupo – almost every passer-by shot the boys a suspicious look.

'Let's move closer,' Luke said, stepping out of the car.

They crossed the street and walked towards the post office – a nondescript concrete building. An old lady pulling a shopping cart towards the supermarket stopped in her tracks as they passed, open hostility in her bloodshot eyes.

'Why is everyone staring?' Toni said. 'I feel like a monkey in a zoo.'

'Let's go in there,' Luke said, pointing at a café diagonally opposite the post office.

The bell above door gave a bright *ping*. A matronly figure in a white coat was stacking her wares into the display cabinet: chocolate cakes, macaroons, pastries of different kinds laden with marzipan, nuts, raisins and glazed cherries…A separate cabinet was devoted to chocolates and pralines. Her hair was a teetering stack of artificial curls, like a beehive. She touched it with her fingertips, as though worried it might collapse, and fixed the boys with a toxic scowl.

'*Bitte.*'

'*Zwei . . .*' Luke pointed at a plate of glazed doughnuts and made a sign for 'two' then took a couple of cans of Fanta from the drinks cabinet.

'I was getting peckish, actually,' Toni said, taking a huge bite. He went on, with his mouth full: 'Doughnuts the size of bread loaves. Love it.'

'Make it last.' Luke slipped his wallet into his pocket and took off his baseball cap. He noticed a magazine rack in the corner of the café and fetched a couple of issues of *Der Spiegel*. 'Look at this,' he said. 'German newspapers and magazines. Loads of facts, hardly any photos.'

'It's all right for you, you speak the language.'

'Well, I understand a bit.' Luke felt a flush rising to his cheeks; he hadn't meant to brag. 'Can't say I speak, really.'

'Nine o'clock,' Toni said, peering across the street at the post office, where a cluster of old ladies stood waiting. 'And already there's a queue.'

'Can you take off the shades, please? We're indoors. You look like a prat.'

'That may be.' Toni took another bite from his doughnut. 'But I'm undercover.'

'Look, they're opening . . .'

A clerk unlocked the glass door of the post office and held it open while the old ladies swayed inside.

A young man had appeared behind the service desk at the café owner's side – he looked like he could be her son.

Luke went over to him and asked a few questions about the nearest hiking trails. The youth spoke good English.

'Bow-tie alert,' Toni grunted in his low voice. 'Get over here, quick.'

Luke hurried back to the table, where Toni had cupped his hands against the window and was staring in the direction of the post office.

'Stop gawping!' Luke said. 'You're drawing attention to us.'

'Is it him?'

Luke picked up his drink and leaned his chin on his hand. He could feel the stares of the café-keeper and her son on his back. Outside, there was no sign of the Audi, but a white-haired man dressed in olive-green hiking gear had stepped from the passenger seat of a dented old Mercedes 4x4. Under his jacket he was wearing a checked shirt with a bright-red bow tie and a pair of glasses on a chain.

'It's him,' Luke said.

The man strode into the post office. A younger guy got out of the vehicle too, lit a cigarette and rested his elbows on the bonnet. He had the agile, focused bearing of a professional athlete or soldier.

'That's an early model of the Mercedes G-Class SUV,' Toni said. 'Also known as the G-Wagen. Originally built for the German military. A real bulldozer to drive.'

'So you've driven one?'

'Well, not as yet ... But I know a thing or two about cars. The driver looks kind of mean, by the way.'

'Stop pointing!' Luke pulled Toni away from the window. 'And get ready to drive the Lupo. Bow tie is back.'

'What's in the envelope?'

'Nothing. Junk mail.'

The white-haired man had re-emerged from the post office and was crossing the street, a large envelope in his hand. His driver tossed down his cigarette and opened the front passenger door. Wintermann dropped the envelope onto the seat, slammed the door shut – and headed straight for the café.

'I can't believe it.' Luke glanced around. 'I'll hide in the loo. Let me know when he's gone.'

He sprang to his feet, bumping into the lady sitting at the next table. 'Sorry... *Entschuldigung*...' Luke muttered, putting the baseball cap onto his head as he sidled through the small café.

The toilet was at the back. Luckily it was unoccupied. Luke rushed past the hand basin and locked himself into the cubicle.

Then he thought of something. *What if Wintermann wanted to use the toilet?*

The bell chimed as the front door opened. With a thrashing heart, Luke listened. No one came. The only sound was the dripping tap and the booming of his own pulse in his ears.

Then there were footsteps and someone began washing their hands at the sink.

Luke bunched his fists.

The person outside stepped up to the cubicle and rattled the door handle. Standing in the tiny space, holding his breath, Luke kept as still as he could.

The unseen person gave an impatient grunt, ran more water from the tap and left. Had it been Wintermann? Fearing his legs were about to collapse under him Luke lowered himself onto the closed toilet seat. What now? It was impossible to return to the café where the man would surely recognise him.

His breathing had just about returned to normal when the door opened again and someone used the sink once more, then knocked on the door of the cubicle.

Luke had decided he wouldn't open the door, no matter what.

More knocking.

'Achtung!' A low voice rumbled. *'Heil Hitler!'*

'You idiot!' Luke rushed out of the cubicle and shook Toni by the front of his fleece jacket. 'Has he gone?'

'He's in the newsagent's.' Toni chuckled. 'You all right? You look a bit white.'

They went back to their table just in time to see the German clambering back into the passenger seat of the chunky, dented 4x4, which immediately pulled out into the street, swung a U-turn and went hurtling back towards Oberstbrunn.

Luke and Toni sprinted out into the street and jumped into the Lupo.

'Follow that car,' Toni said in a B-list film voice as he turned the key in the ignition.

'Don't get carried away,' Luke said. 'Go slow. We're attracting attention as it is.'

The matron in her white coat and beehive hair stepped out onto the pavement in front of the café and squinted after them with her hands on her colossal hips.

19

Applying his considerable willpower, Dietrich Grimmer waited until he was back in his chalet before he tore open the yellow envelope that had been sent to him by the new tenant at the villa in Faleria. He didn't want Achim to see the contents – whatever they were. He used the small, eagle-headed letter opener that had once belonged to his father, just like the hard wooden chair in which Grimmer was sitting, still dressed in his hiking jacket.

His small study was barely big enough to contain the massive oak desk he'd picked up in a Salvation Army flea market many years ago. The walls were lined with shelves constructed out of bricks and wooden boards. He'd had the same 'temporary' shelves since his hungry student days. Some of the same books too. And the same dreams, still unfulfilled.

Through the small, draughty window a bleak forest of fir trees could be seen, and beyond it, the clean white slopes of the Austrian Alps. Built by Grimmer's father in 1936, when Hitler was at the height of his power in Germany, the place had never been renovated, and it showed.

Viewed from the outside, the study window was in the gable of the small Alpine chalet. The dark-brown timbers had been left visible in the whitewashed walls, in the so-called *Fachwerk* style.

Small and run-down though it was, the chalet was located in a peaceful spot. Grimmer's father had been a man who valued being left alone. Dietrich had recently reinforced the privacy of the place by installing a steel-wire fence and an automatic gate. Bergstein, the nearest village – where the letter had been waiting – was six kilometres away.

Grimmer turned his attention to the books on his shelves, running his fingers over their spines, wondering which of them, if any, held the answer to his questions... His library contained literally thousands of books, stored here and in various crates, boxes and chests in the outbuilding. Most of them had belonged to his father and, by the age of fifty, Grimmer had read every one of them. Once, the collection had filled him with pride, but in recent years, he'd begun to resent the waste these books represented, shuddering at the thought of the hours he'd spent turning their pages as he pursued his research and calculations. Until the breakthrough and the discovery of the Caravaggio, he'd had nothing to show for years and years of work. Now he wasn't sure he wanted to go any further.

Again, seized by a strange compulsion, he looked at the canvas pinned to the wall beside his desk and immediately felt a surge of unease in his abdomen. The three mountains, the garish yellow squiggle representing the sun, the half-legible signature... *Adolf Hitler, 1913*...

Who would ever think of calling the painter of such rubbish, the author of such crimes, the cause of a nation's everlasting shame, 'The greatest German'?

He returned the letter opener to its place in the drawer, put his hand into the envelope and pulled out the contents: a brochure from an Italian garden centre. That was all. Nothing to worry about! Relief swept through him. Then a sense of foreboding caught hold. *Why had the new tenant at the villa in Faleria forwarded this?* The man had spoken of an express letter, but this was just an advertisement! It made no sense whatsoever. You'd have to be an idiot to take the trouble to forward junk mail that wasn't even addressed to anyone in particular. Had the new tenant got things mixed up and sent the wrong document?

Whichever way he looked at it Grimmer couldn't help feeling that something was wrong. He decided to be on his guard, more than ever. Fighting his weariness and the crippling sense of dread, he forced his mind to focus on his quest once more. He took off his jacket and tramped down the creaking stairs into the small living room. On the wall was a photo of an Alsatian in a cardboard frame. Trudi had been his loyal companion for ten years. When she died he'd decided never to get a new dog.

Grimmer took a blackened key from its hook in the hallway and stepped outside. At the top of the yard, built into the slope of the mountain, was a small and ugly concrete building. He trudged up to its door and unlocked it. A damp smell wafted from inside. He felt for the switch and a dusty bulb lit up in the ceiling. The place was cluttered with all kinds of junk: bicycles, wooden crates, chairs stacked onto a heavy dining table, a dusty gramophone perched high on a narrow wardrobe. Outmoded clothes hung from rails. Grimmer turned to lock the door behind him then sidled through the crowded space to the very back, moved a wooden crate and pulled aside a dusty curtain to reveal a second door.

He reached inside his pocket and chose a small modern key from a ring attached to his belt with a chain. The second, well-oiled lock opened without a sound. He turned a switch and the neon lights blinked into life overhead. He stepped over the concrete threshold and closed the little door behind him, locking it, then turned to the steel filing cabinet beside the door, which opened with yet another key.

The Schwartzberg location had, unfortunately, been a waste of time: just an oil depot, as the sign outside had said. Staring over the vast reservoir brimming with oil, a pool of bottomless darkness in the man-made cave deep inside the mountain rock, Grimmer had felt like an animal lured into a trap by some cruel hunter. For how much longer would his father torment him from beyond the grave? Perhaps understanding his master's despair, Achim had had the sense not to ask any more questions. They'd simply closed the door of the depot, securing it with a heavy stone, leaving the broken lock lying on the ground, then left.

Grimmer returned his attention to his surroundings. It was several minutes before he found what he was looking for. The sight of the pair of volumes at the bottom of an old chest made him shudder, and he had to make an effort of will to carry them into his house.

It was a signed edition. He'd never actually read this notorious two-part book. But if his father had really thought Hitler was his greatest countryman, if that was the secret message, Grimmer now had no choice but to read it. Locking the outbuilding behind him, hastening back to the chalet like a man weighed down with guilt, he sat in his armchair and opened the first book.

It was *Mein Kampf*, Volume One, published in 1925. A cloud of dust and mildew wafted from the pages. Grimmer had only read a few paragraphs when he suddenly felt his stomach contract and he had to rush to the bathroom, where he folded himself almost double and vomited copiously into the toilet bowl. He remained there for several minutes, kneeling on the floor, head aching, legs still tired from the long, fruitless climb to Schwartzberg...

Vater, Vater, siehst du mich?

With a crunch Toni engaged the handbrake. For a moment a cloud of dust danced around the Lupo, then the mountain breeze swept it away. They'd stopped suddenly, two hundred metres up a small track that climbed from the main road towards a small half-timbered chalet. The white-haired man's car had been driven into the yard of the house, which was hidden from the road by a tall fir-tree hedge. Dense forest grew on the higher slopes beyond the house. The fir trees looked like scrawny giants filing up the mountain.

'Why here?' Luke was furious. 'They'll see the car!'

'Relax. We're tourists, admiring the view.'

The roof of the chalet was covered with moss, and the chimney leaned to one side. The exposed timbers reminded Luke of Tudor houses he'd seen in York. There were no other houses in sight.

Toni locked the car and they slipped into the undergrowth, which hid them from view as they advanced towards the fir trees.

Luke noticed that his pulse was racing – maybe it was the thin air as much as the tension of the moment. Moving cautiously they climbed the slope, pushing aside the ferns that covered the forest floor. In a few minutes they were above the house and had a good view of the sloping square-shaped yard. The angular, clapped-out old 4x4 stood in the driveway. There was not a soul in sight.

Luke took his bearings, imprinting the main features of the landscape into his memory. The track ended at the front of the house. Two windows in the gable looked over the yard and there seemed to be a large room with glass doors downstairs. At the top of the yard, close to the boys, stood a small windowless outbuilding, fashioned from ugly concrete blocks. Towards the right, between the house and the outbuilding, was a ramshackle woodshed and a bin shelter.

Luke took his miniature binoculars from the pocket of his fleece and scanned the yard. A cast-iron sundial jutted out in the middle of the lawn; decorated with mythical beasts of some sort, it looked much older than the house. Luke had once done a school project on sundials. The sun and planets interested him because of his middle name – Copernicus – and his parents had always encouraged his interest in astronomy.

'Creepy spot,' Toni whispered.

Luke nodded. The run-down house with its forbidding steel-wire fence and the dark forest surrounding it seemed somehow unnaturally quiet and lonesome. It was as though the blue sky overhead belonged to another world.

'I just saw someone upstairs. Behind that attic window.'

'Really? Let me see.'

Luke handed the binoculars to his friend. 'We'll wait here until they go somewhere. Then we'll have a closer look.'

'But they've just been to town,' Toni said, peering through the binoculars. 'And, besides, how do we know there's no one else in there?'

'I bet it's just the two them. The house is tiny.'

'Your guesswork will be really comforting when we run into a third and a fourth guy armed with bazookas.'

Luke knew Toni was right. First they had to wait for the white-haired man and his driver to leave and then they had to somehow satisfy themselves that there was no one else around. And then what? Breaking in was not an option. Or was it?

His knees were getting stiff from crouching, so Luke sat on the ground and leaned his back against the trunk of a fir tree. The thick layer of pine needles under the ferns made for a comfortable seat.

'No movement.' Toni joined Luke beside the tree. 'I suggest we go back to the village for some lunch.'

'You can't be hungry already!'

'I'm bored.'

'Bored? Get your mind round this: if they hadn't returned the Caravaggio to the Vatican, we'd probably have found it right here, in that house.'

'Assuming they even stole it in the first place, which I don't believe for one second. This whole hare-brained investigation of yours is a waste of time.'

'Catching the thief is even better than recovering the stolen picture. If you have the nerve.'

'Nerve? I came all the way from Finland, remember,'

Toni said, pulling a face. 'And why are these old paintings so ridiculously valuable anyway?'

'It's the logic of the market,' Luke said. 'Mass products are for sheep like you, but when someone a little more sophisticated wants to stand out, he needs something rare. And the rarest possible thing is an object that's unique. A one-off.'

'There are tonnes of old paintings. Huge museums full of the things.'

'But each one is irreplaceable. Besides, this Caravaggio was quite a character.'

'How so?'

'His full name was actually Michelangelo Merisi da Caravaggio, but he's known by the name of his home district. Same as Leonardo da Vinci – the Da Vinci part isn't his surname but the place where he was born.'

'You're starting to get on my nerves.'

'You're a film buff, aren't you? Movie directors are really into Caravaggio. They copy his use of light and shade. And get this – he didn't just get paint on his hands, but blood as well.'

'Blood?' Toni's mouth fell open.

'Blood,' Luke said darkly.

'What do you mean?'

'He had a bit of a short fuse. One day, in the middle of some ball game, he quarrelled with his opponent and basically topped him. He was sentenced to death but he fled from Rome all the way to Malta in disguise.'

'Really? A painter who could fight?'

'And when Caravaggio painted David holding the severed head of Goliath he gave Goliath his own features as a sign of penance. Then he went crawling back to Rome to ask the Pope's forgiveness, but he died in murky circumstances. Was it malaria, or was it murder? No one knows. He wasn't even forty.'

'There you go,' Toni muttered. 'Bet he wished he'd known Aikido.' And he launched into a long account of the life and mysterious death of Bruce Lee.

20

Lieutenant Marcello Bari liked to say that the *Polizia di Stato* cracked all crimes eventually – if the politicians let them.

He closed the personnel file provided by the Prefecture for the Economic Affairs of the Holy See and leaned back in his chair. He knew in his gut he was on the right trail.

'The personnel file isn't much help,' he said fixing his eyes on Director Simonis. 'But I've received an anonymous tip-off that's likely to clinch this.'

Simonis narrowed his eyes. His leather chair creaked under his weight. It was hot again in central Rome and the mid-morning traffic had created clouds of dust that found their way into the conference room.

'Is your source inside the Vatican?' Anna Buretti asked on behalf of the Ministry of Culture.

'You bet.' Bari smiled. 'And before I say a word more, I want a pledge of confidentiality from everyone present.'

He received instant nods from both the members of the crisis group that he'd invited. Only one – Cardinal Falcone – was missing. Bari knew he could never discuss the information he was about to describe in the presence of the curator of the Vatican Museums.

'I've received concrete information from a source I trust,' Bari began. 'It concerns an official in the Prefecture for the Economic Affairs of the Holy See. Sebastiano Lagos, an ordained priest. A Jesuit, to be precise. A Spaniard.'

Buretti and Simonis glanced at one another.

'To be blunt, this Father Sebastiano is an addicted gambler facing financial ruin. And he's been acting strangely these past few weeks, appearing and disappearing at all hours.'

'Makes me think of that Jesuit oath,' Simonis said grimly. '*The ends justify the means.*'

'My brother is a Jesuit,' Bari said sharply. 'And he tells me they have no such oath.'

'What, you're defending this man?'

'Compulsive gambling is an illness. An addiction. It can deprive you of all sense of responsibility. Father Sebastiano is a regular in Rome's betting shops and casinos.'

'Must be quite a sight,' Buretti put in. 'A priest in a casino!'

'He wears a disguise.'

'And where can we find this fellow?' Simonis demanded.

'He's officially on sick leave with back problems,' Bari said. 'I'd imagine he's either at home or perhaps in Monte Carlo.'

Simonis sprang to his feet and strode up to the window.

'Let's bring the Jesuit in for questioning. But keep a low profile. No *carabinieri*,' he said, turning to face Bari. 'Be as discreet as you can until we know more. This business could shake the very foundations of the Vatican.'

Father Sebastiano's hands were trembling uncontrollably. He had to stand on his toes to reach the framed reproduction of *The Torment of Saint Anthony* by Michelangelo. He'd drawn the curtains and it was dim in his small bedroom. He rested the picture frame on his bed and detached the brown envelope that was Sellotaped onto the back of the cheap poster. It contained a thick wad of purple 500-euro notes.

He went into his kitchen and counted the money one last time, making two uneven stacks on the table. Sun streamed in through the skylight above the sink. He lived in a former maid's flat in one of the smart apartment blocks in the upmarket Parioli district.

He gave a start. What was that noise? Something rustling behind the wall? He pricked up his ears, holding his breath, but heard nothing more.

His nerves were frayed. He was in no fit state for this kind of thing... But what could he do? He looked at the two stacks of cash. The one that would clear his gambling debts was much bigger than the one he'd be able to keep for himself... The loan sharks would come calling that very evening. They'd be mighty surprised when he finally paid up.

The telephone burst into life and Father Sebastiano dived across the room to answer it – his creditors were impatient men and often gave it just a couple of rings before hanging up. On no account should they be given the impression that he was trying to hide. Not any more. No need to, now. He looked at the money again, over a hundred thousand euros. Incredible. What if he just picked it up and left? He could start a new life.

Too risky. These shady men were completely merciless. They knew he was a priest and that he cared for his reputation, and if he tried to flee without paying his debts, they might do anything.

But the caller wasn't one of them. It was Rudolfo, a Franciscan monk, Father Sebastiano's young colleague.

'*How is your back, Father Sebastiano?*'

'So, so,' he replied. 'I'm resting it.'

He could hear from Rudolfo's voice that this wasn't just a sympathetic call. Something was up. Something bad.

'*I wanted to let you know…*' Rudolfo hesitated, as though embarrassed. '*Some Italian police officers showed up at the office. Fraud inspectors, in fact. The cardinal had authorised it, but, still, I found it strange. What are things coming to if the Holy See isn't allowed to manage its own affairs?*'

'Thanks for…letting me know,' Father Sebastiano said in a croaky voice. He'd broken out in a cold sweat.

'*I hope you feel better soon, Father.*'

'So, what are you working on today, Rudolfo?' Father Sebastiano said, desperately trying to lighten the tone of his voice.

'*The draft budget for the Apostolic Nunciature in Paris. I'm starting to get the hang of things, I think.*'

'Splendid. Thank you for your call.'

Father Sebastiano cut the line and sank to the floor, burying his clammy face in his hands. His heart was beating so fast inside his ribcage it frightened him. Were the Italian police after him? Had someone reported him? It was impossible. No one knew what he'd been up to… Or did they?

He staggered back into the sun-drenched kitchen and drank a glass of water at the sink. Where would this all end? Suddenly, the visits from the creditors – one tonight, the other tomorrow – no longer seemed that frightening.

What was the threat of violence, or even death, compared with the disgrace he'd face if he was caught with his hand in the Pope's coffers? He was a thief. A dirty thief.

The thought of escape came back to his mind. The plan he'd idly sketched suddenly seemed vivid and attractive. There were plenty of planes from Rome to Madrid, and from Madrid it was a direct flight to any number of cities in Latin America.

He remembered the solemn promise he'd made to the white-haired German. Quickly he dashed off a text message to the emergency number he'd been given. **Police asking questions at prefecture. Unclear why.**

He'd saved the number under the word '*Tedesco*' – German. He didn't even know the white-haired man's name. He pressed 'send' and cast away the mobile, sitting down on the floor and clutching his face, fighting for self-control.

He sat perfectly still for a moment. Then he rushed to his wardrobe, took down his little suitcase and began stuffing it with clothes. He threw in his cassock as well; it might come in handy.

Then the buzzer rang. Someone was at the front door downstairs. He took a step towards the entry phone mounted on the wall, then stopped. Best not to answer.

He zipped up the suitcase, hoisted himself onto a chair and pushed open the skylight. He looked out and his head began to spin. It was a short leap from the sloping tile roof over to the one next door – but with a suitcase? At his age? Who was he kidding?

He clambered off the chair and staggered through the flat and down a short flight of stairs to the landing where the lift was. The stairwell echoed with sounds – everyday sounds that now terrified him: brisk steps on the ground floor, the clatter of the lift's sliding doors, the hum of the cables. No one spoke. Squeaking as it went, the lift travelled towards him.

He swung on his heel, ran back up the stairs and opened the door leading onto the roof terrace. His sweaty palm slipped on the door handle. The warm wind swept over his face. He kicked the suitcase to the side and closed the door as quietly as he could.

The terrace was small, five by five metres. A chimney coated with tin stood in the corner of the flat space. The tiled roof sloped steeply downwards towards the rain gutter. He took a hesitant step, then another, grabbing hold of the chimney for support. The sheet of tin made an ugly sound.

He closed his eyes for a moment, then opened them and stared hard at the terrifying slant he somehow had to negotiate. It felt much steeper than it had looked. Some of the tiles were broken, or sitting askew. It would have been a short walk to the edge where he could jump across to the next roof, but his hard heels might slip at any moment, sending him tumbling to his death.

His limbs felt numb and rigid. His head was spinning, faster and faster, and it didn't stop when he closed his eyes. He opened his eyes once more and, at that moment, he lost his balance, letting go of the chimney, half rolling and half sliding towards the edge of the roof.

21

Police asking questions at prefecture. Unclear why.

Grimmer read through the text three times then deleted it. His cheeks felt hot, or was it just the glow from the fireplace on his face?

'Who texted?' Achim said, emerging from the kitchen with a ham sandwich on a plate.

'Just an ad from the service provider,' Grimmer lied. 'Don't worry.'

'I always said we should have silenced that slimy priest.'

Grimmer gave a tight smile. The remark threw him for a second; it was as though Achim had been reading his mind. The young man was no fool. It was perfectly true that killing Father Sebastiano as soon as he was no longer needed would have been the safest option. But that wasn't how Grimmer worked.

'Don't worry,' he repeated picking up the phone. 'Father Sebastiano doesn't even know my name, or your name for that matter. He has no idea where we are. And I respect him for having sent us a warning.'

'So it *was* from him?'

'Yes, it was.'

'What did he say?'

'Just to be careful.'

Grimmer removed the SIM card from the phone and tossed it into the fire then reached for a poker, burying the little piece of plastic in the orange coals, where it melted into nothing. Another risk, however remote, neutralised.

He went upstairs and Achim followed wordlessly at his heels. Grimmer leaned over the old map with a magnifying glass.

'It's just seventy kilometres to Todspitze from Salzburg,' Grimmer said, tracing the route on the map with his slim finger. 'We'll be there in an hour. Let's hope we're luckier this time.'

'I see you've been reading the Führer,' Achim glanced at the books beside the armchair. 'Learn anything new?'

'Nothing whatsoever,' Grimmer said. 'Heaven knows why so many people fell for that monster. Including...'

'Including who?'

Grimmer had to steady himself against the desk. He was feeling sick again, sick and dizzy. 'Including, it seems, my own father.'

'Todspitze,' Achim said, eyes on the map. 'Doesn't that mean...?'

Grimmer nodded. 'Yes. It means "Death point".'

The remote-controlled gate opened and the olive-green 4x4 emerged from the yard of the small wooden chalet. The gate closed behind it and the box-shaped car went charging down the track towards the road to Austria. Crouched under the fir trees, Luke and Toni watched it go.

'They're in a hurry by the look of it.' Luke said. 'Have you seen the size of that gorilla at the wheel? He looks like a hired assassin.'

'He's not that big,' Toni said rolling his shoulders. 'In Aikido it's agility that wins. But if they're criminals, there's only one sensible thing we can do. We tell the police.'

'I tried that already. They weren't interested in my findings. There's no point calling them again until we have proof.'

Luke led the way down the mountain slope, through the trees to the new-looking steel-wire fence surrounding the house. Toni followed at some distance, with a reluctant air, glancing left and right. The sky was overcast and the blanket of grey cloud hid the peaks of the mountains. There was almost no wind.

The wire fence was only about two metres tall – and the large eyes of the mesh almost invited you to climb. Within seconds the two boys were on the other side in the small, sloping yard.

Luke felt a sharp tingling in his arms. They were now in breach of the law, trespassing on private property. At the top of the sloping yard, a little above the chalet, stood the cheaply constructed outbuilding, its unpainted concrete walls an ugly shade of grey. He skirted the chalet, approaching the front door, and his heart missed a beat when he saw the warning sticker: a picture of an Alsatian with the words ACHTUNG, HUND – BEWARE OF THE DOG underneath. Another sticker warned of an alarm system. He scanned the walls, but there was no sign of a security camera. And if there had really been a dog inside, it surely would have barked by now?

'I wonder what's in here,' Toni called from the top of the yard. He was fiddling with a padlock on the door of the outbuilding.

Luke jogged over. 'What are you doing?'

'Bet you I can pick this lock.'

'Is that a good idea?' Luke said.

'You want to check out these guys, or not?'

'Yes, but—'

'This place would be ideal for storing stolen goods.'

Luke felt they were at a crossroads. They'd come this far, but to discover something concrete they had to take more risks. Luke bit his lip. Could he trust his intuition? What if the white-haired German was just a law-abiding citizen?

'Child's play,' Toni said waving the picklock he always carried around.

The reinforced door slowly swung open, letting out a stale, musty smell.

'No alarm here, then,' Luke said, sighing with relief. His curiosity was starting to get the better of him. 'The house itself has a heavy-duty security system.'

'They're bluffing.' Toni pulled out a Mini Maglite torch. 'My dad's got one of those signs. He says it's as good as an alarm, and cheaper.'

Toni stepped inside the murky outbuilding. The beam of his torch danced in the gloom. Luke followed, threading his way between stacks of heavy oak chairs with red seat cushions. At the back stood a huge table and a dresser with glass doors, all made of the same dark wood, in the same ponderous style. A collection of old lamps hung from a chain to one side. There was a small desk in the furthest corner, laden with stacks of old cardboard boxes, bursting with books.

Suddenly Luke felt something warm brush past his ankle. From the corner of his eye he saw a pink tail flash into the shadows, and he heard an angry, high-pitched squeal that made him go cold all over. He knew at once what had touched him. He stifled his scream, pretending to cough.

'Looks like we have company,' he said as casually as he could.

'What company?'

'Rats.'

'Yuck!' Toni shrieked. 'Where?'

'They won't hurt you. Main thing is there's no Rottweiler, or anything.'

Luke moved closer to the desk, squeezing between the furniture. He was intensely aware of one thing: if the old man were to return now they'd be trapped. The outbuilding was totally chaotic and made him feel claustrophobic. Where was the famous German sense of order? It looked almost like the place had been over-stuffed on purpose.

'I just saw something move under that table,' Toni said. 'I can't stand rodents!'

Dust tickled Luke's nose. Fighting the urge to sneeze, he put his hand inside a ripped cardboard box and picked a book at random. The title was printed in heavy Gothic script. He spelled out the words with some difficulty: *Die Hanse und der Deutsche Ritterorden.* The pages inside were heavily annotated in dark pencil. Luke knew nothing about the Teutonic knights, and the tiny, blotchy engravings of castles and shields and maps didn't make him want to learn more. He began coughing. The dust from the old book smelled strangely unwholesome.

'Luke, let's get out of here.' Toni pleaded. 'It smells . . .'

Suddenly there was the sound of a car on the main road in the distance. They both froze. The sound grew louder, and then faded as the vehicle continued on its way without turning.

'Come on,' Toni said dashing towards the door, from which bright daylight streamed.

'Relax. It's a road – cars pass,' Luke said, but he hurried after his friend, just as eager to get out.

Before he could reach the door he tripped, bumping into a clothes rack, and knocked down a heavy greatcoat on its hanger. He quickly bent over to pick it up. On the left sleeve was a red band. He hung the coat on the rack and lifted the sleeve closer to his eyes – and immediately felt an ice-cold hand clenching his insides.

'Toni! Check this out.'

Reluctantly Toni returned with his torch and shone its beam on the large black swastika decorating the sleeve. Luke grabbed the torch from his friend's hand and pointed the bright beam on the clothes rack, which turned out to be crammed full of old uniforms, leather coats and military cloaks.

'I can't believe it,' Toni gasped, pointing in horror at something. 'I never thought I'd see a real one.'

There was a wild look in his eyes. He wasn't much of a reader, Luke knew, but he'd watched thousands of films and TV programmes about the Second World War.

'These are *real* SS uniforms,' Toni stuttered, studying the jagged insignia. 'Himmler's boys...And Kaltenbrunner's...A pretty mean bunch of guys, pretty mean, I tell you.'

'I know who the SS were,' Luke said.

He pointed the torch upwards at the peaked caps on a shelf above the rack of dove-grey uniforms. Some were wrapped in brown paper. He stood on his toes and took down a black cap decorated with a skull and crossbones and the letters 'SS', like twin bolts of lightning. As he replaced the cap he lost his balance again and leaned on a brittle cardboard box, from which a cascade of old magazines came sliding onto the floor.

'That's *Heimat*,' Toni said. 'Popular Nazi mag.'

Luke crouched down and turned the pages of one of the magazines. He flipped it over and shone the light on a small, yellowed sticker on the back cover. It had the name and address of the subscriber:

Heinrich Grimmer
Molkereiweg 7
München

'You know what I think, Toni?' Luke whispered.

'You think this stuff belonged to some big fish Nazi. And that his name was Heinrich Grimmer.'

'Toni...' Luke continued in a whisper, then had to clear his throat. 'When I Googled the painting that was stolen from the Vatican I found an article that said it had once been in Nazi hands.'

'Strange coincidence.' Toni stiffened. '*Shh!* Listen.'

They both stood completely still for a minute as another car approached, but, it too, drove past on the main road at the bottom of the track.

'Shall we get going?' Toni said. 'I sense you want to get online, fast.'

'A good library would be better. But the internet will have to do – assuming there's anything in public sources about this Heinrich Grimmer. Wasn't there a computer in the lobby at the guest house?'

'Yeah, the landlord was playing Patience when we arrived.'

They slipped out into the sloping yard and Toni replaced the padlock. They clambered over the fence and prepared to retrace their steps, Toni leading.

'Wait,' Luke said.

'What is it?'

'Just a quick look,' Luke said, rushing round the steel-wire fence to the front gate.

He looked at the letter box, an ornate tin affair painted with flowers. The name plate was oxidised copper. It didn't say *Wintermann*.

It said *Grimmer*.

And the name of the subscriber to the Nazi magazine had been Grimmer. Heinrich Grimmer.

22

Legs dangling over nothingness, heart pounding in terror, Father Sebastiano could feel his grip loosen on the gutter at the edge of the tiled roof. It was a miracle he'd managed to grab hold at all, he'd been skidding so fast, and he knew for certain he didn't have the strength to climb up again. The seconds crawled and the terror of death expanded as the sharp pain in his hands and wrists and shoulder sockets steadily intensified.

He could hear the alarmed shouts of the onlookers gathered in the street below. He twisted his neck and saw a whole mass of people . . . A wave of fresh horror washed through him and he clamped his hands even harder on the metal gutter, fearing he might faint.

'Polizia!' yelled a voice from somewhere above.

He raised his eyes and saw a man in civilian clothes crouching on the ridge of the roof showing an official badge. Father Sebastiano felt his chest fill up with a different shade of fear, or was it just shame? He closed his eyes and the past few months and years sped through his mind in a mad, rushing stream: the wins, the losses, and then the debts, ever more enormous, ever more impossible to pay. The brutal, swinish faces of the moneylenders and the debt-collectors, murderous men with unspeakable backgrounds, always banging on his door.

It was all over now. He was finished. Why not just let go and have done with it? But suicide was a sin...

'We have some urgent questions,' said the plain-clothed officer who'd scuttled down to the roof edge with no trouble at all. 'It concerns a certain painting.'

Father Sebastiano was too scared to grasp the offered hand – it meant letting go of the gutter.

'Help me!'

'It's all right.' The police officer calmly grabbed him by the wrist. 'You're safe now.'

Slowly, painfully, Father Sebastiano raised his knee over the edge of the gutter. The officer pulled him upwards, and he was able to clamber onto the roof, moving forward on his knees, grazing his shins on the uneven tiles. To his dismay the officer then let go of his hand, leaving him to his own devices. He crawled upwards like some slow reptile, grabbing the tiles with his hands, trembling all over.

'Wait...'

The police officer turned impatiently, offering his hand once more.

Feeling sick to the stomach and sweating profusely, Father Sebastiano inched his way up the roof. He couldn't quite reach the offered hand yet, but he was no longer right on the perilous edge, so he tried to rise to his feet and as he did so he slipped yet again, crashing onto his face, hitting his breast bone, hard. He was sliding, feet first, towards the edge... He heard a roar of alarm...

Stabat Mater dolorosa, juxta Crucem lacrimosa, dum pendebat Filius...

Almost without thinking he'd begun to pray.

Again he caught the gutter with his hands, now raw and bleeding. Down in the depths below the excited spectators murmured, waving their arms. He had no strength left. None. Then the worst possible thing happened: the gutter began to give way under his weight, screeching as it bent. Something fell, striking him on the cheek, a screw or some other fastening. And now time froze as he realised that he was definitely falling, backwards, with a stretch of gutter still clamped in his hands, towards the crowded street and certain death below.

His lips kept moving as he hurtled through the air, down, down, down...

Quando corpus morietur, fac ut animae donetur paradise Gloria.

Amen.

And then he hit a grey surface that seemed to balloon around him. The impact winded him and there was a sound like an enormous sigh. Several firemen surrounded the inflatable rescue mattress they'd positioned in exactly the right spot under the eaves of the block of flats. Coming slowly round, Father Sebastiano had two thoughts inside his head: he was alive, but he wished he wasn't.

'I'm Lieutenant Marcello Bari.' A man Father Sebastiano had never seen before extended his hand.

The priest rose unsteadily to his feet. A gasp went up in the surrounding crowd when they saw his dog collar. There were mobiles in several outstretched hands, filming him, but he didn't even try to cover his face; it was too late for that. What had a priest been doing up on the roof? He knew that was what the spectators must be thinking as he followed Lieutenant Bari into a police car... His mind was racing with such speed that he thought he might go crazy, shock blending with shame, shame merging into fear. But all these feelings were as nothing compared with another sensation that washed through him.

Relief.

As soon as the doors slammed shut and the car shot forward he started talking. Lieutenant Bari didn't even need to prompt him. It all came pouring out: the horse races, the athletics meets and the football matches. The bets he'd placed at the bookmakers and online – modest at first, then quite high, then cripplingly enormous, as he'd scrambled in vain to win back all he'd lost. The loan sharks. The pawn shops. The sleepless nights. The fraud he'd committed against his employers – and his God. The antique mixing bowl he'd stolen from the Vatican Museum and sold to a Chinese collector whom he'd met one cold January evening in a car parked behind the Coliseum. He talked and he talked, and Bari just listened, recording every word on his dictaphone.

Father Sebastiano was still talking when the car swung past the Palazzo Quirinale and slipped into the underground garage. Bari made a note or two with his free hand, perking up visibly when the priest mentioned the orchid petals he'd received from a white-haired man he'd met through a shady art dealer, and who was accompanied by a young man who had the air of a bodyguard.

'Petals?' Bari repeated. 'Where was this man from?'

'Germany.'

'What did he want?' Bari asked as the car came to a stand-still in the silent garage and the driver switched off the engine.

'The floor plan of the Vatican Museums, including the areas closed to the public.' Father Sebastiano lowered his head. 'And full details of the security system: cameras, alarms and motion detectors.'

His head still bowed, the priest closed his eyes for a moment, then recovered his composure and continued talking, explaining how he'd already sold the petals to a dealer in the perfume industry using the contacts that the German himself had provided.

No, he didn't know anything else about the man.

'Are you sure? Do you have a phone number, an address, or something?'

'Just a mobile number for emergencies.' Father Sebastiano swallowed. 'I was supposed to warn him if anything went wrong.'

'And did you?'

'I texted him earlier to say...you'd been to the Prefecture.'

Lieutenant Bari swore loudly, his face darkening, then touched Father Sebastiano's arm.

'Sorry,' he said. 'You've been very helpful.'

As they marched up the stairs, Father Sebastiano heard Bari speak to the officer at his side.

'The things these priests get up to! Madonna!'

The beer cellar in the basement of the Gasthaus Grosch was teeming with customers. Locked in grave conversation, they clutched the handles of their bucket-sized glasses, occasionally glancing up at the football match that flickered on the television screen.

Panelled in dark wood, the dimly lit cellar was decorated with stuffed stag heads, copper cowbells and fading photos of workmen labouring in the now-defunct salt mine nearby. The landlord, a red-faced, burly figure in a leather vest, stood washing glasses behind the bar, his face partly obscured by the thick blue smoke from his cigarette.

The computer offered for the use of guests was located in a former telephone booth in a dark corner. Luke cleared the history and scooped up the sheets he'd printed. Using the internet was free, but printing a page of A4 cost one euro a pop – not cheap considering that the result was barely legible. Luke handed over a twenty-euro note at the bar, receiving almost no change, and, instead of a smile, a grunt and an unfriendly scowl.

There had been just the one Grimmer in the local phonebook, a man called Dietrich. Luke's throat tightened with excitement. For he now knew Dietrich Grimmer's home address – and it matched the location of the chalet.

So the white-haired man wasn't Hans-Martin Wintermann but Dietrich Grimmer. Heinrich Grimmer's son. The son of a Nazi.

Luke felt the stares of the locals on his skin as he weaved his way between the tables. The smell of beer, cigarette smoke and sweat was so thick it almost made him gag. Someone made a remark that triggered an eruption of booming laughter, and Luke was sure he knew who the butt of the joke was...

Back in their small room upstairs, Toni lay sprawled across his bed, leafing through the material Luke had told him to read – the stuff about the Caravaggio's link with Nazi Germany.

'You won't believe this,' Luke said, waving the papers he'd printed. 'Guess who Heinrich Grimmer used to work for?'

'The Nazis.'

'And guess what his job was?'

'Tailor, specialising in bow ties?'

Ignoring Toni's attempt at humour, Luke sat at the desk and started reading, pencil in hand. Heinrich Grimmer didn't have much of an internet presence, but the bits and pieces Luke had found on various historical websites corroborated each other. He could barely believe it. Heinrich Grimmer had been the head cashier of the Reichsbank, with direct responsibility for the Nazis' immense gold reserves.

Throughout the war the Nazi leadership had systematically stockpiled immense quantities of precious metals, including gold, depositing it in various Swiss banks. But the vast bulk of the gold reserves, as much as a hundred tonnes of bullion, had remained in Germany in the dying days of the Nazi regime until it was packed onto thirteen train carriages and a convoy of lorries, and hidden in Kaiseroda potassium mine near the village of Merkers, in the state of Thüringen. By the time Berlin fell to the Allies the gold was already safely stored in the mine shafts, half a kilometre underground.

As the Americans pressed ahead into Germany, crossing the Rhine, the Third Army commanded by General George S. Patton came surging across the plains of Thüringen. The Nazi leadership immediately realised that the gold was in danger and tried to transfer it back to Berlin, but it being Easter, the railway timetables didn't allow the operation to go ahead. By the time the Americans rolled into Merkers, all the Germans had managed to salvage was 450 sacks of banknotes.

At first the Kaiseroda mine meant nothing to the

liberating forces, and the immense treasure buried there might never have come to light had it not been for a lucky coincidence. Two American military police had offered a ride to a couple of local women. As they sped past the mine gates, one of the women commented: 'That's where they put the gold.'

When they checked out the mine, the Americans also found artistic treasures from various museums – works by Raphael, Rembrandt, Titian and Dürer, as well as ancient Egyptian masterpieces.

Luke tried to keep his voice calm as he gave Toni a summary of what he'd read.

'It all fits together a bit too neatly,' his friend responded. 'But you've got a strong imagination, I'll give you that.'

'Which part did I imagine?' Luke stepped up to the sink to dab cold water onto his hot cheeks. 'Heinrich Grimmer was in charge of the Nazis' money bags and treasure. And the Caravaggio once belonged to the Nazis.'

'And?'

'And now his son, Dietrich Grimmer, already an old man, is involved in stealing the Caravaggio back from the Vatican. That closes the circle.'

'Nice story,' Toni said. 'Pity it makes no sense whatsoever.'

'You don't think it's a weird coincidence?'

'I'm more interested in cash than I am in coincidences,' Toni said. 'And I doubt I'll be seeing any.'

'The fact is, the Nazis hid tonnes of gold right here in the Alps.'

'I know. And the Yanks found it. I've seen a film about it. Two films, actually—'

'Do you mind shutting up for a bit? I'm trying to think.'

'Quiet, everyone! Luke is *thinking*,' Toni cackled, then swept Luke's papers onto the floor, folded his arms under his head and closed his eyes.

Luke tried to organise his thoughts. Toni was right. No doubt the gold had long since been recovered. But still. This was a mystery worth investigating.

'Toni, I've changed my mind. I think we should try to get inside Grimmer's chalet,' Luke said. 'Not the out-building, but the house itself. We have twenty-four hours left.'

'By the way, have you texted that Miss Hart yet?'

'She beat me to it. But I texted back saying we were hiking,' Luke winked. 'And we were, in fact. In that forest where we watched the chalet. So, what do you think? Shall we go back?'

'Let me get this straight.' Toni spoke without opening his eyes. 'You're suggesting breaking into someone's home? An outbuilding is one thing, but a private house is serious stuff.'

'We're investigating a crime. Let's at least drive back there and see if they're still out.'

Toni sat up on his bed, shaking his head.

'While you work up your courage I need to go online again,' Luke said. 'I need to check some facts.'

23

Dietrich Grimmer took a strong painkiller, fighting the headache that was like a mechanical presence inside his skull. He could barely speak, such was the crushing disappointment. Todspitze had turned out to be another dead end. Sure, it had once been the site of a Nazi storage depot, but nothing was left of it now, and the inhabitants of the nearest village were unwilling to talk about the past.

Achim had driven them straight to the next location, Elend, but there too they had drawn a blank. Yes, the place had once been a vast underground warehouse, but it was now completely flooded, and a local man had told them it had been that way since the 1950s.

Schwartzberg. Todspitze. Elend.

Three locations, three disappointments.

During his long research, Grimmer had found many references to still-to-be-discovered Nazi secrets – bunkers and depots and hiding places that were unrecorded on any map. Some said Eichmann and others had hidden enormous riches at such sites. But maybe it was all fiction?

In one corner of the room stood an old-fashioned microfiche-reader that he'd bought in the 1960s. So long ago already... He couldn't bear to think of all the lonely hours he'd spent on that machine, poring over the micro-films stored in rows and rows of small grey cardboard boxes on the top shelf.

Mein Kampf, Volume Two, published in 1926, lay on the floor beside the desk. Dietrich Grimmer held his temples. The painkiller wasn't working. He closed his eyes.

He hated the Nazis. He always had. Hitler's ideas and his war machine hadn't just destroyed the enemy. It had destroyed Germany itself, slaughtering innocent men, women and children, and blighting the name of a whole nation for generations to come. When the end finally came, the cowardly dictator had killed himself, leaving behind a wasteland of flattened cities, countless miserable orphans, a people with their heads bowed in shame.

Up until these last few days Dietrich Grimmer had always believed his father had never fully embraced Nazi ideology, even if he'd been forced to put his mathematical talents at its service. How could he have avoided it when Hitler took over the bank that employed him, and when Eichmann then picked him out in person? Although Dietrich Grimmer didn't know what lay at the end of the trail, he'd always assumed it would be some proud gesture against the Nazis. His mother had spoken of the mathe-matician's determination to provide for his family. All the son needed to do was keep faith with his severe yet upstanding father, and all would be revealed and redeemed in the end.

Grimmer tried to slow down his breathing. Had he really been wrong for all these years? Had he been terribly, terribly wrong?

What if the trail his father had set him was just a joke, a taunt that had lured him into a wild-goose chase that lasted a lifetime ... only to end in humiliation, a worthless painting and a dead man's salute to the worst dictator in human history?

Der größte Deutsche. The Greatest German. Adolf Hitler.

Did he have to agree? Dietrich Grimmer asked himself with a cold shudder. Was that the last hurdle? Did he somehow have to show that he agreed with his father's opinion? Was that the price he had to pay for his inheritance? Did he have to become a Nazi?

Vater, Vater ...

And again his eyes turned to the three mountains that loomed up in the ugly landscape painting pinned to the wall. Why couldn't he stop looking at it? Was there something familiar about it? He felt as though his head was about to explode. Scrabbling among the chaotic heaps of books and maps on his desk he searched for his medicine tube, doubling the dose, slipping yet another tablet under his tongue. Then, with a tremulous hand, he reached for the glasses that hung on their golden chain and put them on, turning to the final chapter of *Mein Kampf*.

But he couldn't concentrate. He studied the painting once more. And this time, all of a sudden, it triggered a faint memory. The shepherdess, the three mountains, the sun. Where, where in heaven's name had he seen them before?

He leaped out of his chair, dragged the stepladder to one end of the shelf and began emptying it, piling the books on the floor. Then he flicked through them, one by one, without reading a single word, searching frantically.

A new question burned in his mind like acid. How had Hitler's painting come into Heinrich Grimmer's possession? Had the Führer given it to him in person? Most likely not: Hitler's artistic career had fizzled out in his youth, long before he rose to power.

The search seemed hopeless – there were so very many books – but for once, Grimmer struck it lucky almost right away. Tucked inside an old biography of Carl Friedrich Gauss, the world-famous German mathematician, was a yellowed invoice from an antique dealer in Vienna. Grimmer knew it was in Vienna where, as a young man, Hitler had unsuccessfully tried to become an artist: he'd twice applied to the art academy and been rejected for lack of talent.

The composition of the painting was sketched on the back of the invoice. It was dated during the war. And the buyer's name was one that Grimmer abhorred almost as much as that of Hitler himself. A small business card was paperclipped to the document. On the card was written: '*For Heinrich Grimmer, with all good wishes, Adolf Eichmann.*'

So Eichmann had given this painting to Grimmer's father, who in turn had incorporated it into the trail of clues and hints that he'd left his son. But why? What was the point? With shaking hands Grimmer put the invoice back into the book and replaced it on the shelf. He felt more bewildered than ever, and terrified of what he might yet discover.

Luke's fingers leaped over the sticky keys of the keyboard in the basement of the Gasthaus Grosch. Toni was hovering at his side, providing shelter from the curious glances of the locals. On no account did Luke want them to see what he was reading on his screen. Another laugh had gone up in the smoke-filled room when the boys had reappeared, and every now and then one of the burly drinkers would cast a contemptuous look in their direction. There was something brutish about these stocky, flushed, low-voiced Alp-dwellers with their thick accents and their big fists.

Hadn't Bavaria been the heartland of the Nazi movement? And hadn't Hitler been especially popular in southern Germany? What would these men, whose grandfathers and fathers had lived during the war, make of his research?

'Let's go,' Toni said. 'I don't like it here.'

'Just a minute. No one's going to hurt us.'

Luke was running searches in different languages and on different browsers and search engines – desperate for a few more details about Heinrich Grimmer's role in the Reichsbank. What did a bank's head cashier actually do? Could he personally get his hands on the Nazi loot? And why had he decided to live in this remote spot in the Alps after the war? Was it in order to be near some secret stash that no one had discovered?

'Come on, Luke!'

The more he read about the dying days of the German Reich, the more he realised how important the Alps had become in the closing stages of the war... At the end of April 1945 Hitler and his general staff took cover in the Führerbunker in Berlin. Some of his most trusted SS officers headed to the Alps, carrying arms and gold, preparing for a final stand. Had the head cashier, Heinrich Grimmer, been a member of that inner circle?

'*Trink, trink, Brüderlein trink!*' the local red-necks burst into song. '*Lass doch die Sorgen zu Haus.*'

The whole bar was standing, belting out the song. The peasants clinked their massive glasses, splashing foamy beer all over the floor. The landlord came striding from the back room, dressed in lederhosen and a Tyrolean hat with feathers on it. A round belly protruded between his leather braces, and his fleshy neck carried an equally round bald head. He shook hands left and right, grinning, slapping backs, then lowered his bulk onto a stool at the head of the table, letting out a loud grunt. His wife rushed over carrying a large beer mug with a metal lid.

With a clatter of chairs and rumble of laughter, the drinkers sat down as one man. Someone grabbed the landlord by the elbow and began explaining something. Eyes rolled under bushy brows as the men scowled in the direction of Toni and Luke. The boys glanced at one another. For the first time Luke feared for his safety in this place. It was as though the hatred that they'd somehow aroused was coming to the boil. Even the ordinary German couple sitting at a corner table looked scared.

It was hard to concentrate, but he forced himself to return his attention to the information on his screen. When it came to Nazi treasure, the greatest unsolved mystery was the disappearance of the gold linked with Adolf Eichmann. When the first American troops had arrived in Altaussee in Austria on 8 May 1945 the Nazi stronghold at Blaa Alm had been found abandoned. But the US Army never found Eichmann's gold. It had simply vanished without a trace, and scores of historians had scoured the archives in vain to find out where it ended up. Eichmann himself had been executed in 1962 after

Israeli special forces had kidnapped him in Argentina and brought him home for trial.

'I'm leaving!' Toni hissed.

'Just one more second.'

Luke continued reading, gripped by the article. Several historians had come to the conclusion that Eichmann's gold and other valuables had been hidden somewhere around Altaussee, in an area no larger than nine square kilometres. And in 1982, in a small mountain hut nearby, several kilos of gold coins had indeed come to light...

The hut in question was a mere thirty kilometres from Bergstein.

One of the drinkers walked past, close, and moments later Luke suddenly realised that everything had gone quiet. Hunched over their beers, the men glared at the young foreigners through the hovering veils of cigarette smoke. Had the man seen the page Luke was reading?

'Well?' Toni said. 'Before we get lynched.'

'You're right. Let's go.'

'Make sure you log off properly. And delete the history. I don't trust these guys.'

Luke covered his tracks with a few rapid keystrokes, quietly wondering whether any of the assembled peasants even knew how to use a computer. As he followed Toni outside he could feel the aggressive stares of the locals burning on his back.

'I wouldn't come here on holiday,' Toni said. 'What a bunch of hicks.'

As they walked briskly towards their small car Luke felt strangely oppressed by the darkness gathering over the lonely Alpine landscape. Although it was spring time, and the weather was mild, there was a hint of gloom in the air, a deathly, barren tinge. All was well while the sun shone at the foot of these gigantic geological formations but as soon as the light was taken away all life, all colour and all warmth faded too. And the sun set early here, plunging behind the towering mountains to the southwest.

'I heard about this deep valley somewhere in the Alps where they're planning to install a series of giant mirrors on the upper slopes, to reflect sunlight down into the valley,' Luke said, doing up his seatbelt. 'No more solar deprivation.'

'Well, those guys in the bar were certainly deprived of something.'

Toni swung the car onto the main road. They passed a small garden centre, its yard full of stock: soil and fertiliser in plastic sacks, rakes, spades and wheelbarrows, and a locked cage full of multicoloured gnomes.

Some of the oncoming cars had Austrian licence plates. Grimmer's chalet was near the border.

'So you really think you can get us inside?' Luke said, lowering his voice instinctively.

'Trust me,' Toni winked, patting his trouser pocket. 'It's no big deal.'

'You seemed kind of nervous last time we were there.'

'You seemed a bit jumpy yourself, Luke, my boy.'

'It'll be fine. We just need to be sure they're not home.'

Luke's mind was on the material he'd read online. He was finding it hard to hold all the information in his head.

'Strange to think this is where the Nazis came running when they lost the war,' he said gesturing at the dark valley ahead.

'I know,' Toni said darkly. 'The Allies expected years of guerrilla warfare, but it didn't happen.'

The dying embers of the sun blazed like fire behind the jagged crest of the mountains. The oncoming cars were few and far between, but they all had their lights on and kept appearing and disappearing on the winding road before swishing suddenly past.

'Call me thick, but I didn't quite get the link with the theft from the Vatican,' Toni said. 'Run me through that one more time, would you?'

'I never said I had any proof.' Luke paused. He was getting tired, and as his excitement wore off he was less certain about his suspicions. 'I just think there are too many coincidences.'

A white Mercedes 4x4 overtook them, sweeping past at great speed.

'Wasn't that them?' Luke said. 'It's the same car.'

'Relax,' Toni said – but he slowed down all the same, letting the other vehicle get ahead of them. 'Theirs was olive green, remember? And that's an M-series, whereas theirs was a G-series.'

Luke took a swig from the water bottle. He knew his mental capacities were starting to be affected by his fatigue; he could neither see nor think straight, and his nerves were on edge.

They didn't speak for the next few minutes. Soon they passed the turning leading up the forested slope to Grimmer's chalet. They hid the car and made the final approach on foot. It was much harder in the dark, and without Toni's little torch it would have been impossible. They advanced between the trunks of the fir trees, feeling their way along the soft carpet of pine needles.

The lights were on in the tiny chalet. With its mossy roof and fretwork decorations, the place looked like a gingerbread house. The green 4x4 stood parked in front of the door.

'That settles it. Let's go back.' Toni sounded almost relieved. 'They're home and they're hardly likely to go anywhere tonight.'

'Unless they go out to eat,' Luke said. 'You should have seen how late people were eating in Italy.'

'This is Germany, boy. *Deutschland*. They *invented* the early night.'

'Let's wait a bit.'

Toni started telling a long and complicated account of some war film he'd seen. He always talked when he was nervous. Luke let him natter on. The minutes crawled. The wind whispered in the dark trees.

'*Shh!*' Luke squeezed his friend's arm. 'Look.'

The external light had been turned on.

The door opened and Grimmer stepped out with his young companion, both men casting looks in different directions, as though preparing to fend off an attack.

For a terrifying instant the younger man seemed to be staring straight into the forest where Luke and Toni were hiding. Luke felt a cold shudder pass though him. The boys were both wearing bright fleece jackets but it was dark, and Luke's reason told him that the man could see nothing whatsoever among the dense trees. He was painfully aware of how lonely this place was. If they were caught here they'd be completely helpless.

The men skirted the chalet and came into the front yard, where another lamp hooked up to a motion sensor suddenly bathed the 4x4 in a bluish haze. They got into the vehicle, the young one taking the wheel as before, and the heavy old car roared off down the track and turned onto the road heading for Bergstein.

'Let's see some more of those lock-picking skills, then,' Luke said. 'But make it quick.'

They climbed the fence as before and crept closer to the chalet. Luke felt unnaturally alert. His legs had gone a little wobbly, but he tried to hide it, knowing that the slightest sign of hesitation would put Toni off the whole enterprise. They reached the door. Luke stopped to listen.

'You sure this is a good idea?' Toni said, pick in one hand, the small torch in the other.

Luke glanced at the picture of an Alsatian on the door. 'We'll soon see.'

'Wait!' Toni pulled Luke's hand off the doorbell. 'Are you serious? What if there is someone else inside? Or a dog...?'

'There's only one way to find out.'

Luke pressed the button. A surprisingly loud buzz sounded inside. Then there was silence. He rang a second time. Then once more to be sure.

No reply. Clearly there was no one at home. And no dog.

He glanced at Toni, who came forward with his pick. Luke tried the handle, not imagining for a single second that the door would be unlocked – but to his astonishment it was.

How was it possible? Could it be a trap of some sort?

They tiptoed into the small chalet. The hall smelled of waxed furniture, mildewy books, old carpets and dust. Toni wordlessly handed Luke the torch, and they moved deeper inside, taking slow steps across the creaking floor.

*

Grimmer hated eating out, but he knew that Achim, having grown up in poverty, took a childlike delight in choosing food from a menu. Besides, Grimmer himself needed to get out of the chalet and to forget the sight of all the dusty books and maps and manuscripts that littered his study floor.

'Are we close, boss?' Achim asked, staring through the windscreen at the winding road. 'Tell me honestly.'

The lights of the village of Bergstein glowed a short distance ahead.

'Very close.' Grimmer gave his assistant a friendly clutch on the shoulder and tried to smile.

'Where shall we eat?' Achim asked as they entered the village. 'At that guest house again?'

'They serve excellent bratwurst. Or would you rather drive to Teisendorf to that Turkish place? You choose.'

'Here is fine.' Achim pulled up in the street opposite the Gasthaus Grosch.

'*Verdammt!*' Grimmer said, feeling his pockets. 'I left my wallet.'

'I'll go back to fetch it.' Without the slightest sign of annoyance, Achim refastened his seatbelt once more. 'You go ahead and order for both of us.'

'The usual? Spinach, but no sauerkraut?'

'Yes please, boss. And plenty of roast potatoes.'

Achim swung a U-turn and accelerated back out of the village.

Grimmer stepped into the beer cellar and chose a table in the corner. He poured himself a glass of water from the jug on the table and began writing furiously in his notebook. He was usually good at solving problems in his head, and would amuse himself by completing complex mathematical calculations over a period of days without writing down so much as a single formula. But right now his mind was a tangled mess.

'Good evening.' The landlord wiped the table with a cloth. 'Just the one of you tonight?'

'Two.' Grimmer flipped over his notebook. 'You're doing good business, I see?'

'If the foreigners had any money, I would. We have these two boys staying – heaven knows what they think this place is. An internet café?'

'Boys? From where?'

'England, maybe. Foreigners. Driving around at all hours. And Valpurga found *this* in the waste-paper basket in their room.'

The landlord pulled a crumpled and torn piece of paper from his pocket. When he saw what was printed on it Grimmer almost cried out in surprise, but he checked himself. It was a picture of a painting by Albrecht Dürer. The caption read: *Tracing the rightful owners of artworks looted by the Nazis.*

Achim pressed the accelerator and the powerful 4x4 surged past the sign for Oberstbrunn, nearing the turning that led up through the forest to the chalet. He was secretly pleased to have an excuse to go back; he had a nasty feeling he'd forgotten to lock the door behind him.

It was the kind of lapse that drove the boss up the wall. This way, Achim would be able to cover his tracks. Never the most patient of men, Herr Grimmer had been on a particularly short fuse lately and it wasn't a good time to provoke him.

24

Luke paused when he reached the top of the small staircase. The narrow beam of the torch licked the wooden walls. Toni had stayed downstairs, 'keeping a lookout', ready to make a quick escape if the men returned.

The attic was a narrow space lined with bookshelves that reached all the way to the ceiling. There were two rooms. A colossal mahogany desk sat in the centre of the first room, with two old-fashioned office chairs, one on either side. The desk was littered with maps, index cards, yellowing journals, and thick books in leather bindings. There were more books on the floor, stacked in towers, some opened and lying face down. It was as though someone had decided to read them all at once.

He wiped his hands on his trousers and carefully picked up one of the books on the desk, shining his Maglite on the front cover. The title was in German, but he understood what it meant: *Mathematical Puzzles for the Hitler Youth*. He turned to the flyleaf, which gave the name of the author: Heinrich Grimmer.

Footsteps climbed the stairs. Toni was getting lonely...

'Found anything?'

'Maybe.' He showed the book to his friend. 'Look at the dedication.'

'What does it mean?'

'*For Dietrich, Merry Christmas! Berlin, 24 December 1944. Father.*'

'So that confirms that the white-haired guy is the son of the Nazi.'

'I guess.'

Luke was thinking, did that mean Dietrich Grimmer was also a Nazi?

'We're kind of trapped up here if someone returns suddenly,' Toni said. He looked pale in the glare of the torch.

'Just a few more minutes.'

Emboldened by his discovery Luke turned his attention to the bookshelves. Some of the publications were modern – science journals, chess journals, mathematical-research journals, all addressed to the same subscriber: Dietrich Grimmer. At least when it came to his intellectual interests, the son had followed in the footsteps of his father.

A small sliding stepladder was attached to the bookshelf, which could be used to reach the books at the top. Luke climbed up the rungs and peered over the top shelf. There was a long cardboard tube behind the row of books. He grabbed it and quickly climbed down again, pulling out a large photocopy.

'I can't believe it...' He spread the paper on the floor, but it kept curling up again. 'Check this out, Toni! What did I say?'

'What is it?' Toni held down one corner of the large sheet with his hand.

'Don't you recognise it?'

'Is it . . .?'

Luke nodded. It was a photocopy of Caravaggio's *Burial of Christ* – the painting that had been stolen from the Vatican.

His pulse accelerated. It was scary to see his suspicions confirmed . . . It was terrifying.

At that moment there was the sound of a car on the track. Luke and Toni rushed towards the stairs to begin the climb down, but it was too late; keys clinked against the lock outside.

'I double-locked it,' Toni said in a reedy voice. 'So we couldn't be taken by surprise.'

'*They'll* be surprised, if they remember they left it unlocked . . .'

The front door swung open and the lights were switched on. Luke and Toni crept back up the stairs as silently as they could. Luke scuttled into the space under the big desk and Toni slipped behind a cupboard in the corner. They were useless hiding places – if someone sat at the desk or went to the cupboard they'd see the intruders at once . . . But there was nowhere else.

Luke held his breath. Hurried footsteps pounded straight up the stairs. A light was switched on and the steps came directly towards the desk. He was already sure he'd be caught now, but miraculously the person didn't come round to his side of the desk. The steps passed on the other side and then simply turned and left. Within seconds the visitor had reached the bottom of the stairs once more . . . There was the sound of the front door being meticulously locked. Then the car started and set off again.

At once Luke clambered forward and stood to his feet.

'What was that all about?' he whispered, switching on his torch.

'It was the bodyguard. He took something from the desk and then just left.' Toni came forward from the shadows. 'Come on, Luke. Let's go!'

'Just one last look,' Luke said, fumbling among the papers. 'Keep guard downstairs, if you want.'

'Too right, I want. It's a miracle we weren't caught just now. I'm waiting outside, do you hear? Not inside.'

'Fine. I won't be long,' Luke said. 'Leave the door ajar and whistle if you hear something.'

His hands were shaking as he tried to make a systematic scan of the papers and publications piled up on the desk – journals, maps, notebooks... Toni's footsteps went down the stairs then the front door opened and closed. Somewhere in the dark forest an owl hooted among the whispering trees.

Luke swung round the torch; the beam was already flickering a little and had developed a yellowish tint. He saw a picture pinned to the wall: an ugly-looking landscape painting, and beside it, a piece of an old map with a black triangle drawn on it.

Achim Voynovych drove the 4x4 to the bottom of the track and some way along the road, then pulled up to make a call.

'There's someone in the chalet.' He didn't want to confess that he'd left the door unlocked so he chose his words carefully. 'They must have broken in...'

'You didn't enter?'

'I did, but I pretended not to see them. Burglars,

probably. One was hiding behind the cupboard and the other was under your desk.'

'*Let us think,*' Grimmer said calmly. '*As we only have two choices: let them go, or—*'

'That's what I figured. I wasn't sure what you wanted.'

There was a pause as the boss reflected.

'*We can't let them go. They might have seen something. Do what you need to do – I'll get a taxi right away.*'

Achim stepped out of the car, locked it and strode back along the road, keeping close to the trees, ready to take cover at any moment. When he'd passed the turning he slipped his Sig Sauer pistol from his armpit holster and checked the clip: full, naturally. Moving in silent bounds, very fast, he climbed through the forest towards the chalet.

PART THREE

25

Luke was clutching a sheet of paper with a small scrap of fabric attached to it. He'd found it inside a transparent plastic document sleeve lying on the desk.

There was a series of tiny Gothic characters on the dirty little patch of material, written with a fountain pen, which spelled three words and a series of letters:

Schwartzberg-Todspitze-Elend
5-6-20-8-20-17-22-23-6-5-6-24-23-21-3-9-6

The number 8 was enclosed in a jagged circle, like a sun. The numbers and a series of letters had been copied onto the sheet in a kind of grid, followed by a name and a question mark...

5	6	20	8	20	17	22	23	6	5	6	24	23	21	3	9	6
d	e	r	g	r	ö	ß	t	e	d	e	u	t	s	c	h	e

Der größte Deutsche =
Adolf Hitler?
Luke knew the words meant 'The greatest German'. Hitler's name was underlined several times. The question mark was thick, and the dot under it had spread into the

sheet of paper, forming a dark stain. Luke brought the patch of fabric close to his nose. It was like sackcloth, but even rougher. The smell of linseed oil jolted his memory and he instantly realised what he was holding: a piece of canvas. He'd once been given a set of oil paints for Christmas and set up a studio in the spare room at home in Brussels, where he tried to learn the real techniques, stretching the canvas on its frame and priming it with gesso. He'd begged to have the paints, and his mum had finally relented, but his enthusiasm had been short-lived. The paints and a couple of unfinished daubs still lay gathering dust somewhere in the family home in Brussels. The memory made him feel ashamed. He didn't like quitting.

Was the scrap of canvas somehow linked with the theft in the Vatican? *How?* It couldn't be a piece of the stolen Caravaggio – the lettering was too modern, and distinctly German. And, besides, the Caravaggio had been returned, apparently undamaged, probably against a ransom, or so the reports in the press assumed.

Luke couldn't get his mum out of his mind, and he gave his head a shake, a silly habit of his when he wanted to change focus. One thing was certain: she'd have been shocked and amazed if she could see where he was now. His whole body had gone taut with excitement and fear.

He returned his attention to the photocopy of the Caravaggio, spreading it over the floor once more. There was a small rectangle in the corner. It was around the same size as the small patch of canvas with the writing on it. Luke began to roll up the photocopy in order to slip it back inside its tube and when he did so, he suddenly noticed something on the back of the picture: another rectangle, in exactly the same place as the one on the front, with the same writing on it.

Schwartzberg-Todspitze-Elend

5-6-20-8-20-17-22-23-6-5-6-24-23-21-3-9-6

What did it mean? Had the scrap of canvas been attached to the back of the stolen Caravaggio?

Luke had always loved secret codes, puzzles and mysteries... His favourite code was a simple one named after Julius Caesar, which involved simply shifting letters left or right in the alphabet, yielding what looked like a random sequence. To crack the code the receiver simply needed one number. '3,' for example, meant that 'A' was replaced by 'C,' 'B' was replaced by 'D' and so on.

The ancient Romans had also invented a technique where you tattooed words onto the scalp of a slave, then waited for his hair to grow back before sending him on his way to deliver the message. A barber would be on hand at the destination to reveal the hidden words. Not as quick as an encrypted email, but safer.

Except for the slave, who was probably killed.

There was a sound downstairs. Luke froze. Wasn't Toni supposed to be on the lookout? Luke was sure he hadn't heard a car, just the murmur of the forest and the regular hooting of an owl. But now footsteps were tramping up the stairs once more, and they didn't sound like Toni's...

Luke switched off his torch and stood in the darkness, heart hammering against his ribcage. The timbers of the stairs creaked as the person approached. Luke felt the hairs stand up on his neck.

Without even thinking he sank to a crouch and scuttled back to his hiding place under the desk. A switch was flicked and the lamps of the bronze chandelier came on, flooding the room with light. He saw a pair of legs. Black shoes.

A man walked towards the cupboard, stopped, then turned. Luke could feel his pulse at his jaw and in both his arms. Now the shoes were coming towards the desk. Had he been seen?

Too scared even to breathe, Luke clenched his fists, driving his nails into the skin of his palms.

The man dropped to a crouch and peered under the desk, pointing at Luke with a black pistol. *It was Grimmer's driver…* He didn't look at all surprised to see Luke. But boy, did he look angry. He said something in German.

Luke clambered forward on all fours and rose to his feet, raising his arms towards the ceiling.

The man had stepped back but he now charged forward, barking a phrase in German.

'Do you speak English?' Luke asked in the politest voice he could muster. '*Sprechen Sie Englisch? Bitte?*'

'What are you doing here, you little thief?' the man replied in heavily accented English. 'Do you know what we do to thieves?'

'I'm not a thief.'

'Where is your friend?' the man snapped. 'There were two of you before.'

'What friend? I'm on my own.'

'Don't lie to me. I'm not stupid.' The man was almost shaking with anger. 'Where is your friend?'

Toni peered at the chalet from behind the large dog kennel at the top of the fenced yard. He'd taken cover as soon as he'd seen the familiar figure in the leather jacket

204

arrive, gun in hand. Moving swiftly, the man had bounded up the front steps and into the chalet before Toni had time to whistle – and within seconds the lights had been turned on upstairs.

This was bad, really bad... Luke was trapped, and Toni felt like it was his fault. But what could he have done? He was unarmed, whereas the man had a gun. Luke and he had taken a mad risk by coming to this place at all, and here they were now, facing the consequences.

The sun had sunk behind the mountains, so quickly it felt like it had been switched off. Toni tried to figure out what he should do next, but his mind was a blank. At least the young man didn't know of Toni's existence – unless Luke had told him. Maybe there was some way of surprising him?

Maybe he could hide behind the bin shelter? From there he'd see the front door. He gathered all his courage and crept along the edge of the chalet, keeping away from the squares of light that shone through the upstairs window. Congratulating himself for this small, almost meaningless step he sat on the cold grass and leaned his back against the wooden bin shelter. Where was the white-haired man?

At that moment a diesel engine approached from the direction of the road, labouring up the track. Sick with fear, Toni listened as the vehicle pulled up outside the house, a door opened and shut, and footsteps scraped across the gravel towards the chalet. Then the car drove off.

Forcing himself to move, Toni put his head round the side of the bin shelter and saw the white-haired German standing at the front door, listening. In his hand was a pistol. Without making a sound the old man opened the door and glided inside.

Great. *Two* gunmen. Luke was toast.

Toni fumbled in his pockets and pulled out his phone, gripping it in two hands – he was shaking so much he was worried he might drop it. What was the number for the emergency services here in Germany? He didn't have a clue, and had no idea what address he should give, for that matter. Would they even speak English? No, he knew who the only person he could talk to was. He dreaded the call, but it had to be made. With shaking fingers, he picked out Luke's home number in Brussels and listened to the distant ringing.

Luke's dad would know what to do, Toni told himself, but how would he ever explain what had happened? He was almost relieved when there was no reply and no answering machine.

He fumbled in his pocket and felt the shape of his picklock. What if he could somehow disable the 4x4? That way, at least, the men couldn't drive off with Luke as their prisoner...

Upstairs, inside the chalet, Luke was sitting in a leather armchair beside the fireplace. There was no fire, yet he felt hot and could barely breathe. The chair creaked at the slightest movement.

The white-haired old man paced the floor, his steps almost soundless on the oriental carpet. His bodyguard – whom he addressed as Achim – stood at the top of the stairs, blocking off the only escape route, arms folded, a black pistol in his right hand. Grimmer had begun interrogating Luke patiently, almost like some polite official, starting with his name, place of birth, address. Luke had quickly decided against pretending to be someone other than he was; he'd just get confused and infuriate the German even further.

'I've seen you before,' the old man said. 'In Italy. What are you doing, following me across Europe? Sending me junk mail? This is the second time you have invaded my privacy. What do you want? What is your name and what is your friend's name?'

Luke swallowed. He'd hoped in vain that Grimmer wouldn't recognise him from their previous encounter outside the villa in Faleria.

'Answer my questions.' Grimmer's voice remained soft and calm, but there was a steely glint in his eyes. 'Why did you break into my house? Are you looking for something in particular?'

Luke lowered his gaze to the floor. His right foot was shaking slightly, tapping against the carpet. He moved it. The chair creaked.

He gave Toni's name.

'Thank you,' the German said. 'And what do you want?' His upper lip quivered, as though he was suppressing anger. He looked at his watch several times and dabbed his temples with a handkerchief. There was something terrifyingly emotionless about his focused, deliberate bearing.

But the bodyguard slouched against the bannister was even scarier. He kept shifting impatiently. His leather jacket and pumped-up muscles made Luke think of a gang member or a mercenary.

'I want to know what an English boy is doing in my house. I am in the middle of a very important project and your presence here fills me with great worry.' The old man licked his lips, shaking his head slightly. 'Great worry.'

He spoke excellent English, but pronounced each word with such excessive care that it came out mechanically, as though he were a robot. Luke took a deep breath. He had to say *something*.

A bright glow suddenly lit up the window: something had triggered the security light outside. Then there was a loud wailing sound. *A car alarm* . . . In a flash, Achim went slinking down the stairs, noiseless as a cat. Luke heard the front door open.

Moments later he was back. He tossed a picklock onto the desk.

'The other one tried to break into the car,' he said. 'He escaped into the forest.'

'Why didn't you . . .?'

'I couldn't.' Breathing hard, Achim looked his boss in the eye. 'There were cars passing on the road. A shot would have been heard.'

'*Verdammter idiot*,' Grimmer hissed, swinging round to face Luke, eyes flashing with anger. 'I have better things to do than to chase small boys off my property.'

He pointed at the phone on Luke's belt.

'Ring your friend and tell him to get over here. He has five minutes. If he wants to see you alive again.'

Luke took the phone from its holster. 'My friend doesn't have a phone,' he said.

'Don't take me for a fool.' Grimmer's hands were shaking slightly. 'Show me a teenager with no phone and I'll show you a donkey with no ears. Phone him, now!'

Achim stepped closer, nodding approvingly.

'Put the loudspeaker on so I can hear what your friend says. And if he doesn't come back right away, too bad for you. My friend here will take you up into the forest and shoot you in the temple.'

26

A chilly wind streamed down the valley from the east. Toni felt cold sweat dribble along his spine. Expecting a bullet in his back at any moment he'd rushed up the slope among the trees, thinking it was safer there than down on the road where he'd be an even easier target...But he'd be a sitting duck here as well. And on the road, he could at least have stopped a car for help...Or he could have driven off in the Lupo...Why hadn't he done so right away? It wouldn't save Luke's skin if he was caught as well...

He crouched down among the ferns and tried to calm his breathing. He wasn't used to running like this. The taste of blood filled his throat.

Suddenly his phone rang. He quickly dug the handset from his pocket and took the call.

It was Luke, ordering him to return to the chalet. If he didn't, something bad was going to happen. The same applied if Toni made the mistake of phoning the police or anyone else. Luke spoke haltingly and his voice sounded high-pitched. His life was in danger. It was obvious.

'OK...I'll come right away,' Toni said and at once the line went dead.

As he stood there among the dark trees, listening to the murmuring wind, Toni wondered if he was about to die. Death felt unreal, yet it was a distinct possibility, he understood that much. One shot each and they'd be lifeless bodies, easily hidden in some remote Alpine ravine where no one would ever find them. Wild animals would tear the flesh from their bones.

Five minutes, Luke had said... Close to tears, Toni began plodding through the trees towards the yellowish glow of the chalet. But he had to try something, didn't he? He suddenly remembered that Luke had given him Miss Hart's number – the teacher had insisted that she be able to contact either of the boys at any moment, and vice versa. Toni dialled the number. He got her voicemail.

'It's Toni, Luke's friend.' He cleared his throat, and wondered whether the sound of the wind in the trees would be audible at the other end. 'We have – we have a problem. If we don't ring you by tomorrow morning at the latest, please come... and look for us. We're in Oberstbrunn. It's a small village east of Bergstein, near the Austrian border. There's a house, a kind of chalet, about one kilometre from the village, in the direction of the border. On the right. It's a lonely place, surrounded by trees. Please... This isn't a joke. And I'm sorry...'

The last word came out as a sob. As he stumbled down the sloping forest Toni cleaned the log on his phone. A minute later he walked into the yard of the chalet and approached the front door feeling like a condemned criminal mounting the scaffold for his execution.

Achim Voynovych glanced at his watch, a fake Rolex bought off a Senegalese street vendor in Berlin. More than five minutes had passed already, almost ten, in fact, and he hadn't heard a squeak from outside . . . He stroked his itching cheek with the cool metal of his pistol, standing stock still behind the front door, ready to act. The seconds dragged. Had the other boy run away?

At last he heard timid footsteps outside. Achim flung open the door, and a boy, or a young man dressed in a fleece jacket and walking boots stumbled back, falling onto his bottom on the gravel.

'Hands up!' Achim hissed. 'Get in the house.'

Holding his arms in the air, blinking fearfully, the youth struggled to his feet.

'Go straight up the stairs. You know the way, you nosy brat.'

The lad didn't say anything in reply. Eyes glistening with fear, he began climbing the narrow stairs.

Luke glanced at Toni who shuffled into the study on stiff legs, arms upraised, face the colour of ash, followed by his scowling captor. The sight filled Luke with guilt; the whole trip had been his idea, a very bad idea, and now Toni was paying the price.

With a huge effort of will, Luke dismissed his fear and forced himself to focus on Grimmer who had taken a seat at his desk and was calmly working on his papers.

Whatever else, the man had stupendous powers of concentration. Having issued his five-minute ultimatum he'd immediately immersed himself in his work. He looked like he was wrestling with some problem that had seized his whole attention, preoccupying his mind with the force of an obsession, filling every waking minute.

He looked over seventy, but Luke could see he was in good physical condition. He had narrow hands and the agile fingers of a pianist, and his tall forehead and bright gaze gave an impression of intelligence. He couldn't have been more different from the square-shouldered body-guard with his surly eyes and big muscles. But there was also something hard and frosty about the older man. And something unnaturally intense, as though he was being slowly eaten up from inside.

The younger man seemed used to waiting for his boss's attention; as soon as he saw that Grimmer was working he pushed Toni in the direction of a wooden chair and took up his earlier position at the top of the stairs, pistol in hand, Rolex glinting.

Luke had never seen Toni look so scared. His face was streaming with sweat. Pine needles stuck to his fleece, he was breathing fast and his eyes shuttled left and right. The sight made Luke feel even more frightened.

Again he forced himself to concentrate. There were only two things he could do: think and observe. He tried to read the titles of the books on the floor: mathematical works, books on Germanic mythology, military history. *Mein Kampf*, in two dog-eared volumes ... And several biographies of Hitler ... What was the old man researching? Was it somehow linked with the strange patch of canvas?

'Take our guests down to the cellar,' Grimmer said in a quiet voice, without raising his eyes from his work. 'You know what to do.'

Achim swung his pistol, beckoning the boys towards the stairs. Toni obeyed at once. Luke also got to his feet. His mind was racing in all directions. He'd recently read a book about the murder of the Russian royal family in a Yekaterinburg cellar…He saw the firing squad, rifles spitting death…Did Anastasia survive? Only in legend…As for Luke and Toni, no one would ever know what had happened to them. When they were missed, it would be too late.

Dragging his feet, Luke paused beside Grimmer's desk. He pointed at the scrap of canvas, then at the painting and the map pinned to the wall.

'Is there a secret code in that painting?'

Grimmer narrowed his eyes. 'No, not *in* the painting – what do you mean?'

'There's a pattern.'

'What pattern?'

Luke swallowed. 'The map has three locations, and in this painting there are three hilltops.'

'And?'

'The three place names – could they be three hills or summits? Or three places in the mountains?'

'Schwartzberg, Todspitze and Elend…' Grimmer took off his glasses, put the frame between his lips and narrowed his eyes. 'They are indeed places in the Alps, but I've searched all three and found nothing. I hadn't seen the link between the painting and the code. You're sharp. Although it's probably irrelevant. But go on. Have you noticed anything else?'

Encouraged, Luke continued: 'Well, there's another link between the code and the picture.'

'What do you mean?'

Luke pointed at the squiggle that represented the sun on Hitler's painting. Then he pointed at the sun shape that was carefully traced around the number 8 on the patch of canvas. He'd understood that it corresponded with the first letter of the word '*größte*'.

'Yes, number eight is circled, or the letter "G", if you will. I saw that right away,' Grimmer said. 'But I didn't know what to make of it.' He snatched a magnifying glass off the desk and pushed Luke aside. 'As you say, the letter is circled with a jagged line, which could be a rudimentary sun symbol, but why should that have anything to do with the sun in the painting? Most landscapes have suns, don't they?'

'True,' Luke said, doubting his own ideas. He didn't know what to make of the link either – if it even was a link. He needed more time to think.

Grimmer put his fingertips to his temples and stared intently at the painting, then at the code written on the sheet of paper, then at the painting again.

'No, no!' he shrieked in the end. 'We're just floundering here! Your guesswork is leading me astray. *Verdammt!*'

'But you said the three mountains made sense.'

'Maybe I was wrong.' Grimmer threw up his hands. 'My father was a mathematician, do you hear? A great mathematician! He set me a mathematical riddle, not some stupid picture puzzle! I'm sure this whole thing has a clear mathematical solution, if only I can find it!'

'A mathematical solution?' Luke bit his lip, hesitating. He could almost feel the neurons firing in his brain, the adrenaline coursing through his veins... Then he asked the question that was on his mind. 'I'm sorry, but why do you think Adolf Hitler was the greatest German?'

Grimmer gave a violent start. He stepped closer to Luke. His blue eyes flashed behind the glasses. The words came out in an angry snarl and his upper lip curled, showing yellow teeth: 'Who said I thought Hitler was the greatest German?'

'You did.'

'What?'

'You've written it down on that sheet of paper.'

'It's not *my* opinion! It was the answer to the riddle!'

'What do you mean?'

'My father left a trail of secret messages. They led to a painting by Hitler, with the coded message on it that refers to 'the greatest German'. In my father's view, Hitler was the greatest German. So there. Hitler was a mesmerising speaker. Many people were fooled by him during the war.'

'Then why is there a question mark after "Hitler"?'

'Well, the code didn't explicitly say "Hitler", but he painted that awful picture, so the meaning is obvious. Isn't it?' A note of anguish and shame had crept into the old man's voice. 'My father made a tragic mistake. And it looks to me like this whole code is nothing more than a sick tribute claiming Hitler was the greatest German.'

'And what if the code is suggesting that the greatest German was someone whose name began with "G"?'

'You mean, like my name?' The old man gave a dry laugh. 'Well, my father, Doctor Heinrich Grimmer, was a proud man with a brilliant mathematical mind, but he wasn't fool enough to imagine he was the greatest. My country has a proud mathematical tradition. Our mathematicians are the greatest in the world!'

Luke turned his eyes to the ugly picture painted by Hitler, and as he did so, his heart rate accelerated wildly. He stared at the glaring yellow brushstroke at the top of the canvas, representing the sun. It was unmistakable once you noticed it: it was also the letter 'G'. And it had obviously been added to the painting – it was in a much brighter colour than the rest.

'Isn't that also a "G"?' Luke pointed at the sun.

Grimmer froze. He grabbed the glasses that dangled from his neck on a chain and perched them on his nose for a better look. His Adam's apple bobbed up and down. He loosened his collar, as though he was having trouble with his breathing.

'*Mein Gott,*' he said in a hoarse whisper. 'It's obvious – how could I have missed it? And that's also why the receipt was in Gauss's biography!'

'What receipt?'

'The receipt for this painting.'

The old man rushed to a bookshelf and took down an old volume, slamming it onto his desk.

He grabbed Luke by the shoulders and shook him, staring hard with blazing eyes. 'I have it! It's Gauss! "G" stands for Gauss! You're right, boy!'

To Luke's amazement the old man gave him a bear hug.

Achim came forward.

'Everything OK?' He shot a menacing look at Luke.

'Of course!' Grimmer leafed through the book on his desk. 'Carl Friedrich Gauss. The Greatest German! Of course!'

The old man was completely white.

'You two wait here,' he said with a glance at Achim and Toni.

He blew dust off the book and strode up to the wall, ripping down the map and leaving the painting where it was, then went skipping into the adjoining room, Luke on his heels. There was a new sprightliness and vigour to the old man's gait, as though he'd grown younger, or put down some heavy burden.

The other room was furnished with dark, antique chairs with deep-red seat cushions, wallpaper with a brown and gold pattern, heavy, moss-green curtains and richly patterned oriental carpets that were pleasantly faded. Luke watched Grimmer leafing feverishly through the pages of his book. Dust mites danced in the beam of the lamp beside the armchair. The old man sat down.

'*Princeps Mathematicorum*,' he chuckled. 'Of course... Luckily, Gauss's writings are not voluminous. I'll soon get to the bottom of this. *Pauca sed matura* – that was his motto.'

'What does it mean?'

'Few, but ripe. Gauss never published anything half-baked. If only we could say the same of his modern successors.' A kind smile appeared on Grimmer's face. 'How much do you know about Gauss?'

The old man was suddenly like a different person – all warm and friendly – but Luke didn't drop his guard. The armed thug was still lurking in the next room and nothing important had changed. From the corner of his eye he could see Toni straining to hear what they were saying.

'Not much.' Luke tried to play for time by prolonging the conversation. 'But I like maths. Gauss was a child prodigy, wasn't he?'

'Indeed he was. Do you know the story of 5050?'

'No.'

'Gauss was only a boy when his teacher asked him and

218

his classmates to add together all the numbers from one to one hundred. It was supposed to take them ages, but Gauss had the answer in the blink of an eye.'

Luke couldn't believe it. 'He did it in his *head*?'

'Easy. 100 + 1 is 101. 99 + 2 is 101. 98 + 3 is 101. And so on, fifty pairs of numbers, each pair adding up to 101. Total: 5050.'

'That's neat,' Luke said, a grin of pleasure spreading across his face. 'That's really *cool*.'

Luke noticed that his smile brought a chuckle to the old man's lips. But his good mood vanished at once when he glanced through the doorway and saw Toni sitting in the other room peering uncertainly towards them, and Achim at his station at the top of the stairs. The young man looked tense – as though he were longing to use the pistol in his hand.

27

'We now know two new things,' Grimmer said, gazing at the yellowed map on which Schwartzberg, Todspitze and Elend were joined, forming a perfect triangle. 'One, the code refers to Gauss. Two, it points us to these three places, yet none of them is the right one—'

'There's also a third element. The sun,' Luke cut in. 'We don't know what that means, either.'

'Indeed. Very good. So how do we bring this information together? And how do we do it quickly?'

'We go online,' Luke said, pointing at the MacBook Air on the small table.

'Online? You think so?' Grimmer had opened the thick, leather-bound biography of Gauss, but he closed it. His frown melted into a doubtful smile. 'Well, why not give it a try?'

He watched as the boy's fingers danced on the keyboard and the touch pad, conjuring up an image of the planet Earth on the screen, then splitting the screen in two.

'This is Google Earth,' the boy said. 'Can you spell out the names of those mountain tops for me? I thought we'd start by getting the exact coordinates.'

Grimmer spelled out the names: *Schwartzberg. Todspitze. Elend.* He was having trouble controlling his voice. He'd thought of hiring an expert to help him in his search, but then dismissed the idea for two reasons. The first was that he didn't trust outsiders, and couldn't think how he could seek help without revealing his secret. The second reason was that he firmly believed he could solve the riddle without any help from computers.

As he watched the boy typing, a memory of his childhood piano lessons flashed into his mind. His mother had taught him. Pushed into the background by his domineering father, who only believed in hard reason and iron discipline, she had not been a very affectionate parent to him and had died young. But the weekly piano lessons, conducted on Sunday mornings when Heinrich Grimmer visited a coffee house to read the newspapers, were a sweet memory. A rare kiss was the reward that little Dietrich would receive for playing a new piece without mistakes. Sometimes his mother would sing in her bright soprano voice, accompanying herself on the piano as she went through her favourite songs, always ending with *Der Erlkönig*. Set to music by Franz Schubert, the famous poem by Goethe told the story of the Elf King enticing a feverish child at the moment of death...

'What's the boy doing?' Achim said in a low voice. 'He broke in here, remember?'

Startled, Grimmer jumped back then waved his subordinate away. 'Leave us alone.'

'You're not letting him go online, are you?'

'It's all right. He's an intelligent boy – he won't do anything stupid.'

'*Intelligent!*' Achim spat the word out. 'That's a word you've never used about me. I just hope *you're* intelligent enough to know what you're doing.'

The young man glided away with a dark expression on his face. The insult hung in the air, but Grimmer was too excited to react. His eyes bore into the screen of the MacBook. The boy worked with astonishing speed. It was hard to keep track of what he was doing. A perfect triangle had formed over a map on the screen, joining the three Alpine locations that Grimmer had fruitlessly visited.

'Now I'm going to Google "Gauss" and try to find out some more about him,' Luke said.

'Go ahead,' Grimmer said reluctantly. 'Although I have to say I'm not personally a great fan of computers – or the internet. They make people lazy.'

'It's just mathematics, applied in practice,' Luke said. 'Google is based on these amazing relevance algorithms.'

He narrowed his eyes, concentrating fiercely. There were plenty of web pages about maths, many of them exclusively devoted to Gauss. Born on 30 April 1777, in the Duchy of Brunswick, he'd died on 23 February 1855 in Göttingen.

The childhood anecdote that Grimmer had told was mentioned many times: Gauss had been just seven years old when he'd pulled off the trick of adding together all the integers from one to one hundred. His most famous book was *Disquisitiones Arithmeticae*, published in 1801, which concerned number theory. Gauss had been such a perfectionist that he hadn't ever published many of his most interesting ideas – some said this had slowed down the development of mathematics by half a century.

'Maybe there's a link between Gauss and the sun,' Luke said. 'Was he interested in astronomy?'

'Of course.' Grimmer leaned closer. 'He once found a lost planet – Ceres. And, of course, he invented the heliotrope.'

'Isn't that a flower?' Luke asked. 'A flower that turns towards the sun?'

'Same word,' Grimmer said. 'But Gauss's invention was a geodetic surveying instrument. It uses the sun's rays reflected by a mirror to measure positions over huge distances. You turn it and bounce the sun's rays off in the direction you want. Very useful for performing large-scale triangulation surveys. Gauss invented the instrument for the geodesic survey of the state of Hanover, but the heliotrope also led him to one of his greatest discoveries: the *theorema egregium*. You might say the sun and the heliotrope played a central role in his career.'

Luke nodded.

'The *theorema egregium* is rather fascinating,' Grimmer continued, warming to his topic. 'It means "remarkable theorem" in Latin.'

Luke kept nodding as the old man launched into a complicated description of the theorem. Luke couldn't follow the details, but by Googling 'Gauss' and 'heliotrope' he soon came across a picture of that instrument and some articles about the surveying work that Gauss had performed.

'Gauss's theory had major implications for cartography,' Grimmer was saying. 'It explains why no map is perfect. You can't accurately represent the surface of a sphere on a flat sheet of paper.'

'Yeah, I've heard about that.' Luke turned his attention

to the map he'd made. 'You said there was nothing in any of the three places?'

'No, and I'm surprised my father cited three in the first place.'

'I have an idea.' Luke bit his lip. 'Maybe it's simpler than that. Maybe it points to just one location.'

Luke printed off the image from Google Earth, grabbed a ruler and a pencil, measured the mid-points on the sides of the triangle, and then split the triangle three ways. Within seconds he'd located the point in the exact centre of the triangle. He compared it with the piece of old map pinned to the wall. Grimmer leaned over his shoulder for a closer look, and Luke felt a prickly shiver travel through him from head to toe. For there was a small mark in the centre of the triangle, a single letter, written in faint pencil.

'I think this might be where you want to look,' he said, handing over the map, his cheeks red with excitement.

Grimmer removed the pins and held the page of atlas in his hands. The marking was so tiny it would have been impossible to notice unless you knew it was there. But there it undeniably was. Luke could barely believe his eyes. The exact centre of the triangle, a spot where two waterways met near a small lake, was marked with a tiny sun, inside which was the letter 'G'.

Time seemed to stand still. Luke's heart felt like it was about to burst out of his chest. Surely he was right – surely the letter 'G' marked the place that the old German had been hunting for? But what was the significance of the sun symbol around the letter?

Grimmer appeared to be frozen to the spot. Luke wiped his palms on his trousers. The old man stared at the map in his hand. In the adjoining room Toni was still sitting in his chair, biting his nails, no doubt longing to know what Luke was up to. Achim continued to glower from his station at the top of the stairs.

'You could be right...' Grimmer said in a soft voice. 'It's simple, almost too simple, but you could be right.'

For one second Luke forgot his fear, melting into a triumphant smile. Grimmer looked up and returned the smile, then slowly shut the heavy book. He stared at Luke, obviously thinking hard, weighing the options and, as he did so, his gaze went cold once more, as though in the midst of his joy he'd remembered something unpleasant.

'What are you looking for?' Luke demanded, pointing at the map. 'Is something hidden in that place?'

Achim shifted his feet, as though warning his master not to answer.

'Treasure, I hope,' Grimmer said, dabbing his forehead with his handkerchief. 'Hidden treasure that my father stole from the cursed Nazis.'

'But wasn't he also...?' Luke didn't know how to finish his sentence. 'You know...'

'Was my father a Nazi?' Grimmer said in a half-whisper. 'It is a question I've been asking myself for a long time. And the answer, I'm happy to say, would seem to be no. No, he wasn't. He detested Hitler. And he fooled him, by the look of it.'

'How do you know?'

'This location, in the centre of the triangle, is not marked on any of the known Nazi maps. But as you saw, the other three depots give its exact coordinates. I think my father tricked his paymasters, Adolf Hitler and Adolf Eichmann. My father hated them.'

Luke nodded. 'But he loved Gauss.'

'All mathematicians love and revere Carl Friedrich Gauss.' A happy smile spread across the old man's tired features. 'My father was a difficult man. But I think I could have agreed with him on this point. Gauss is indeed the greatest German. Yes, perhaps even greater than Kant, and greater even than Bach.'

'What about Klose?' Luke said.

'Who?'

'Miroslav Klose. The only player in history to have scored five goals in successive World Cups.'

'I don't understand.'

'Sorry, it's just a joke. He's a footballer.'

'A joke? My father didn't tell jokes. I've never told them, either,' Grimmer said crisply. 'They seem to me a waste of time.'

The old man sat deep in thought for a moment then suddenly called out in a loud voice. 'Achim!'

'Yes, boss?'

The bodyguard appeared instantly at his master's side.

'We're done here. Take these boys into the cellar.'

'Shall I . . .?'

'Not yet,' Grimmer said. 'Later.'

'We don't need witnesses.'

'Indeed we do not. But the younger boy might still be useful to us. We've cracked it, Achim! We've cracked the code!'

Luke decided this was as good a moment as any to play his card. 'By the way, if anything happens to me or Toni, my dad will hear about it.'

'What are you saying?' Grimmer's eyes narrowed. 'Don't try and fool me. I warn you. Don't even *try.*'

'I wrote an email when I was online. When you were looking at the map.'

'I knew it.' Achim threw up his arms in disgust. 'Why did you let him use the computer?'

'I didn't send anything,' Luke said. 'I just saved it as a draft in my Hotmail account. But if I go missing, the police will get the password and look at it.'

'And what . . .' the old man adjusted his bow tie with a trembling hand, 'does this email contain?'

'Your name, the coordinates of the location in the middle of the triangle and the address of this house.'

Dietrich Grimmer bunched his fists, squeezing hard, until his tendons hurt. The dizzy mixture of relief, shock and sublime joy he'd felt when the code had finally been broken had suddenly been swept away and was replaced with a much darker feeling: rage.

The little English brat was blackmailing him. Shamelessly. Grimmer was on the brink of attacking Luke with his fists, but what would be the use of that? The boy had him cornered. And there stood Achim, eyeing his master with open contempt.

The anger stung like poison, coursing through Grimmer's veins, but this was not the moment to release it – that had to wait. Taking a long, calming breath, he joined his fingertips and turned to the one resource he'd learned to rely on: logic.

Analyse, he told himself. *Reflect. Think.*

There had to be some way out of the impasse – there always was, if you looked carefully. Treat the situation like a mathematical problem . . . Numbers had no feelings. Untainted by emotion, inhuman, abstract – only numbers were reliable. He had to be inhuman too if he was to find a way out of this trap, and find one he would.

Achim cleared his throat, shifting his athletic body restlessly.

'The boy's trying to trick you, boss.'

'Shut up.' Grimmer closed his eyes and pinched the bridge of his nose with his slim fingers. 'I'm thinking . . .'

Achim was important to him, almost like a foster son, but Grimmer had often wished the young man had been more intelligent – more like himself, and more like this maddening English boy. As his fury slowly subsided and lucid reason took over once more, Grimmer couldn't help but admire the pluck that the boy had shown. Someone like this would have been a perfect associate. Someone older, of course, but someone with curiosity and sharp reason and innate intelligence . . . Yes, that was the phrase, *innate intelligence*.

But where was his own innate intelligence right now? The more he thought about it, the more hopeless it all seemed. Eliminating both boys would have been the cleanest and most efficient option, but that was out of the question now. On the other hand letting them go was equally impossible. He could never allow them to talk, revealing what they knew.

Maybe he was wrong. Maybe there was no way out. He reasoned and reasoned. But reason wasn't helping. What remained? Madness? Defeat?

He opened his eyes and glanced at Achim, who was fiddling with his mobile, texting someone. Who? He had no friends . . .

The beginnings of yet another headache pulsed inside Grimmer's skull, and he quietly slipped his hand into his pocket, feeling for his medicine tube. Seated at the desk, the boy waited, alert but calm.

The thought stole into Grimmer's mind like a gentle whisper. He had to accept how bad this situation was. If he let the boys go, the police would come after him and everything would be ruined. How could he ensure the boys' silence after they were released? He couldn't.

So there was only one option. That made the choice simple – even if it wasn't a pleasant one.

28

An hour later Luke and Toni sat silently in the back seat of the 4x4. Grimmer was in the front passenger seat. The LED of his forehead lamp cast a blue glow onto the scrap of map on his knees. Looking sullen, concentrating fiercely behind the wheel, Achim was slowly negotiating the hairpin turns as the car climbed the Alpine slope towards Knittelhofen.

Not a word had been uttered inside the car for more than half an hour. They'd passed Wengsee ages ago and crossed the river Aich by an old bridge. Huge, lonesome valleys yawned on either side of the road, lost in darkness. Directly ahead, the twin peaks of Waldkofen poked at the sky like a two-pronged fork.

Luke wasn't enjoying the burning sensation in his abdomen. Panic wasn't far away. By helping the old man crack the code, had he sealed his own fate? And Toni's fate...? He should never have talked his friend into joining him in Germany at all. Luke didn't like the way Grimmer had gone silent, sitting in his seat, peering at his map and casting cold glances out over the dark mountains, his joyless face mirroring the desolation around.

The higher they climbed, the steeper the Alps appeared to become. It was as if the silent car was a pressure cooker, ready to explode with the unspoken tension, anger and fear... The moon flashed behind the clouds, like a lighthouse giving a last warning to a ship headed for the rocks, then lost itself in the night sky.

'I don't know if you get it,' Luke said suddenly, trying to keep his voice firm. 'But unless I phone my dad tomorrow morning he'll call the police,' Luke said. 'That means you'll get caught – it's only a question of time...'

'Calm down, will you?' The old German twisted round in the front passenger seat and glared at the boys. 'You two are irrelevant.'

'Seit rühig, bleibe ruhig, mein kind, in dürren Blättern säuselt der wind...'

The words from Goethe's *Erlkönig* soothed Dietrich Grimmer's nerves. When he'd been the same age as the maddening English boy was now he'd known the entire poem by heart... That was how often he'd heard his mother sing it. *Be still, be at peace my child... It is just the wind whispering in the dry leaves...* The words of the father of the delirious child who was being called by the Elf King... Grimmer felt as though some strange, unearthly being was calling him to this moment. A voice that offered an escape from the trap he found himself in.

The boy was insufferable, a real pest, like most children, yet Grimmer also felt as though he recognised something of his former self in the cheeky, quick-witted, tenacious Luke. He wondered what he'd one day become? It all depended – Grimmer knew from bitter experience – on whether his confidence was nurtured by his parents. Or whether he was belittled and discouraged.

With an almost physical jolt, he suddenly felt the old, half-forgotten regret flash through him. *He could have been a great mathematician.* But his upbringing, his father's attitude, had killed his self-belief. The father had failed, so the son had to fail also. And so Dietrich had become just a bank clerk, a successful, first-rate bank clerk, but a bank clerk nonetheless. He'd been so brilliant in what he did, so over-qualified for the mechanical task of managing accounts, that he could easily have defrauded his employer many times over. He'd thought of it, once even drawing up a detailed plan and acquiring a South American passport for his new life – but he'd quietly buried the idea. He was a man of honour and honesty. The passport he'd kept regularly updated, however. It was in his breast pocket now. And he owned a flat in Paraguay.

Unmarried, childless, he wondered how he should use the years that still remained? Rich at last and liberated from his long obsession, he'd be free to do whatever he wanted and to live where he pleased. He glanced into the rear-view mirror and saw the pale faces of the two boys. What would it have been like to be a father? Had he had a son, would Dietrich have done a better job than his own father? He was sure he would have. But it was now much too late for anything like that.

Again the words of Goethe's strange, bittersweet poem came into his mind, casting his thoughts back to his school days in Flügenbach, where he had been a timid pupil with no friends and a mind like crystal.

*

Luke noticed that Grimmer kept glancing at him in the mirror. The old man's lips were moving, as though he were reciting words to himself... The cold, rational treasure-hunter had seemed scary enough, but a mumbling nutter was even worse – nutters were unpredictable.

He decided it was best to continue protesting, if only in order to show the German that they wouldn't submit to their fate just like that.

'Stop the car. Let us out! You can't—'

'Luke, Luke...' Grimmer said with an exhausted sigh. 'You know as well as I do what this situation means. I can't afford to let you talk.'

Luke's stomach clenched. The man was right: Luke had known all along, yet he hadn't wanted to admit it to himself. The situation was simple: *the worst was about to happen.*

He shot a look at his friend beside him, and wished he hadn't, for Toni's face was white with terror. With an immense effort of will Luke slowed down his breathing and stilled his swirling thoughts.

'I can't let you talk.' The white-haired man was leaning between the seats again. 'And that is the key to everything. Get thinking. Based on that fact, how can we come to an understanding to our mutual benefit?'

'What are you saying?' Luke's voice was faint as a whisper. 'Are you offering some kind of deal...?'

'Let's negotiate.' The old man adjusted his lamp, fixing his eyes on Luke, a flicker of a smile crossing his face. 'You can have a small share of the treasure – provided you swear to silence.'

The boys glanced at one another. Luke fought to control his facial expression – he feared that the German might change his mind if he showed his relief – but it was too late. Beside him, Toni was already grinning broadly.

The old man watched them closely. The smile was still there, as though he were enjoying a game. His hair had turned silver in the glow of the blue light of his forehead lamp.

But then Luke saw, in the rear-view mirror, the eyes of the younger man at the wheel and the expression in them made his blood run cold.

'Well? Aren't you excited?' Grimmer said, his voice almost merry. 'Give me a guarantee that you'll be silent, and you'll be rich. Provided, of course, that we find something.'

'Well that's the problem,' Luke said. 'What guarantee can we give that would satisfy you?'

'I'll take your word – and obviously you must do something about that foolish, foolish email you wrote.'

'So we become your accomplices, is that it?'

'There can be no accomplice where there has been no crime.'

'You're a criminal.' Luke felt Toni's elbow in his side, but he continued. 'You stole a painting from the Vatican.'

'And returned it, undamaged,' Grimmer shot back. 'For a small fee.'

'Extortion was a crime, last time I checked.'

'Stop insulting him,' Toni hissed.

'I never took a single penny for myself,' Grimmer said. 'I could have but I didn't. All I was interested in was the hidden message from my father.'

'You don't expect me to believe that?'

'Believe what you like. The money was used to pay the

234

men who performed the raid. I made sure the Caravaggio was returned safely. My conscience is clean.'

'Does he have to know everything?' Achim shot a disapproving glance at his master. 'How about I drive us all to a police station while we're at it?'

'What men?' Luke said.

'Italian *Mafiosi*. Greedy, stupid men, and a disgrace to their own country. One of them has been caught already, a clergyman employed by the Vatican, although you won't have seen *that* in the news. The Italian police are confident that they'll soon nab the whole gang. But I won't be caught. Not unless you denounce me to the authorities.'

'What makes you any different from the men who work for you?'

'The fact that I have never profited from any crime. This whole quest is my family's way of settling its scores with the Nazis.' Grimmer spoke with loud assurance. 'My father was tasked by Eichmann to hide a cache of gold in one of the pre-built Nazi depots. That might have been a crime. But my father tricked him by hiding his gold in a depot that was omitted from all the secret registers and maps, a place so secret that not even Eichmann knew about it. My father was a good man. He despised the Nazis; I know it now, for sure. You helped me see it.'

'In England we have laws about treasure troves. Finds have to be reported to the authorities, and if they're historically important they belong—'

'One, this isn't England. Two, what we are about to unearth has no cultural or historical value whatsoever. Grow up!' Grimmer wagged his forefinger, finally losing patience. 'Stop splitting hairs and give me your word of honour, or you can forget my offer.'

Again Luke felt Toni's elbow prodding into his side. It was true, of course, that this was no time to wind up the old German, but Luke couldn't help it: he hated fuzzy reasoning.

'But—'

'I am no criminal. *Verdammt!*' Grimmer exploded. 'I am a mathematician. I'm only interested in my father's legacy. I have spent my whole life looking for it!'

The old man's eyes glistened in the blue LED light. There was a pause. Then he chuckled and continued in a milder voice: 'It's beautiful, don't you see? My father used his intelligence to defeat the Nazis...A great mind is stronger than the most brutal tyrant! Reason prevails!'

The car had slowed down slightly and was skirting a small Alpine lake. The black surface of the water held a rippling reflection of the moon. As the road began to climb once more Achim changed into a lower gear and pressed the accelerator, sending the old 4x4 roaring up the slope, powered by its Mercedes engine.

Luke noticed that Toni was quietly fiddling with his door handle – pointless because the child lock was on and the doors and windows in the back were impossible to open from the inside. He'd already tried.

The offer was tempting. Very tempting. Why not accept a chunk of the treasure and worry about the rights and wrongs of ownership afterwards? If Luke and Toni emerged rich out of this situation they could always make a charitable donation. Besides, Luke honestly felt he deserved some sort of reward. Had he not kept at it when everyone told him to drop his investigation? Had he not helped Grimmer to crack the code?

'You *idiot*,' Toni whispered beside him. 'Why didn't you just say yes?'

Luke shrugged his shoulders. Toni's fear, which shone like a light from his pale face, infected him as well. Did they have any choice but to accept the old man's offer? Refusing it, or sowing doubt in Grimmer's mind, would be suicidal.

He cleared his throat. 'So could you tell me more about this . . . treasure?'

'Not until we find it,' Grimmer said, without looking round, eyes drilling into the map on his knees. 'What I'm offering is one per cent. Provided you forget about me and never speak of me to anyone for as long as you live.'

Luke knew he was talking to an intelligent man and that honesty was the safest course.

'Like I said. Let's say I give you my word. How could you ever be sure I'd keep it?'

Luke knew there was no point trying to trick a man like Grimmer. Everything had to be out in the open. Everything had to be clear.

'I could help you with that,' Grimmer said softly. 'You see, if you failed to keep your word I'd come after you and eliminate you without a second's hesitation.' The voice was polite, almost affectionate. 'Rest assured, I have the means, and I have the contacts to kill you both, whenever I choose – all I need is a reason.'

Achim glanced round, as though to lend force to these softly spoken words.

Luke could feel his back begin to sweat. The implications were obvious. The deal on offer was conditional

– keep quiet, or die…Luke and Toni could talk to the police and reveal everything they knew. But if they were killed soon afterwards, they couldn't identify Grimmer in a court of law.

Luke stole another look at Toni, whose face suggested he couldn't quite follow everything that was being said.

'Just one per cent,' Luke said. 'After I helped you crack the code? Are you kidding?'

'*Verdammt!*' The old man hissed, throwing up his hands. 'Do you know how many years I've spent on this search? I started decades before you were even born.'

'Nevertheless, you were completely stuck before I helped you—'

'I'd have got it eventually!' Grimmer interrupted, voice trembling with fury. Then he paused. 'At least, I think I would. But let me be honest. Not everyone is honest, but I *try* to be. It is true, undeniably true, that your intervention saved me precious time. *Three* per cent. My last offer.'

The road ended at the edge of an Alpine meadow but Achim continued along a rutted track; the Mercedes 4x4 felt unstoppable, like a tractor or a Jeep. The swollen moon was almost blindingly luminous against the black sky. Luke examined his surroundings and noted, with a fresh burst of fear in his innards, that there was no sign of habitation in any direction. No lights. No houses. Nowhere to run. Up ahead, through the window of the jolting vehicle, the terrain looked rocky and inhospitable, and strangely lifeless.

'How much would three per cent come to?' Luke said. 'Give me a ballpark figure.'

Grimmer didn't reply.

The car swung from left to right, see-sawing violently as it powered along the overgrown track, tufts of grass brushing the chassis.

Luke clenched his jaws together, gathering his courage: he was in a tight spot, but then, so was the German. 'Five per cent,' he said. 'I honestly think it's a fair share considering my contribution. And I'll need to split it with my friend Toni here.'

The old man turned round again, staring in disbelief, shaking his head. His white hair glowed in the moonlight, and there was a fanatical shine in his eyes as he suddenly broke into a dry laugh. 'You have quite a nerve, don't you?'

'Five per cent.'

'It's a deal. And now you give me your word of honour that you'll never tell anyone a single thing about what we're about to see.'

'But if it's a significant sum how do we explain where we got it?'

'Will you stop?' Grimmer sighed. 'First: yes, it is a significant sum. Secondly, you'll just have to wait before spending it, won't you?'

'I could always pretend I won it,' Luke said. He was grinning now – maybe this would all end well, after all. 'At online poker, for example.'

The car came to a halt at the bottom of a slope that was so steep it was impossible to climb, even on foot, at least without ropes. Achim killed the engine, and silence filled the big car.

Grimmer reached for a notebook in his breast pocket, ripped off a page and began writing on it in fountain pen.

'I'll take your word of honour about your silence, but

239

I want your signature for the five per cent,' he said. 'And should you break your word, I will make very, very sure this contract is seen by the authorities.'

Luke took the text and skimmed it quickly. He didn't like the idea of a contract – his father had taught him to be careful with his signature.

Having today assisted in an operation to find an unknown quantity of hidden treasure dating back to the end of the Third Reich, we, the undersigned, are to receive five per cent of the full value of the sum total recovered.

'We don't have all night,' Grimmer said. 'Sign. Both of you.'

'Five per cent of what?' Luke said, taking the heavy fountain pen from Grimmer's hand. 'I'd like to know before I sign.'

'I'd like to know as well, but I don't!' Grimmer snapped. 'I think it's gold bullion – but to be honest with you, I don't even know that for certain.'

'But—'

'Sign, or else!'

Luke felt a strange, needle-like sensation travel up and down his limbs, a swarming, electric tingle . . .

Were they about to find this treasure? Was it gold? A stash of Nazi gold?

He returned his attention to the handwritten contract, which now took on a new meaning – a horrible meaning. By signing, wouldn't he be giving his allegiance to this strange German?

What, he asked himself with a fresh blast of dread, would a document like this mean in a court of law? Would it implicate Luke and Toni in Grimmer's crimes? Or was the old man simply playing games with them –

fooling around with worthless bits of paper just to scare them? Achim sat hunched over his telephone, texting.

Luke made his decision. With a swift, determined gesture, he signed. Frowning darkly, Toni followed suit, just as Luke expected him to do. Then Grimmer snatched back the document and carefully folded it in four. Luke could have sworn he saw a smile on the man's face as he opened the door and slipped out into the cool air.

29

They crossed a small meadow, from which the mountain soared up almost vertically, forming a wall of rock. Grimmer and Achim led the way, talking in muted voices. They didn't seem at all worried that Luke and Toni might try and do a runner.

Nor was escape the first thing on Luke's mind. Now he thought about it, five per cent of a hidden treasure sounded like an attractive prospect.

Achim and Grimmer were both wearing small lamps strapped to their foreheads and Achim was swinging a massive black torch that reminded Luke of a truncheon, and which cast a beam that was as bright as a car headlight.

'Give me that,' Grimmer said. 'You're wasting the battery.'

The old man switched off the torch and the small party advanced by the light of the little headlamps. As his eyes got used to the dark, Luke was able to examine his surroundings. A fast-flowing mountain stream foamed and bubbled in the distance, glowing in the moonlight. Curiously enough, it met another stream under the rock face, forming a strange forking waterway.

Grimmer and Achim stopped. Luke glanced at Toni and they joined the German and his assistant, who were studying the old piece of map.

Grimmer's eyes glinted with excitement. 'This is it.'

After they met, the two streams ran into a small Alpine lake, but a very deep one by the look of it. Luke had visited Lake Geneva several times, and his dad had explained that it was so deep it contained more water than all the lakes of the UK combined.

Grimmer gave his assistant a friendly slap on the shoulder and beckoned for Luke and Toni to follow. He charged forward, heading for the streams, a boyish spring in his step. Luke and Toni brought up the rear.

Suddenly the German stopped again and clicked on his torch, playing its beam on something directly ahead.

Next to the stream on the right-hand side, at the foot of the rugged wall of rock, was a hole. A dark hole.

Luke's breathing quickened. The beam of the big torch leaped about in the thin, scraggly vegetation that clung to the rock. For a few moments the German stood stock still, listening. Then he advanced once more, taking slow, cautious steps – as though dreading he might step on a mine or into some deathly trap. Luke and Toni fell back, peering left and right. An eerie silence enveloped the desolate place.

They gathered at the cave mouth which, Luke immediately realised, was not natural but man-made. He knew the Nazis had built countless bunkers and storage depots in the Alps during the war. Once, on holiday in Switzerland, he'd seen some that were still in use; they'd had sturdy steel doors fitted with modern locks and well-oiled hinges, and freshly painted ventilation shafts.

But this place looked derelict. Abandoned. Luke and Toni followed Grimmer and Achim inside. Regular in shape, like a pedestrian underpass, the cave made a sharp right turn. The torch beam swept the flat gravel floor littered with the remnants of old campfires, squashed beer cans and broken bottles. Some graffiti artist far from home had even sprayed a tag on the wall. There was no sign of any further door or other passage deeper into the mountain. If anything had ever been hidden here by the Nazis, it had surely been found and spirited away decades ago.

Luke saw Achim cast a disappointed look at Grimmer. But the old man didn't seem discouraged in the least. He was gazing up at the back wall of the cave, stroking it systematically with his torch beam.

'I've been in caves like this before.' Grimmer narrowed his eyes, staring at the wall. 'They have their secrets. Maybe there's a hidden mechanism somewhere.'

'But look at all this junk,' Achim blurted out. 'We're not the first to find this place.'

'We are the first to make a systematic search,' Grimmer said. 'This cave was never marked on the German maps. My father's code was the only trace – and now we are here.'

The old man searched and searched, caressing the walls with his hands, sweeping the torch over every inch of the ceiling and the floor, but he found nothing aside from rubbish. Not only the floors were covered in it – even the recesses in the walls were full of junk. There was a small hole on the southern wall clogged up with old tins and newspaper. Hikers must have taken shelter here.

After half an hour Grimmer suddenly stopped his

search. He'd moved about with the energy of a young man, but he now shook his head slowly and seemed to shrink before their very eyes, as though his real age had suddenly caught up with him.

'Well,' he muttered, catching his breath. 'I guess I was wrong.'

He blinked once or twice, and with a bowed head ambled towards the door, a defeated man.

'Let's not give up yet,' Achim said with surprising gentleness, as though trying to comfort his boss. 'Maybe we should come back in daylight?'

'Daylight?' Grimmer snapped. 'What use is that? We're in a cave, you idiot!'

Anger flashed in Achim's eyes.

As they all began filing out in silence something clicked in Luke's mind. Daylight. *Sun.*

He returned to the hole stuffed with newspaper and began clearing out the contents. He saw at once that the hole widened outwards... He followed the others into the moonlight and sidled along the wall of rock, searching ... He saw a dark niche, which seemed to be at exactly at the same spot as the small round hole inside...

'Can I have some light over here for a second?' he said.

With a puzzled frown Grimmer handed him the torch.

Luke rose onto his toes and aimed the beam into the niche in the wall. There was more rubbish inside.

'Toni, hold this.'

Toni took the torch, and Luke began frantically gouging out the rubbish, tossing it all onto the ground: cans, bottles, more newspaper. He was sure now. The niche narrowed inwards until it became the hole that he'd seen inside.

'What are you doing?' Grimmer demanded.

'Look,' Luke said. 'If it was day, the sun would shine through here into the cave.'

Grimmer understood at once. He looked up at the dark sky.

'That's south,' Luke said, peering at the compass on his watch. 'Toni, can you point the torch so it shines all the way in?'

Toni held the torch high above his head, pointing it into the niche.

'What for?' he muttered. 'What's going on?'

'Wait and see,' Luke said, rushing back inside with Grimmer and Achim.

The cave was almost completely dark. Only a narrow spear of light entered through the hole, projecting a round tablet of light high on the back wall, as though marking a spot. A pair of pale hands shifted in the light – Grimmer was pressing and feeling the cold rock where the light hit.

Luke knew the Egyptian pyramids contained light shafts that were calibrated to the movements of the sun. Once a year, and once a year only, the rays of the sun struck down at the right angle, shining inside. 'How do you know you have the angle right?' he said, his mouth dry.

'It's a deep hole so the sun can only enter at one angle, no matter where it is in the sky,' the old man replied in a hoarse whisper. 'Achim, I need something to mark the spot. Then we'll examine it with the torch.'

'I don't have a pencil,' Achim said helplessly. 'My pockets are empty.'

'Think of something!' Breathing hard, standing with his arms upraised, Grimmer kept his fingers pressed against the stone in the circle of torchlight, as though holding this last clue in place, terrified that it would dissolve and vanish, hiding its secret for ever.

Luke searched in his pockets and found a packet of chewing gum. He chewed hard and squashed the ball of gum onto the wall in the precise centre of the circle.

'We're ready here, Toni!' he called.

They waited until Toni came bustling in, panting, the big torch in his hand throwing shadows along the walls. Grimmer grabbed the torch and aimed the beam up at the small white fleck on the black stone.

Luke let out a gasp. Carved on that very spot was a small symbol, shaped a little like a bottle top: *the sun*. The old man ran his fingers over the shape, pressing and probing, but nothing happened.

'What if we jolt it in some way?' Grimmer's voice was thick with agitation. 'We need a plank of wood, or something.'

They looked about, but there was nothing suitable to hand.

'What about this?' Achim broke the silence.

He stepped into the light with a round rock the size of a huge apple in his hand. The old German hesitated for a moment then gave a small nod. They stepped back as Achim prepared to launch his missile. He threw it hard, missing the target by a metre at least, and the rock fell on the floor, rolling to one side. He picked it up at once and tried again, hitting the spot perfectly.

Nothing happened. Not at first. But then, after a silence that lasted a second or less, there was a slight creak and a slab of stone came loose. Like a dictionary falling off a shelf, it just dislodged itself from the wall and came thudding to the ground.

'Step back!' Grimmer's voice echoed in the darkness.

As he scuttled towards the exit, Luke heard a heavy, hollow rumble deep inside the mountain behind the rock wall. A second slab fell. Then a third and a fourth. Like a collapsing mosaic made of thick rectangles of stone, the entire back wall of the cave disintegrated, crashing to the floor.

There was silence. Dust shone in the torch beam. Behind the rock, a rusty surface had been revealed.

It was a door.

Luke took a long, deep breath. A big round combination lock was embedded in the door, which gave it the appearance of an old-fashioned safe. A small tin sign was affixed next to the lock. Grimmer staggered forward and dropped to his knees.

'What does it say?' Luke asked.

In the old man's eyes shone a feverish light. He held the beam of the torch at an angle up to the sign and translated the words for Luke and Toni's benefit.

'Attention! Entering a false combination will result in the irreversible destruction of this passageway.'

'Irreversible?' Luke stared at the rusty old sign. 'What does that mean?'

'It's a threat. And not an idle one.'

'Are you ... sure?' Luke swallowed. 'We don't want to get buried alive.'

'I'm sure.' Grimmer chuckled. *'Einfacht ist schön.* Simple is beautiful.'

'The same code again,' Luke said in a half-whisper. 'The code you found on the painting.'

'Five ...' Grimmer grasped the dial and turned it. 'Six.'

Then he turned it the other way.

'Two.' He wiped his hands on his trousers and glanced up with a crazed leer. 'Do you trust me, boys?'

Luke and Toni glanced at one another. The German didn't seem to expect an answer. He was going to carry on to the end, no matter what...

'Zero...' The old man paused, then grasped the dial once more and slowly turned it again. 'Eight...'

When he reached the last digit there was a loud *clunk* deep inside the door. He seized the handle and tried to turn it, but it didn't budge. Not even a fraction of an inch.

'Help me...' he hissed at his assistant. 'Achim!'

Achim went forward, and the two men joined forces, applying all their strength, forcing down the handle. With an unearthly sound, a sound somewhere between a screech and a creak, the door opened at last...And what a door it was: at least three metres high, two metres wide and a good half-metre thick.

Without a word Grimmer and Achim glided through to the other side, as though drawn by a magnet. Achim glanced behind him, waving his pistol in a commanding gesture, but it wasn't necessary – Luke and Toni followed eagerly. The mystery of what lay behind the door pulled them forward like a physical force. All four of them were in the grip of a power that was stronger than they were.

They came to a large double door that looked flimsy compared with the armoured entrance they'd just passed through. Achim seized a rock and struck off the rusty padlock with a single blow, then slid aside the old bars at the top and bottom of the doors. Grimmer pushed the right-hand door with his palms and it swung open, hinges squealing like a cat...

A small whimper escaped from the old man's lips as he stumbled on, entering a cold, dank space.

To the left the floor sloped upwards. To the right it sloped downwards towards a large wooden gate. It was like a road tunnel, broad and tall, easily big enough to accommodate a large truck. The shifting light of the torch revealed regular stone walls. The deep cavern smelled of rock, dust and metal. Grimmer hastened to the gate and ran his hand along the seam in the middle.

'This is the exit,' he said. 'I can feel a draught.'

Luke could feel it too.

The old German studied the gate closely then turned on his heel and began climbing the slope, heading deeper into the mountain. The others followed without a word. Further up ahead the passage was lost in darkness.

Now, Luke thought to himself, would be the right moment to try to escape . . . Grimmer and his bodyguard were far too excited to pay the two boys any attention. But some weird force, born of the fascination of the mystery that was about to be revealed, made him follow the old German towards the dark heart of the mountain, which swallowed them like insects. A few steps behind he could hear Toni's walking boots scraping along and his friend's heavy breathing.

Dark and light played on the walls of the passage and gave sharp outlines to the silhouettes of the men advancing ahead of him. Dark and light, good and bad. Were they all headed towards darkness and evil? Luke asked himself. *Surely not,* pleaded a voice inside him. *If the treasure no longer has an owner, and if no one even knows it exists, what's wrong with trying to recover it?*

They came to a second wooden gate. It was bolted but

not locked. Achim shot the bolts and opened one side of the gate. Rust pattered onto the dusty stone floor from hinges that no human hand had disturbed for decades. The beam from Grimmer's headlamp cut a swathe of light into the slanting hall-like space ahead. Toni had found his miniature Maglite in his pocket but its beam was ridiculously faint in this huge space.

Suddenly Luke heard his friend let out a gasp. And he saw why at once ... Lined on the floor ahead stood row upon row of ceremonial flags decorated with the notorious Nazi symbol: a white circle on a red background, in the middle of which sat a tilted swastika. Though faded, the blood-red colour of the standards seemed to retain an animate glow, as though the spirit of Hitler's hysterical followers lingered here still. Luke shuddered, wondering whether these were the actual flags that the Nazis had carried at their mass rallies in Nuremberg. Eagles with their wings outstretched perched on the tips of the flagpoles, as though waiting for someone to bring them back to life.

Eyes wide with fear and fascination, Toni grabbed the closest standard and shook dust from it, causing the whole thing to topple over with a crash. Grimmer swung round and pointed his torch at Toni's face. The boy blinked in the glare, his cheeks flushed with embarrassment, and he bent over to lift up the flag, coughing from the dust.

Grimmer was standing over a large crate. Luke glimpsed the contours of yet another eagle on it, caked with grime. The German grabbed a crowbar that was leaning against the crate and quickly levered off the metal clasps that were screwed to the lid. It was easy. The rotten wood splintered at the slightest pressure.

'And what do you imagine this crate contains?' Grimmer said in a low voice, dabbing his brow with a handkerchief.

'The Arc of the Covenant?' Toni said. 'Like in that old Spielberg film.'

Luke felt like kicking him in the shins.

'Much as I enjoy the films of Steven Spielberg, I'm afraid we have something altogether more real here.' Grimmer handed the crowbar to Achim, who stepped forward and wrenched off the lid of the chest.

Luke took a step closer and saw dark steel inside.

'Oiled, cleaned and ready for use,' the German said, touching the shiny barrel of one of the old machine guns. 'An arms cache for the guerrilla war that never happened.'

Grimmer and Achim led the way past a whole stack of similar crates. An immense subterranean warehouse had been carved into the rock. On its rough-hewn walls their shadows grew into giants.

Luke and Toni glanced at one another. Luke was sure they were thinking the same thing: this was probably their very last chance to escape. But, no, nothing would stop them now. They were entitled to five per cent of whatever treasure lay hidden in this strange mountain vault. The German had given his word. Could they trust it? With an unpleasant shudder, Luke thought how easy it would be to hide dead bodies in a place like this if Grimmer suddenly decided he wanted to get rid of them... Yet he instinctively believed the white-haired, mild-voiced old gentleman.

Twenty metres ahead, at the top of a slope, stood yet another gate reinforced with iron studs and bars. There was a door set in the gate with a yellowing cardboard sign nailed to it, which said simply: EINTRITT STRENG VERBOTEN – Entry strictly forbidden. There was no keyhole on the oak door, and no lock. Just a handle.

Grimmer grasped it, eyes blazing with an almost religious fervour, and opened the door.

Luke suddenly felt like he didn't have enough air in his lungs; his head started spinning and he thought he was about to topple over. He leaned against the door frame and took several deep breaths.

Toni took his arm. 'You OK?'

'Fine.'

They came into a vast underground chamber carved deep inside the rock, much bigger than the one before. Tall as a cathedral, the place must have been forty metres from floor to ceiling, and perhaps ten metres wide and fifteen metres deep. Right in the middle of the floor stood an unreal sight: a pair of Opel Blitz trucks, pre-war model, painted black, and covered in a layer of dust so thick they looked like they'd been coated with soft felt. The dust also covered the windows and windscreen of the cabs. The air was very dry, and Luke could see no trace of rust on the vehicles. A few shallow crates were lined up on the back of each truck.

Toni let out a delighted whistle, eyes round with excitement. The two trucks seemed to be in mint condition. Luke felt a gleeful smile begin to form on his lips. The shallowness of the crates and their small number could mean one thing only: the contents were incredibly heavy.

One of the heaviest substances in the universe is gold. Luke had never been particularly interested in precious metals, but at this moment the idea of that noble element, that loadstone of human vanity and greed, held an irresistible fascination for him.

Grimmer skipped up onto the back of the nearest truck, moving with surprising agility, like a young man. Achim climbed up onto the other vehicle.

Gold... The word pulsed inside Luke's brain like a mantra. He suddenly remembered a surprising fact he'd learned in his physics class. One litre of gold weighed 19.3 kilos – over nineteen times the weight of a litre of water. And gold was incredible malleable. A single gram could be stretched into a thread more than two kilometres long... A wondrous substance! Universally worshipped, everywhere lusted after, there was something mysterious about it, something eternal. In uncertain times, the rich always invested their wealth in gold. Gold was for ever. It could be trusted.

'Sixteen crates,' Grimmer said, straightening his back. 'Fifteen kilos in each. That makes two hundred and forty kilos in total.'

'Just four crates here,' Achim replied in a disappointed voice. 'Sixty kilos in all. The rest is just files and rubbish.'

'Very well.' Grimmer nodded with approval. 'So we have three hundred kilos of gold.'

Toni stepped up onto the running board of the nearest truck and began scraping the grime off the side window, keen for a glimpse of the original 1930s interior. He managed to clear a small patch, pointed his torch – and let out a blood-curdling scream.

'There's someone...' He ran away from the truck and grabbed Luke by the arm. 'There's someone in there!'

'Don't be ridiculous.' Grimmer clambered off the back of the truck. 'Achim, open this door.'

The young man pulled out his pistol. Standing with his back to the cab, he grasped the door handle and glanced at his boss. Grimmer also reached for his weapon and, holding the large torch in his other hand, gave a small nod. Achim tried to open the door with a sudden wrench, but it was jammed and he had to put away his weapon to force the handle. At last he managed it. With an ugly creak, the door opened.

'What the hell...?'

They all drew back instinctively. Toni covered his mouth with his hands. Grimmer stepped up and shone his torch into the cab.

Seated behind the wheel was a man dressed in an SS uniform. In the shadow of the peaked cap, empty eye sockets stared... His long teeth seemed to leer back at them in the shifting light of the torch. There was a hole in the side of the pale-brown skull.

'The mystery thickens,' Grimmer said. 'But this man cannot harm us now. Looks like he's completely mummified.'

'The other cab's empty,' Achim called from the direction of the truck behind.

'Let's continue with our work,' Grimmer said, beckoning Luke. 'Help me.'

Tearing his attention away from the skeleton, Luke clambered up onto the bed of the truck. The old man had already prised the lid off the top crate. The gold bars inside shone brightly in the light of the torch. Grimmer took a bar into his slim hands and held it up for Luke to see, wordless triumph in his eyes

With a shiver Luke recognised the symbol stamped onto the bar. *A swastika*. The ancient Indian symbol of the sun, irreparably tainted by the Nazis.

'My father must have planned this for years ... You see, he was involved in the building of the secret depots where the gold was hidden when Germany lost the war,' Grimmer said, returning the heavy bar back into the crate. 'Gold and arms. Top secret.'

Luke couldn't remove his gaze from the glowing yellow metal. There was an eagle stamped onto the side of the bar too, and an inscription: *Reichsbank 1936*.

'How much?' Luke said, struggling to form his words, embarrassed and confused. 'How much is each bar... worth?'

'The current price on the world market is around 1,700 dollars an ounce. An ounce is thirty-one grams. And the experts say the price likely to climb higher.'

Luke swallowed.

'Higher?' he said.

'Much higher. Thousands of dollars.'

Luke was crunching the numbers inside his head. One kilo of gold was worth around 55,000 dollars. Five per cent of three hundred kilos was fifteen kilos. So the share that had been promised to him and Toni was worth 825,000 dollars.

He stared at the gold, mesmerised.

Grimmer was watching him. A thin smile appeared on his lips. 'Don't worry. Five per cent is yours – a promise is a promise.'

'Congratulations.' Luke smiled. 'You've cracked your father's riddle.'

'Indeed.' The old man beamed back. Then he glanced at his watch. 'But it will all have been for nothing if we can't get the gold out of this place.'

Working with sudden urgency, as though worried that someone would come and wrest the prize from his hands at the last minute, the old man began emptying the crate. He kicked it with his heel, and the board came loose revealing more gold bars.

Luke was wondering what Grimmer's plan was for transporting the bullion out of the cave. Wouldn't it be simpler to drive the 4x4 inside and to load it up here? The passage was easily wide enough.

The German paused to catch his breath and added another remark.

'If you knew how many years I've spent on this trail... And how many times I... doubted my father... But I kept going.'

Luke nodded. Few people seized the opportunities that came their way. Even fewer kept trying when they failed at something. Grimmer hadn't given up – and he'd kept faith with his father, even when it had seemed that he'd been just a crazy Nazi taunting his son from beyond the grave... He'd spent his whole life on this quest – wasted it, some would have said – yet here he was, with his reward, at last.

And Luke too had shown his mettle when he'd followed his investigation through and when he'd trusted his intuition, even when others mocked him, when fear threatened to immobilise him – and when danger loomed.

The old man patted him gently on the shoulder. Luke smiled.

'We need to get out of here as fast as we can.' All emotion had suddenly drained from the voice, which was businesslike and cold as before. 'Achim, let's go.'

Silence.

Grimmer stiffened. He craned his neck, looking left and right.

'Achim?'

The torch beam danced about like a sword in the dark, cavernous space. Then Grimmer switched it off. In the sudden blackness, Luke could hear him breathing heavily, faster and faster.

'Achim, where the hell are you?'

But there was no reply.

'What's wrong?' Luke hissed.

'*Shh!*'

Grimmer waited a little longer then switched his torch back on, lowered himself off the back of the truck and glanced wildly about him. Fury darkened his features.

Luke jumped down too. The stone pillars cast weird shadows on the brick walls. There were dark nooks behind the pillars where you couldn't see properly.

Where was Achim? And where, for that matter, was Toni?

'Toni!' Luke suddenly yelled, but there was no reply.

His voice echoed off the walls, dying away, leaving an eerie silence.

'Achim!' Grimmer roared. '*Verdammt!*'

30

Luke began to make his way round the second truck, sidling between it and the rock wall through a gap no wider than a metre. His foot caught on something soft and he almost fell on his face.

It was Toni.

Luke dropped to a crouch and somehow managed to roll his friend onto his side. He peered behind him and into the dim space ahead. He listened. Nothing.

Toni was breathing normally and showed no external injuries. But something was wrong, seriously wrong. Toni wasn't in the habit of taking impromptu naps, not in the middle of a tense situation, famously drowsy though he was early in the morning. Luke ran his hand along Toni's neck, feeling for a pulse. Suddenly he felt something rough under his fingers between Toni's shoulder blades: a small, hard protrusion, clearly not a normal part of the human body.

Luke fished in his pocket and switched on the LED on his key ring. The object on Toni's back was a tiny metal spike no thicker than a rose thorn, with a red tail.

Luke pulled it out and held it on his palm. He swallowed. He knew exactly what the object was. He'd seen darts like this – and the guns that fired them – in a brochure his father had picked up at a defence and security exhibition in London. The police used them to incapacitate violent offenders. Not unlike a Taser gun, the darts delivered a non-lethal electric shock, buying the police the time to handcuff their suspect.

But Toni wasn't just incapacitated. He was out cold. Luke felt the back of his friend's head and, just as he'd expected, found a large bump there. There was no blood but it was clear Toni had either received a ferocious blow to the head or hit it as he fell.

Had Achim attacked him? Why? Luke peered under the truck and sprang back, almost crying out in fright. He knew at once what it was. Another skeleton, still in its uniform...

The second driver.

The first had been shot from close range, so perhaps this one had tried to crawl to safety under his vehicle ... Suddenly Toni let out a low moan. He tried to raise his head. Though his eyes stayed shut he was clearly struggling his way back to consciousness. Luke saw at once his friend wouldn't be up to much for some time, and was certainly unable to defend himself. So much for his martial-arts training; even a black belt in Aikido wouldn't be much use if you were caught by surprise.

There was a crunching sound as something disturbed the gravel on the other side of the truck. Lowering himself to his knees, Luke rested his palm on the ground to peer under the vehicle past the mummified skeleton. A pair of legs, black jeans and boots...

Achim was back...

The man was standing stock still, as though listening or waiting for something.

'Achim!' Grimmer called out again, his voice cracking slightly.

Still the young man didn't answer.

Why not?

Suddenly two more pairs of feet could be heard, moving at a brisk pace, approaching along the wide passage that lead down towards the open air.

'I'll show you!' Grimmer swore loudly and climbed back up onto the truck.

Luke scuttled forward until he reached the front wheel and peered round it.

Two men were standing at the gate. Dark, Italian-looking. And Achim was bounding across the gravel towards them.

A shot rang out. The bullet whistled, deflected off the wall and went buzzing past like an enraged insect. The three men instantly disappeared through the gate, half-closing it behind them.

'Achim! Lorenzo! Giuliano!' Grimmer yelled. 'You can't do this to me!'

Luke tried to help Toni up into a sitting position, ready to cover his mouth at any moment should he start talking.

'Achim!' the old man pleaded. 'Have you no honour?'

Luke had no idea what was going on, except that the old German had lost control of his team – and that it made him very, very angry.

'Come out, you rats! Or don't you dare to?' The shrill voice echoed in the confined space. 'Well then, how do you like *this*?'

Another bullet went zinging past. Bits of grit pattered

from the ceiling. Luke noticed that the shots from Grimmer's pistol bore no resemblance to the rounds fired in movies, which always rang out loudly and were accompanied by a bright muzzle flash. The pistol in the old man's hand simply shuddered as the weapon kicked, a little wisp of smoke accompanying the bullet on its way. The report was crisp and brief, and the weapon's quiet efficiency was somehow much more frightening than any Hollywood sound effect.

Luke cowered beside the front wheel of the truck, protecting himself from the ricochets, which he knew could even kill the shooter himself in a confined space like this.

There was silence behind the gate. Then a fist hammered on the wood and a voice with an Italian accent yelled out: 'Listen up, Grimmer! You thought we were all a bit stupid, didn't you? Who's stupid now?'

'Achim's on our side and there's nothing you can do about it,' called another man. 'Throw down that pistol and put your hands above your head or we'll shoot you full of holes.'

Grimmer responded with two more pistol rounds. The shots echoed off the vaulted ceiling. Spent cartridges fell onto the ground beside Luke's feet as the old man reloaded. An acrid smell of cordite drifted through the stale air.

Suddenly there was a barrage of gunfire from the direction of the gate. A figure darted into view, fired and withdrew. It was the bald, chinless weirdo from the Sistine Chapel. Luke wasn't sure what the weapon was but its noise completely drowned out Grimmer's pistol.

Undeterred, cursing aloud on the back of the truck,

Grimmer returned fire, striking sparks off the walls. More cartridges pattered to the ground. Luke pressed himself flat against the floor.

Kneeling behind the gate, peering through the gap between its two doors, Achim calmly took aim, tracking the bright spot of bluish light on the back of the truck. He knew what the light source was, having bought it himself in a large camping shop near Munich. It was a headlamp strapped over his boss's forehead. But the light kept bobbing and shuttling erratically. From time to time it disappeared altogether as Grimmer crouched down to reload behind the cab.

Switching sides had been a calculated move, and one he'd made weeks ago, after careful consideration. Achim didn't like the Italians with whom he'd thrown in his lot, and he felt stinging remorse at having to betray the old man, yet what choice did he have? He didn't trust Grimmer to reward him in the end. The man was obviously indifferent to wealth, well off as he was. But Achim was virtually penniless. No house, no job, no prospects – he couldn't afford not to cash in on this operation. Lorenzo and Giuliano at least understood the value of money. Grimmer had been his mentor, it was true, and a generous one at that, but wasn't it only proper and fitting that the apprentice one day outgrew his master?

Once upon a time Achim had felt almost like the old man's son – but he now understood he'd always be just a hired hand. Immersed in conversation, congratulating one another for their clever interpretation of the secret code, Grimmer and the English boy had seemed to forget his very existence. Although it had been Achim who'd discovered the patch of canvas bearing the code in the first place! No matter what he did for Grimmer he was just the muscles, it seemed. Today's events confirmed what he'd always suspected: the old man viewed him as a brainless fool.

Big mistake.

Achim steeled himself for what he had to do.

Soon he'd be free. Rich and free. All it would take was one well-aimed shot.

Luke's mind was racing. How would they ever get out of this place? And how many more men were waiting behind the sturdy gate? He glanced at Toni, who had come round at last and was blinking blearily, clutching his head. Luke hoped his friend would be able to walk; he was much too heavy for Luke to carry.

Suddenly the gate slammed shut with a loud crash, and after the diminishing echoes had died out a deathly silence filled the vaulted rock chamber. A single thought thudded in Luke's consciousness. A single, shocking fact.

They were trapped.

The only exit was closed. Whichever way he turned he saw just solid walls: rock, brick, concrete. The Alpine wind, cold and bracing, seemed a distant memory, and so did the sight of the blue sky and the blazing sun.

He couldn't breathe. Perhaps another half-century and more would pass before anyone found them here. By then they'd all look like the two dead drivers . . . A crazy thought came to him: maybe the gold was cursed? Within days they'd happily exchange the lot for a bottle of water or a loaf of bread . . .

Again Grimmer's voice cried out from the truck. Luke

put his forefinger to his lips, warning Toni. He couldn't see the gate properly in the dim light and he knew the shooting might start again at any moment.

The back of the truck pointed towards the wall opposite the door, away from the gunmen, and the German took advantage of the temporary cessation of hostilities to leap down.

Moments later he was at their side... Breathing hard, he flourished his Sig Sauer pistol. Luke could see the strain on his face.

'Is he OK?' Grimmer nodded at Toni.

'He'll be fine,' Luke replied, showing the dart in his hand. 'He just caught one of these.'

'Better than catching a bullet,' the old man said.

'There's another body under this truck.'

Grimmer knelt down to see for himself, then straightened his back and dusted his knees. 'That must be the second driver...'

'What do you think happened to them?'

'I have a hunch. But we'd better deal with our own situation now. Those men have us trapped, but we'll show them what we're made of.'

Luke wasn't hugely comforted by the words of the mysterious old German. It was crazy – the man was undoubtedly a criminal, and a bit of a nutter to boot, but he obviously respected Luke, and seemed to be taking the situation quite calmly having got over his tantrum. His eyes were on the big gate, a dark shape in the dimness ahead.

'Who are they?' Luke said. 'What's going on?' His voice came out a bit reedy, but that couldn't be helped.

'They were my associates. Just a pair of small-time

crooks from Italy,' Grimmer said. 'They snatched the Caravaggio for me from the Vatican. It would seem Achim has gone over to their side.'

'How can we ... get out?'

'Good question. Go and see if there's anything useful in the other truck.' He gave a thin smile. 'A small canon, for example, that could blast a hole into that gate.'

Luke took a deep breath then dashed back to the other vehicle. A small ladder led from behind the driver's door to the loading platform. He scampered up, dreading the sound of a gun shot at any moment. The corroded rungs, rough as sandpaper, left flecks of rust on his hands.

This wasn't at all like running for cover on a PlayStation game, he thought as he threw himself down onto the back of the truck. The only sound he could hear was his thudding heart and urgent breathing. He peered over the side and was pleased he couldn't see the gate – that meant the Italians and Achim couldn't see him, either, if they reappeared to shoot some more.

'Nothing there,' Luke said when he returned. 'Just a bunch of paperwork and one crate of gold.'

'A whole truck for just the one crate ...' Grimmer knitted his brow and was silent for a long time. 'I've been thinking, my father must have removed some of the gold before he sealed this place.'

'What next?' Luke said.

'We'll have to negotiate,' the old man said eventually and dabbed his face with a dainty gesture. 'We're cornered.'

'We have a vehicle here, don't we?' Toni suddenly put in. His voice was weird, as though he was finding it hard to shape his words.

'You think these old trucks will start?' Luke said. 'Come off it. You're not thinking straight.'

'Hardly likely it will start with an ancient battery. But look at the floor.'

Luke did as told, and was none the wiser. He glanced at Grimmer who shrugged his shoulders.

'Your friend has concussion, maybe?'

'Maybe.' Toni grimaced as he heaved himself onto his feet. 'But I'll say it again. Look at the floor.'

He scraped at the gravel with his foot. Luke waited for an explanation. Toni took his time over it.

'This floor slopes down towards the gate and it's quite a steep gradient.' He was still slurring his words. 'May I also draw your attention to these large bricks, one in front of each wheel?'

Luke's mouth felt dry. He nodded.

'The bricks were wedged in there to stop this baby from rolling out of here by itself. Even if we can't start the engine, I'd say the weight of this thing will blast us right through that gate.'

Luke and Grimmer both studied the distance between the truck and the gate. It was true there was a gradient, but Luke wasn't at all convinced the gate was far enough away to allow the truck to pick up enough speed to crash through. On the other hand it was just wood reinforced with iron bands, and the truck was huge and heavy. If they got through the first two gates they'd be in the tunnel leading to the third and last gate, the one in the mountainside, and that tunnel also sloped steeply downwards, Luke now remembered. So maybe, just maybe...

'My father thought of everything,' Grimmer said in a half-whisper.

'What?' Luke said.

'Your friend is right. Hauling a large quantity of gold bullion out of this place by hand would be slow work. So my father made sure it could just be rolled out of the gate.'

Luke nodded. He glanced at his friend who was quietly stretching. Toni was sharp, and calm in a crisis – calmer than Luke had been, in fact, ashamed though he was to admit it. He quietly told himself never to underestimate his friend again.

'What about the tyres? They must be completely flat by now.'

'No.' Toni gave the closest one a kick. 'They're solid synthetic rubber – wartime speciality.'

'I'd always wondered about that.' Grimmer smiled at Toni as though he'd noticed him for the first time. 'Why was that?'

'During the war the importation of Asian rubber was disrupted so it was manufactured synthetically out of oil.'

'Can't have made for a very comfortable ride,' Luke said.

'These trucks were built for construction work, not tourism.'

'Let's get ready,' Grimmer said. 'We're not leaving any gold behind so it all needs to be transferred to the front vehicle. I'll keep a lookout.'

Luke passed Toni the small, heavy bars from the four crates. He soon began sweating, from nervousness as much as from the physical effort. Then he turned his attention to the other boxes, which contained musty old files and sheaths of yellowing documents covered in faded typed text. He opened a file at random. The paper was soft and fragile, and there was mould on the documents inside. Then he noticed a pair of slim, leather-bound files that were a different shape from the rest, and was excited to find they contained stamps. An occasional philatelist, he wished he had the time to study them more closely... Could this be the Führer's personal stamp collection, or parts of it?

Luke remembered having read somewhere that Hitler had specialised in the stamps of the British Empire. If so the album might contain some great rarity, such as an 1847 blue or orange Mauritius Post Office stamp, the very first to be produced in a British colony, almost impossible to find, worth millions. He hid one album under his shirt, tucking it into his belt, and flung the other among the papers.

Toni had opened the passenger door of the truck and was placing the gold bars on the floor of the cab. 'What do we do about *him*?' he said darkly, staring at the uniformed skeleton.

'Lift him out,' Grimmer said. 'He won't weigh much.'

Luke and Toni exchanged a glance, but what choice did they have? Toni knelt down to hold the legs, and Luke slipped his arm behind the dead driver's back, preparing to support the upper half of the body.

'On the count of three,' Luke said. He didn't feel like touching the skeleton. However old it may be, it was still a dead body. 'One... Two... Three!'

There was a crunching sound and the head of the body wobbled on the spine, then fell onto the seat. The sleeve of the uniform literally crumbled into small flecks and dust in Luke's grasp. Toni had stood up with the dead man's leg bones in his arms, and he now threw them aside, brushing his fleece frantically, face twisted in horror.

'Yuck!' he gasped. 'I'm going to be sick.'

Gathering all his willpower Luke grasped the torso of the desiccated cadaver and dragged it out of the cab. It was strangely weightless, like a chicken carcass. Then he went back for the skull on the floor and placed it beside the skeleton. Grimmer lifted the peaked cap off the seat and tossed it to the ground, where it dissolved in a puff of dust leaving just a leather frame.

'Why have the clothes decayed like that?' Luke said.

'Fungus,' Grimmer said. 'Look at the walls.'

He shone his torch on the rock, which, Luke now realised for the first time, was covered in strange black blotches, as though the evil that had entered here with the Nazis had caused an illness inside the earth itself.

'We must hurry. We'll only get one chance at this,' Grimmer said. 'Are you both ready?'

'I'll drive.' Toni said. 'If that's OK?'

'Are you sure?' Grimmer wiped dust off the windscreen. 'The driver's seat is the most dangerous spot. They won't hesitate to shoot when they see us coming.'

'Right.' Toni glanced at Luke. 'I'll take my chances.'

'I can drive if you prefer,' Grimmer said with a faint smile. 'I'm old, you know.'

'It's OK.'

'Very well. I'll just check we didn't leave any gold back there.'

Toni pulled himself up and checked that the handbrake was on. He leaned over and chucked out the last thing that remained of the driver: a pair of heavy boots. Then he kicked the bricks away from the wheels before taking his place at the controls of the truck.

Luke climbed in from the other side, sitting in the middle of the cab. Grimmer returned and took the passenger seat.

'Better than that rental, I guess,' Luke said. 'Sure you'll be OK?'

'Absolutely.' Toni buffed the inside of the windscreen with his sleeve. 'You guys might have to push to get us started.'

The cab smelled of leather, dust and oil. It was hard to see the gate, but they knew where it was in the gloom ahead.

Toni glanced at the old German, who gave a small nod.

There was a click as Toni released the handbrake and, almost at once, the truck nudged forward.

'Jammed…' Toni gasped, turning pale. But by wrenching it left and right he managed to free the steering wheel.

Slowly but surely, creaking as it advanced, tyres crunching on the gravel, the truck gathered momentum. Toni bit his lip, staring hard at the target ahead.

As they drew closer the passage ahead suddenly looked much too narrow for the truck to pass. But Luke's reason told him this had to be the way it had entered all those years ago.

'Further left,' Grimmer whispered. 'You're doing well. Now you're too far—'

He didn't finish his sentence, for at that moment the gate cracked open and a shot rang out. Luke and Toni lowered their heads under the dash, but Grimmer leaned out of his window and fired several return shots in quick succession. Toni crunched the truck into second gear. The starter made a whirring sound, there was a loud *clunk*, more whirring, and with a violent sputter, incredibly, the engine started.

'If I was a superstitious man,' Grimmer muttered to himself. 'I'd say you boys changed my luck!'

Now the truck really shot forward, its loud, rumbling engine drowning out the sound of gunshots. From the corner of his eye Luke saw the wooden gate shatter into a shower of wooden splinters. A dark figure dived to one side, and another flattened himself against the wall, howling out in terror, narrowly avoiding being crushed under the heavy vehicle.

Toni stamped down the accelerator and the engine tone rose to a roar. Blue exhaust fumes curled up the walls and into the cab. Then there was a strange sound – it took Luke several seconds to identify its source in the cab: the white-haired German was laughing, teeth showing, eyes shining with glee. Had he gone mad? Or was it just the sweet sense of revenge as he outwitted his treacherous comrades?

'They weren't expecting this,' he chuckled. 'Bunch of traitors.'

They were already almost at the second gate, one side of which was open. The truck charged down the slope. Toni bared his teeth as he wrestled with the wheel.

'Slow down!' Luke shouted.

But Toni did no such thing. He too was now laughing, with a demonic gleam in his eyes. Luke alone seemed to be worried for his life. He drew back in his seat, wishing he'd been buckled in, but, of course, the old vehicle had no belts. Let alone an air bag...

With a deafening *clack*, the side of the gate they'd left closed gave way, flying open and slamming against the stone wall, shattering to pieces.

'One more to go,' Grimmer said. 'Only we don't know what's behind it...'

The truck rumbled down the slope, hard tyres thundering along the stone floor. The last gate was an unknown quantity – what did it open out onto? Luke met Toni's eyes. He gave a small nod. Stopping now would mean losing the only weapon they had: the vehicle's momentum. This was their only chance.

With an almighty, bone-shaking jolt followed by a storm of shattering wood, screeching metal and breaking glass the truck struck the second gate, ramming through. The pinching Alpine wind swept into the cab, flushing out the exhaust fumes. The windscreen lay in pieces all on the cab floor. And still the heavy truck forged on, bouncing and swaying its wild way along a potholed, half-overgrown track that led down the mountain. In the sky a colossal moon hung, its silvery sheen unnaturally bright to Luke's eyes.

Some thirty metres ahead the track swung left to avoid a steep precipice.

Toni tried to engage the brake, stamping down on the stiff pedal.

But nothing happened.

'The pedal feels weird... It's all loose.'

Luke understood at once. The rusty brake cable had snapped.

The truck was racing down the incline now. The cliff edge was only seconds away.

'Use the engine to brake!' Grimmer yelled out.

'I am,' Toni said. He sounded surprisingly calm.

He rammed the truck back into first gear, causing the

engine to judder and complain. The speed reduced fractionally, and with a groaning effort Toni wrenched the wheel, swinging a turn that brought the truck within metres of a sheer drop. They careered on along a flat stretch of mountain track towards a small plateau.

'Look, that's the stream!' Luke shouted. 'And that's where we parked!'

They were heading straight for the spot where Grimmer's 4x4 waited. Using the clutch and the accelerator Toni did what he could to rein in the vehicle's fearsome momentum. They were slowing – but not fast enough.

'Watch out . . .' Grimmer screamed. 'Stop!'

But it was too late.

Luke clutched the edge of his seat, bracing himself for the impact with the Mercedes. To avoid it, Toni's only option now was to drive up onto the bank on the left, causing the truck to tilt fearfully. He almost managed to brush past the 4x4 – until the right bumper of the truck clipped the parked vehicle. There was a deafening bang as the massive truck simply flicked the smaller vehicle out of its path, spinning it round on its axis. All three passengers were thrown violently from side to side, but they were spared the frontal impact that would have killed them.

There was a moment's silence. They looked at each other. Toni had hit the side of his head on his window, but it was just a bruise. No one was seriously injured.

The glove box in front of the passenger seat had swung open. Grimmer peered inside and took out a folded sheet of paper. He glanced at the writing and seemed to stiffen in his seat.

'What is it?' Luke said.

'Later. We must make haste.'

Without a word they filed out of the cab to inspect the damage.

'It's still drivable,' Toni said. 'The bodywork's just a little crumpled.'

Grimmer took out his keys and got into the driver's seat. He turned the key in the ignition and the engine started smoothly.

'Put the gold in the back,' he said. 'Quick! They'll be on our tails soon. I'll keep watch.'

He left the engine idling, jumped out of the 4x4 once more and rushed back towards the cave, pistol in hand, white hair shining in the moonlight.

Luke filled his lungs with fresh mountain air. A feeling of triumph blossomed inside him, but they weren't out of danger yet and he forced himself to focus. The Italians had apparently felt pretty sure of themselves – or they wouldn't have parked their car right next to the 4x4.

'Stop dreaming!' Toni hollered from the back of the truck, his cheeks bright red. 'Give me a hand.'

As they were lugging the first load of bullion into the 4x4 a single shot rang out in the direction of the cave. They froze, waiting.

No more shots were fired.

'If you ask me, that sounded like Grimmer's pistol,' Toni said. 'I reckon he just shot in the air to warn them off.'

'Or he got one in the head himself,' Luke said.

They waited, but there was no further sign of life from the cave.

'Let's get on with this,' said Toni.

Luke's arms and fingers were soon hurting, such was

the dense weight of the gold bars. Luke hoped the 4x4 could handle the weight...Suddenly footsteps came running.

The boys glanced at one another, and were about run for cover when they recognised the silhouette of the old man and the glow of his white hair. It occurred to Luke at this moment that they could have just driven off with the gold, leaving Grimmer to walk home empty-handed. But that would have been unfair. Criminal he might be, but the old man also clearly had a code of honour, and Luke respected that. When someone trusted him, Luke liked to return the compliment. But did a law-breaker deserve loyalty in the first place?

'Let's get out of here before they realise I've gone,' Grimmer said mildly.

'Just one thing first...' Toni dropped to his knees and quickly let out the air from the left front tyre of the Italians' vehicle. Luke took care of the tyres at the back. Soon all four were flat.

Grimmer waited at his wheel, engine running softly. Right then, the old man could have abandoned *them* to their fate, Luke thought to himself, climbing into the front passenger seat. Toni got into the back.

As the 4x4 shot forward Luke felt something shift in the footwell and was horrified to realise it was Grimmer's pistol... Fearing it might go off as the car bounced along the track he quietly picked it up and held it in his hands, barrel pointed to the floor.

'Hope the radiator's not damaged,' Toni muttered, leaning forward between the front seats. 'Or we'll have to walk.'

Grimmer ignored the remark, eyes riveted to the

track ahead. A smile flickered on his face. Soon he slowed down and relaxed visibly. Only one of the headlights was working but it cut a bright path through the darkness.

'Was that you shooting?' Luke said.

'Just a warning shot,' the old man said. 'They were trying to creep out of the cave. Don't worry: no one was hurt.'

Luke swallowed. He hoped the old man was speaking the truth. He didn't like the cold weight of the gun in his hand. If things had gone just a little differently it might have been used against him.

A road sign flashed in the glare of the headlights. Indicating a turn, driving for all the world like some law-abiding pensioner on his way home from church, Grimmer eased the 4x4 onto the main road. The tyres thrummed on the smooth surface.

Luke quietly placed the pistol back on the rubber mat at his feet. He could feel the stamp album hidden under his shirt pressing against his lower ribs. He wondered whether he should show it to the German? Hulking mountains rose up on either side of the road, their shapes lost in the dark sky, but Luke could see lights twinkling in the distance ahead and he took a deep breath, closing his eyes: they were back in civilisation.

31

Luke and Toni stood in Dietrich Grimmer's study on the upper floor of the chalet. Their clothes were shabby, their hands grimy. With bewildered eyes they stared at the three gold bars laid out inside an open leather bag on the oriental carpet. Seven and a half kilos each. Fifteen kilos in total.

Luke's heart was beating to a rhythm he didn't recognise. He knew what was lying there before him, and what opportunities it represented, yet he couldn't quite believe it... Fifteen kilos. 825,000 dollars.

Standing over his desk, Grimmer was calmly slipping documents into his briefcase. Luke caught sight of the cover of an Argentinian passport inside a plastic sleeve. Then, to his surprise, the old man turned round his desk chair and sat down, facing the two boys.

'I have already had the opportunity to read this.' He pulled out the sheet of paper he'd found in the truck's glove box and put on his glasses. 'It will interest you as well. It's in German, but I will translate as I go.'

The old man cleared his throat and began:

'*I, Heinrich Grimmer, declare that I have seized a quantity of gold bullion from the criminal Nazi state, part of which I hereby deposit in this secret location for the benefit of a new generation of Germans. The rest I will arrange to return to the victims of the Nazis. In the course of this operation I have killed two men who were appointed to accompany me on this mission by Adolf Eichmann. Their names are Ivan Balanchuk and Otto Schmitz. No civilised German who knows the deeds these men have committed will regret their passing.*

As this catastrophic war draws to a bitter close, I wish I had done more to resist the dark forces that have overwhelmed my fatherland. I hope and believe that tomorrow's Germans will turn from dreams of world domination, and once more cultivate the life of the mind. To this end, I hereby request that the bulk of the proceeds from this gold be used to fund a scholarship in mathematics at the University of Heidelberg so that the doors of our oldest seat of learning shall remain open to students of modest means, and the noble calling of pure reason may be pursued by youths of exceptional talent. Let us not forget that our greatest compatriot, Carl Friedrich Gauss, was himself of lowly origin. Born in poverty, he rose to be the brightest star in the constellation of German science.

My heart is heavy as I write these words, but, as the father of a small son whom I love more than anything else, I must have faith in the future. One day soon the healing sunlight of civilisation will dispel the darkness that has engulfed my country. Long live Germany! Down with Hitler! Signed, Heinrich Grimmer, Head Cashier of the Reichsbank.'

'Carl Friedrich Gauss,' Luke said in a whisper. 'The Greatest German.'

'Sunlight . . . dispelling darkness . . .' Grimmer said, wiping his eyes. 'I owe you boys my thanks. A gold bar each and one to spare seems to me an apt reward.'

'But the scholarship fund...' Luke said. 'It's more important.'

'There is plenty of gold here, you know. And this letter is reward enough for me.'

The boys glanced at one another and then nodded. Luke was thinking back to the day in Italy when he'd first seen the white-haired German in the yard of the villa and had found him frightening. Right now the man seemed like a kindly old uncle.

'We must hurry.' Grimmer glanced at his watch. 'We have a head start, but only a short one.' He stared straight ahead for a moment. 'I have just one regret. My father once hinted that Hitler's stamp collection had come into Eichmann's possession. But heaven only knows where it is now!'

'Is it valuable?' Toni said.

'Oh, it certainly would be. He was especially interested in stamps of the British Empire.'

Luke looked at the pattern on the carpet and hoped that neither Grimmer nor Toni would notice his flaming cheeks. He felt bad betraying the old man, who seemed transformed by his father's letter. Yet the fact remained that Grimmer had threatened and used him, placing his and Toni's life in danger... And the old man could just as easily have found the album, had he bothered to look.

Suddenly Luke realised that Grimmer was chuckling to himself. In his hand was the other album... So he *had* looked on the other truck after all...

'One for me,' the old man said with a wink. 'And one for you.'

'What?' Toni said. 'I don't follow.'

'I'll fill you in later,' Luke said.

'And now,' Grimmer said in a slightly metallic voice, his clear blue eyes staring right through Luke. 'Go online and delete that draft email.'

Luke had been expecting the demand. So here was another dilemma. Was it still possible that Grimmer was playing an elaborate game? That he'd change tack as soon as the email had been taken care of? Of course it was. Once the message was deleted the boys would no longer have any hold on him. He might just shoot them dead and walk off with their share as well. Luke's instinct told him he had no reason to fear this gentle old man, but he decided to err on the side of caution.

'Fair enough,' Luke said. 'But on one condition. You let my friend leave in our car, and you let him take our share of the gold with him. Fifteen minutes later I'll delete the email and join him. I'll take a taxi, if you don't mind calling one.'

'You don't trust me.' The old man looked hurt. 'That pains me, you know.'

'Sorry.'

'At least let me drive you,' Grimmer said with some annoyance. 'Why waste money on a taxi?'

Luke winked. 'I can afford it.'

Grimmer stared at Luke. His lips were drawn in a tight, thin line, and for a moment Luke thought some violent outburst was coming. But then the old man began laughing, eyes filling with tears, frail body shaking.

'You can afford it!' Grimmer could barely speak he was laughing so hard. 'It's been a long time since I laughed like this.' The old man wiped his eyes. 'I never get jokes – my father, you see, he didn't make jokes.'

'But he wasn't a bad man.'

'No, he was not, and that is the greatest treasure I have found today.' Grimmer cleared his throat. 'Well then, your friend will leave in your car, and I will call you a taxi. You are clever boys. I wish you both a bright future.'

'Thank you,' Luke grinned.

'We have a deal?'

'We have a deal.' Luke shook the old man's hand. 'And good luck to you as well.'

32

Luke stepped out of the taxi by the Gasthaus Grosch. Toni was standing beside the front door holding the leather bag containing the three gold bars. The Lupo was parked across the street.

Luke was pleased to see that the beer cellar had long since closed for the night and no curious eyes would witness their late return. The pastel-coloured house fronts glowed in the yellowish light of the streetlamps.

'Time for some shuteye,' Toni said, yawning.

'Not just yet,' Luke said, watching the tail lights of the taxi as it slowly crawled down the main street of the village. 'Let's talk in the car.'

They waited until the taxi had disappeared from sight before crossing the road to the little Lupo. Luke placed the leather bag between his feet on the floor of the front passenger seat. Toni crunched back the driver's seat with the brisk air of an experienced motorist and rested his hand on the wheel.

It was as though an electric charge radiated from the bag that contained their share of the treasure.

Luke was the first to take the bull by the horns.

'So, what do we do with this lot?' he said.

'Oh that lot,' Toni said. 'We sell it.'

'I mean right now. Maybe we could hide one bar here and take the other two with us,' Luke said.

'They've got those metal detectors at the airport,' Toni said. 'They even found my house keys.'

'I didn't mean carry-on luggage. We'll check it into the hold. One bar each.'

'Is it . . . legal to carry that much gold?'

'I don't see why not. Besides, what other option do we have?'

'We could travel overland.'

'How long would that take?'

'Good point.' Toni cracked his knuckles. 'And what about the third gold bar? Where do we hide it?'

'Somewhere off the beaten track so no one finds it by accident.'

'Good idea. But let's come back and get it soon. As soon as we've, you know, spent the first two.'

'What do you mean, "spent"?'

'We deserve a bit of fun, don't we, after this ordeal? I need a new car, actually, and a new leather jacket.'

'You don't get it, do you?' Luke shook his head. 'If you have a bit of capital, the last thing you should do is spend it. You need to make it work for you.'

'So what's your idea? The stock market?'

'Actually, I was thinking investment betting.'

'*Gambling?* No way.'

Luke felt his cheeks go red. 'Well, we're in no hurry to decide. Let's start driving.'

'Where?' Toni started the engine and put the Lupo in gear.

'That forest before the turning to Grimmer's chalet.

There are no houses and no roads for miles.'

'Great. We manage to escape that creepy Nazi and now we drive right back into his arms?'

'He wasn't a Nazi, or even that creepy.'

'Luke, it's the middle of the night.'

'Exactly. We won't be seen.'

They drove slowly through the sleeping village. A large dark cat went slinking across the road in front of them. There were no lights in any of the houses' windows.

'You know, when we were first here and I didn't believe your theory about that painting...' Toni said. 'Sorry I made fun of you. You did a good job.'

'I couldn't have done it without you,' Luke grinned, somewhat sheepishly. 'Especially the bit with the truck.'

He was already fretting. Where could he hide a gold bar at home in Brussels? How would he ever explain it if Mum or Dad found it?

They soon arrived on the lonely stretch of road with thick forest on both sides. Leaving the car on the verge, near a road sign that would serve as their landmark, they clambered up the mountainside and searched for a hiding place by the light of the torch. Their legs were heavy and the forest seemed oppressive and hostile – Luke kept imagining he could see the eyes of wild animals flashing between the tree trunks.

He was near-delirious with exhaustion and his neck and head hurt, yet a strange nervous energy kept him going. At last they found a large, twisted tree stump. The system of roots was crammed with half-rotten pine needles and earth. Luke scooped out a hole with his bare hands and lowered the extra bar inside.

'Shouldn't we wrap it in something so it doesn't, you know, rust?'

'Gold doesn't corrode,' Luke said. 'Or it does, but very, very slowly. We could leave it here for a hundred years and it would look the same when we came back.'

He rammed a stout branch into the earth next to the stump and broke it off, then covered the bar with pine needles. There was no way anyone could ever guess what was hidden there. But how would they ever find the spot when they returned?

In the end they pulled the red cord from the waistband of Toni's fleece jacket and hung it from a tree branch in a small clearing about ten metres from the stump. Then they clambered straight down the slope and memorised the exact spot where they emerged back onto the road, a few metres behind the car and the road sign.

It was dawn when they arrived at the guest house once more. They opened the front door with their latch key and crept up the stairs as quietly as they could. Luke figured they could sleep until noon before checking out. Toni started snoring right away, but Luke couldn't sleep. At seven, he slipped into the bathroom to ring his dad. He knew it was early, but he felt like he simply had to do it.

'*Luke?*' said Dad's gruff voice at the other end of the line. '*Do you have any idea what time it is?*'

'Sorry, Dad.'

'*What's wrong?*'

'Nothing, nothing. Everything's fine. I just wanted to say I'm OK.'

'*Why wouldn't you be OK?*'

'We thought we might run out of money but, in fact, we're fine.' Luke winked at Toni who had appeared at the bathroom door. 'We're flush.'

'*Glad to hear you haven't spent everything.*'

'My flight gets in at five past nine this evening.'

'*See you tonight then. You woke me up, you know.*'

Luke cut the line, which immediately began ringing. It was Miss Hart, almost sobbing with anxiety.

'*Luke, thank God...Are you OK?*'

'I'm fine.'

'*I had the strangest message from Toni. I only just heard it. What have you boys been up to?*'

'Hiking. How was the skiing? How is Paolo?'

'*Never you mind about Paolo,*' Miss Hart said. '*I want a full account of what you've been doing.*'

She tried to speak sternly, but already her voice was soft with relief. In the background Luke could hear Paolo's voice singing some Italian pop song in the shower.

Miss Hart had good reason to feel relieved; she'd been neglecting her messages during her time with Paolo...If she'd let something happen to Luke, Monty would never have forgiven her.

'*Luke, I'm waiting.*'

'Well, it's complicated. I didn't know Toni had left you a message. It must have been when we thought we had a cash-flow problem, but in fact we didn't.'

Luke deliberately made his account long and complicated, and Miss Hart soon interrupted him, demanding that he show up at the airport a full three hours before departure. Luke decided it was best not to resist. It would soothe Miss Hart's conscience if she could at least pretend for a few moments that she was responsibly looking after him.

*

'Good riddance,' Toni said after they'd returned the tiny car to the rental company. 'Never again. Next time we get a BMW or a Merc, or I'm not coming.'

On the bus to Munich, Luke sat by the window and placed his pack at his feet, where he could see it and feel it. Toni was less worried and soon dropped into a doze in the seat beside him. Luke could have sworn he heard him say 'BMW' in his sleep.

As they approached Munich airport Luke felt the tension gathering in his belly. They were already in sight of the terminal building when the driver had to brake suddenly, sending Toni's head crashing forward against the seat in front.

'Right,' Luke said. 'We're almost there. The moment of truth.'

They found Paolo and Miss Hart kissing and whispering near the check-in desk. The lovers were so focused on their moment of farewell that Luke was sure they didn't notice his nervousness as he handed his heavy pack to the clerk for weighing and labelling. He tried not to stare after it as it went down the luggage belt on its way into the aircraft's hold.

They went through the security check and decided to eat together before heading for their respective departure gates: Paolo was returning to Rome, Toni was flying to Helsinki, and Miss Hart and Luke were catching a flight to Brussels.

'How did you boys get on?' Miss Hart said. 'How was the hiking?'

'Yeah, great,' Luke said, squirting ketchup onto his chips. 'Gotta love those Alps.'

'Yeah,' Toni said nodded. 'All that *golden* sunshine.'

Luke kicked him under the table.

'So you had fun?' Miss Hart said sharply. 'I suppose that's always the main thing with you.'

'Fun's not quite the word,' Luke said. 'I've never walked so much in the space of a couple of days.'

'I'll treasure these memories,' Toni went on. 'I'll treasure them like *gold*.'

Miss Hart turned to Luke. 'What's he on about?'

'Toni's just excited to be going home.' Luke got up, wiping his mouth to hide his grin and pushing away his half-finished plate. 'I'll walk you to your gate, Toni. Your plane leaves before ours.'

'We've got plenty of time,' Toni protested, but Luke pulled him to his feet.

'Better get there early,' Luke insisted. 'Can't you see Miss Hart and Paolo would like a few moments alone?'

They walked through the busy terminal building and sat on a bench near Toni's departure gate.

'That wasn't funny,' Luke said.

'Where's your sense of humour?' Toni said. 'Hear the one about *Goldilocks* and the three Nazis?'

'Keep your voice down.'

'You know, I've been thinking, I would have chosen Michael Schumacher.'

'What?'

'The Greatest German,' Toni said. 'Yeah, my money's on Schumi. Or possibly Heidi Klum.'

'I'd have chosen Copernicus.'

'You're obsessed with that guy. And wasn't he Polish?'

'Depends how you look at it. He was born in Prussia.'

Boarding began and Toni joined the queue. Luke walked beside him until they were almost at the gate.

'See you in the summer, I guess?' Luke said. 'Or maybe before, if we decide to go back for the third bar.'

'Yeah.' Toni winked. 'Meanwhile, look after your dirty washing, won't you? Don't let your mum unpack for you.'

'Same to you. I'll Skype you tomorrow.'

Luke waited until Toni had disappeared into the telescopic gangway. Behind the glass wall of the terminal the evening sun reflected off the fuselage of a Lufthansa jet. It was amazing how easy it was to travel from one country to another – provided you had the money.

Toni and he had the money now – or would have if everything went well on the way home. He couldn't wait for his next holiday. He had the feeling it would be exciting. Just thinking of the many things they could do with 825,000 dollars made his head spin.

And that wasn't all. He put his hand inside his fleece jacket and felt the corner of the strange little album he'd taken from the truck. He hadn't had a chance to study the stamps in detail yet but there were several that looked promising, including a reddish one-penny stamp with the head of Queen Victoria, marked 'Mauritius'.

Maybe the collection was valuable, maybe it wasn't, but he'd share the profits fifty-fifty with his friend.

OPERATION OCEAN EMERALD

ILKKA REMES

The Ocean Emerald is a floating luxury palace. A cruise ship carrying 1,000 wealthy passengers. And a sitting target for terrorists. . .

14-year-old Luke Baron isn't supposed to be there in the first place. He only boards the Emerald to return a lost passport, hoping for a finder's fee and a glimpse of the ship. But before he knows it, he's upset the plans of a brutal criminal gang on board, and has been taken captive.

As the ship sails across the stormy Baltic towards certain Hell, will Luke be able to escape and save the terrified passengers around him? Or are they fast travelling to their doom?

9781849390583 £5.99

OPERATION BLACK COBRA

ILKKA REMES

Luke Baron has agreed to buy a fake driving licence from a girl he's just met online. But when he realises he's made a big mistake and tries to back out, he discovers that Gemma Dolan is in serious trouble with her criminal dad. Trying to protect her, he gets caught up in a terrifying plot to attack an armed nuclear convoy. Who's behind it and what do they want? Luke is starting to like Gemma, but should he trust her? And can he stop the catastrophe that threatens to engulf London, the UK and the world?

'This novel is compulsive, quick reading and will definitely give thrill-seeking teen readers value for their money.' Books for Keeps

9781849391207 £6.99

OUTLAW

Stephen Davies

The rules are there to be broken

Fifteen-year-old Jake Knight is an explorer and
adventurer at heart but this often gets him into trouble.
When a stuffy English boarding school suspends him
for rule-breaking, Jake flies out to Burkina Faso where
his parents are living. He is expecting a long,
adventure-filled vacation under a smiling African sun.
But what awaits him there is kidnapping, terrorism and
Yakuuba Sor – the most wanted outlaw in the Sahara
desert.

'A strong desert setting and a corkscrew of a plot make
this a terrific page-turner.'
Julia Eccleshare, LoveReading4Kids

'Stephen Davies writes brilliantly'
Writeaway

'Exceptional talent'
The School Librarian

9781849390880 £5.99

HACKING TIMBUKTU

STEPHEN DAVIES

Long ago in the ancient city of Timbuktu, a student pulled off the most daring heist in African history – the theft of 100 million pounds worth of gold. It was never recovered but now a cryptic map of its whereabouts has been discovered.

Danny Temple is a good traceur and a great computer hacker. When the map falls into his hands and he finds himself pursued by a bizarre group calling itself *The Knights of Akonio Dolo*, both of these skills are tested to the limit. From the streets of London to the sands of Timbuktu, this high-tech gold rush does not let up for a moment.

9781842708842 £5.99

THE ISLAND OF THIEVES

JOSH LACEY

Buried treasure. Ruthless gangsters. An ancient clue . . .

Our Captayne took the pinnace ashore and I went with hym and six men also, who were sworne by God to be secret in al they saw. Here we buried five chests filled with gold.

Tom Trelawney was looking for excitement. Now he's found it. With his eccentric Uncle Harvey, he's travelling to South America on a quest for hidden gold. But Uncle Harvey has some dangerous enemies and they want the treasure too. Who will be the first to uncover the secrets of the mysterious island?

Praise for other books by this author:

'A delight'
The Times

'Smart and pacy'
Sunday Times

9781849392457 £5.99

The Absolutely True Diary of a Part-time INDIAN

SHERMAN ALEXIE

WINNER OF THE NATIONAL BOOK AWARD

'Son,' Mr P said, 'you're going to find more and more hope the farther and farther you walk away from this sad, sad, sad reservation.'

So Junior, who is already beaten up regularly for being a skinny kid in glasses, goes to the rich white school miles away. Now he's a target there as well. How he survives all this is an absolute shining must-read, and a triumph of the human spirit.

'Excellent in every way, poignant and really funny and heartwarming and honest and wise and smart.'
NEIL GAIMAN

9781842708446   £5.99

EDGE OF NOWHERE

John Smelcer

'More psychological depth than Robinson Crusoe'
Frank McCourt, author of *Angela's Ashes*

This is an astonishing tale of survival based on true
events. When Seth and his dog, Tucker, are washed
overboard from his father's fishing boat during a
torrential storm, they are assumed drowned. But by
good fortune, Seth and Tucker make it safely to one of
the hundreds of islands that line the Alaskan coast.
Over many months, the boy and his dog make their
way, island by island, towards home,
while Seth's desperate father never
gives up hope. Along the way, Seth
learns many hard lessons about
survival, and even harder lessons
about himself.

'Beautiful, literate prose ... it's a
cold desert-island story for our
times.'
Independent on Sunday

9781849391962 £5.99

HAUNTED

**A FANTASTIC COLLECTION OF GHOST STORIES
FROM TODAY'S LEADING CHILDREN'S AUTHORS**

'A chilling slice of horror. An excellent balance of
traditional and modern and a perfect pocket-money
purchase for winter evenings.' *Daily Mail*

Derek Landy, Philip Reeve, Joseph Delaney, Susan
Cooper, Eleanor Updale, Jamila Gavin, Mal Peet, Matt
Haig, Berlie Doherty, Robin Jarvis and Sam Llewellyn
have come together to bring you ten ghost stories:
from a ghost walk around York; to a drowned boy,
who's determined to find someone to play with; to a
lost child trapped in a mirror, ready
to pull you in; to devilish creatures,
waiting with bated breath for their
next young victim; to an ancient
woodland reawakened. Some will
make you scream, some will make
you shiver, but all will haunt you
gently long after you've put the
book down.

9781849393218 £6.99